Four Children for the Emperor
Four Elements in the World
And the dark of Void shall bind them
Blood shall control them all. . . .

A Fifth shall rise in Tainted lands
Bearer of Ancient Names, he calls them
One by one, they come to seek the past
Blood shall rule them all. . . .

A Throne of Steel, a Sword of Honor
Winds of Chance and Change
An Empire stands on the brink of death
Blood shall destroy them all.

THE FOUR WINDS SAGA

WIND
of
HONOR

REE SOESBEE

WIND OF HONOR

Cover art by Stephen Daniele
First Printing: August 2002
Library of Congress Catalog Card Number: 2001097134

9 8 7 6 5 4 3 2 1

US ISBN: 0-7869-2755-0
UK ISBN: 0-7869-2756-9
620-88607-001-EN

U.S., CANADA,	EUROPEAN HEADQUARTERS
ASIA, PACIFIC, & LATIN AMERICA	Wizards of the Coast, Belgium
Wizards of the Coast, Inc.	P.B. 2031
P.O. Box 707	2600 Berchem
Renton, WA 98057-0707	Belgium
+1-800-324-6496	+32-70-23-32-77

Visit our web site at **www.wizards.com**

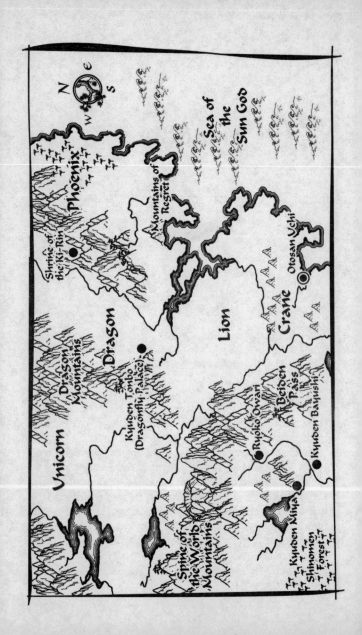

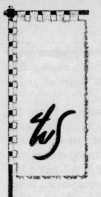

PROLOGUE

High, storm-ridden peaks pierced the sky, tearing open the bellies of clouds that ventured too near. These were the dangerous lands of Rokugan, the untamed mountains of the Dragon. For centuries, they have stood impenetrable, a defense and a defiance of those who would dare assault the mighty mountain clan. For thousands of years, they have been an ominous reminder of the stability of the earth.

As the clouds swept across the sharp teeth of the high rocks, a round-faced young woman opened her arms to the sky. Balanced on one foot against a tremendous wind, she smiled with a gaze of rapture in her eyes. Her long black hair flew about her like a flock of birds, the thin braids hissing like serpents in the vicious cold of the coming storm. Hovering in the air, the broken teeth of a skull chattered at her side, the symbol of Void carved and painted in blood upon its forehead. Its laughter was swallowed by the wind.

The woman closed her eyes in a whisper of passion, feeling a tremor far beneath the ground, hidden among the rumble of the storm. "It comes," she sighed. "It comes, and I am here to see it."

Far in the distance, one of the mountaintops began to glow, an orange-red shimmer that rivaled the fading sun. The woman opened her eyes as if in expectation. A man walked on the road beneath her, his steps strong and intent. His face was cold and lined with the passage of difficult days, but his step was sure. With a laugh, the woman lifted from the mountaintop as if blown by the wind, swiftly floating down to block his passage. Her bloodstained purple robes flickered in the air as the glow rose from a second mountain, and her eyes shone with delight.

"The summoner . . ." the woman whispered, hovering a few feet before him like some twisted wind spirit.

The man covered his eyes from the glowing brilliance of the peaks. "You . . . should not be here. This is my mission, and mine alone."

Her laughter echoed from the high rocks. "I am not here to stop your quest, shugenja. In fact, I seek your master. You have been sent here on a task, and I simply wish to know if it can be accomplished!" She spread apart her hands like an innocent little girl, and the skull at her shoulder howled in mad, cacophonous laughter.

The shugenja scowled, his hand chopping through the air in aggravation. He growled at her, "Leave me. I must go. Already time grows short, Bloodspeaker, and you do not amuse me anymore."

"No, summoner . . . I don't believe I ever did." The woman floated just out of his reach. "But tell me this. When you step into those dark mountains and call forth the Eight who will Serve, where will you lead them? Who calls you that you have come to summon the Swords of Fu Leng?" Her eyes, violet and dark like pools of thick oil, shimmered in the growing light of the mountains.

"I will follow him, as I am bidden, and I offer his secrets to no one. You annoy me, Shahai, with your arrogance."

She laughed then, a clear, pure sound that echoed through another tremor that rocked the earth at his feet. "Go, then, little servant. I will find him myself." She reached to take the skull and hold it to her breast, quieting its raucous cawing with a gentle, adoring hand. "But remember this. You owe me your life. You owe me your soul. The very blood in your veins calls to me and commands that one day . . . you will return the favor you owe, and on that day—" her full lips curved in a rich, supple smile— "the Empire will die."

The old shugenja's eyes fell, and his jaw became firm. "Even the Shadowlands have some form of honor, though it is not that of the Empire." He looked up at her, his eyes sharp and feral. "I do not forget."

Shahai's laughter rang out once more as she lifted away from him into the air. "Good-bye, summoner," she called back. "Enjoy the darkness."

Howling in laughter, the skull freed itself from her grasp as she drifted into the wind.

Shahai looked once more upon the mountains beneath her, reveling in the impending fury of the eruption that was about to occur. As the Summoner of Oni entered a dark cavern, she looked up once more at the brilliant light spilling forth from the mountain's peak. At any moment, the ritual would begin—a ritual of blood and pain such as had never before been brought to life, and the birth of a new darkness, within fire. Eight swords for Rokugan. Enough to tear the Empire to shreds.

Slowly, so slowly . . . the Shadowlands would rise once more. And she—the Queen of the Bloodspeakers—would control them all.

As it was meant to be.

1   FIRE IN THE SKIES

U*tz!* Attack!"

Swords flashed, swift sandals moved in the dust, and a single opponent fell onto the ground, his blade lying at his feet.

The girl's impassive face stared down at her opponent, arms stiff and weapon mere inches from his throat.

"Withdraw!" the sensei shouted, and she moved back instantly. Mutters moved through the judges as they marked neat calligraphy upon their rice-paper scrolls. "Toturi Tsudao!" The judge called. "Kio-ichi, the Tenth stance!"

She altered her footing, sword snapping back behind her left knee in a ready stance as her opponent climbed to his feet. Her amber eyes were impassive, long black braid swaying gently against the backplates of her formal armor. She held her sword with the grace and skill of a master swordsman, a pure spirit of steel. Tsudao was sixteen years old.

"No, Kuchini-san," the sensei said as his other student shakily prepared to fight Tsudao once more. "This time, you are released from the duty to oppose our Golden Tiger. I will fight in your stead."

A murmur of awe and amazement swept through the crowd. Rarely did one of the sensei join a gempukku contest. Never before had they seen such a contest against a member of the Imperial Line. Then again, most of the Imperial Line had been trained with the Crane Clan, and this was a Lion battleground.

"On your ready, Tsudao-san," the sensei called, readying his stance and lowering his blade.

The battleground was silent, and each of the two hundred spectators stood hushed, their eyes frozen on the silent drama that played out before them. Fans did not move, although the day was sweltering, and even the banners on the Kitsu fortress did not to wave in the faint, hot wind. The blue of the sky shone on the blades of the katanas in the competitors' hands, sparkling like sunlight on water.

Tsudao moved, like a striking snake, dropping her knee and striking under the sensei's quickly raised sword. A swift counter, a doubly quick assault, and she stood behind her mentor. With a twist and a lunge, she rolled beneath his sword, rising into her stance between the hilt of his weapon and his chest. With only inches between them, she laid her katana blade against the neck of the finest sensei in the Lion Clan and said, "Surrender."

The crowd burst into awed whispers, their wondering tones carrying as clearly as the rustling of fans in their hands, applauding the perfection of the contest with silent bows of gratitude. Kitsu Yusi stepped back, his old eyes shining with tears. "Never before have I been beaten—on the field of battle or in tournament against my betters. And yet, you have defeated me on this, your gempukku day." Turning his katana over and placing it at her feet, the old Lion smiled. "I have lived enough, and need no greater thought to turn my eyes to heaven."

The head judge stood, raising her hand in the Matsu family style. The crest of the Lion shone on her enameled helmet as she cried, "We, in the name of the Champion of the Lion, do commend and praise this student. We find her worthy!" With that announcement, cheers erupted from the crowd, and Tsudao's serious face broke into a faint smile. The audience surrounded the tournament grounds to watch the Emperor's daughter achieve her second sword in the true style of the Kitsu. Such an event was seen as a blessing, a celebration, and a time for good friends and good cheer. Tsudao looked over the crowd and saw many of her fellow students, but none of her father's guard. Her heart dropped, but she understood. The needs of the Empire must outweigh the desires of the Emperor.

The student bowed to her teacher, then once more to the judges, and stepped from the field. Lifting her hands to her head, Tsudao untied the thick cords beneath her helmet.

"Tsudao!" A young man, also in armor, pushed his way through the crowd to her side. With the camaraderie of close friends, he clasped arms with her, tugging at her sleeve with his fist in a gesture of approval. "I knew you'd beat him," he said with fire in his eyes, "and you did!"

"He should not have fought me, Tanitsu-san. He should have let me beat Yokinchi and not shamed himself against my blade." She shook her head, removing the helmet and running her fingers through the long braid that hung against her back.

"He did it to show them you are worthy." The young man smiled, his Crane-blue eyes sparkling. "But he didn't let you win. You really did it."

Toturi Tsudao, daughter of the Emperor and firstborn heir of the Empire of Rokugan, watched her grinning friend with amusement. "Of course I beat him," she said with mock exasperation. "He was slow."

Laughing, Doji Tanitsu clapped the shoulder of Tsudao's enameled armor. "Everyone is slow to you, Tsudao. The

Dragons themselves would be slow before your blade."

"You're too prideful, Tanitsu!" Tsudao chastised her friend. "The heavens will strike you down for your impudence." She gathered her equipment and strode from the field at his side.

"Maybe they will, but they won't strike me for a liar." This time Tsudao was forced to laugh with him.

"You're a silly boy." She smiled, glad to leave the press of the crowd behind.

"I am, and that's why you love me."

In an instant, Tsudao's eyes narrowed, and her voice grew still. "Do not speak of such things. Even in jest." She looked around to see that their conversation had not been heard. Most of the crowd had remained at the tournament ground, watching the next competitor on the field.

"I can joke about the high Heavens and the Dragons themselves . . . but not your love?" He chuckled, his voice low to match hers.

"The high heavens are not so great as my imperial father's wrath, and the Dragons do not have ears like he does." Tsudao allowed herself a mild smile, glancing up into Tanitsu's pale eyes. "That time is over, Tanitsu. We must let ourselves move on. I am my father's daughter. I must remember that now. I am . . . sorry." Her words were quiet, but her eyes were sad.

For a moment, Tanitsu felt a faint pain, but he smiled to cover it. "Then I will have to live below the clouds and hope for the sun of your smile." Tanitsu laughed as he mocked the supple style of the Crane courtiers that he knew Tsudao hated, and she rolled her eyes in mock frustration.

"Better to say my lips are like sweet icing and my eyes like golden honey." Tsudao shook her head and spat, "You would think I was some kind of pastry."

They both laughed at that, voices raised in pleasant friendship.

"Tsudao-sama!" A sweet, soft voice raised just above the din of the Lion festivals. "Tsudao!"

The two samurai looked back to see a young girl of sixteen, her heart-shaped face smiling and her eyes sparkling, running to catch up with them. She was the same age but seemed younger than Tsudao. Still, she was very serious about her position as the princess's handmaiden and bore her responsibilities with a mature spirit. Although the two had been together from childhood, Kekiesu was rarely informal with Tsudao. The Centipede, Kekiesu's people, treated Tsudao with an almost holy reverence. They were an ancient clan, dedicated to the Sun Goddess for thousands of years. In the past ten years, their clan had suffered a deep blow—their goddess, Amaterasu, the Lady of the Sun, had passed forever into darkness. After her death, a new Sun had risen in the Rokugani sky—a male, which some of the Centipede claimed was heresy and blasphemy to their way of life. They lived with the spiritual struggle of knowing that the goddess they worshipped had been usurped, and her light had forever changed.

Still, the Centipede believed that Amaterasu would come again—and that her chosen mortal heir would usher in a new age. Tsudao had been born with the mark of the sun—golden hair upon her head. Although it quickly turned dark as she grew, the Centipede believed that portents proclaimed her to be Amaterasu reborn. Thus, many of them believed that the imperial princess was the chosen heir of the Sun, destined to take the throne of Rokugan and lead the Empire into a new age of spiritual enlightenment. Kekiesu held to her clan's beliefs, though she rarely mentioned them.

"Too slow, Kekiesu!" Doji Tanitsu laughed, tugging at the maiden's foxtail as she stopped to catch her breath. "I almost had her, and where were you? I could have ravaged the imperial princess! Heavens forbid!"

Moshi Kekiesu frowned at the Crane. "Well, if you were not such a scoundrel that your own house would not teach you its lessons, Doji, then I would not have to worry about you with our princess." She grinned, her words impossible to take as anything other than light teasing.

"I am wounded to the core. My old uncle, Toshimoko—Fortunes rest him—would have hated to cross words with you, Centipede, and so I will not challenge your wit."

"Best that you do not." Kekiesu lifted her chin in mock arrogance. "For I happen to be a very close personal friend of a member of the Imperial House."

Tsudao rolled her eyes, looking for a way to escape their banter. "I know no one of the Imperial House, but I do know a couple of very dirty samurai. One here," she tapped Tanitsu's chest, "and one here." She pointed a finger at her own. "I doubt anyone will take us very seriously until we are clean.

"I think—" Tsudao began, but suddenly her amber eyes took on a strange, golden cast, and she stumbled.

Immediately, Moshi Kekiesu gripped the princess's elbow, bearing her weight so that Tsudao would not fall. She reached across her lady's armor to seize the helm and other equipment, keeping Tsudao standing while the princess's eyes went wide and turned pale.

"The Sun is within her," Kekiesu said as she strained to hold Tsudao upright. "Help me . . . we cannot let them see." Moshi Kekiesu's words were low, urgent, and Tanitsu immediately put his arm beneath Tsudao's shoulder on the other side.

"What is happening?" he whispered, suddenly frightened.

"The Sun is upon her. She sees visions."

At that moment, Tsudao's eyes turned fully golden, and long black strands of hair from her braid blew loose in a sudden chilling wind. The banners above the Lion festival snapped as if in anger, and the audience at the gempukku field let out a collective sigh of disappointment. Someone had failed the trials.

"She walks . . . in darkness . . . the blood stains her hands." Tsudao's words were almost too soft to be heard, and her hands shook violently. Kekiesu and Tanitsu half-carried Tsudao to the shade of a thin oak tree and lowered her to the ground. "The wind carries her. The fire of dawn rises from broken teeth stained brown, heralding the beginning . . . of destruction for the Empire. Eight swords rise in the Shadowlands, led by a single master. Eight . . . and one soft voice, and he who rules them—the Scion of Hantei. The Lesser Houses fall. The darkness takes the Emperor . . . in nightmare, a battle . . . but not an ending."

"Tsudao," Doji Tanitsu said softly, his face showing worry.

"She will come out of this when it is time," Kekiesu whispered. "Be silent. Let none know." She watched as festival patrons passed nearby. "You should not be here. You should not know of such things."

"How long has this been happening?" Tanitsu stared in awe and shock at Tsudao, staring into her unseeing golden eyes.

"Since she was a child. Shh. She comes back to us."

Tsudao's eyes began to water, and she blinked, burying her face in her hands. Impulsively, Moshi Kekiesu put her arms around the imperial princess's shoulders, comforting her in a low tone. "It is over. The Sun has moved on. Her grace no longer shines through you."

"I . . . I couldn't control it. The light was so strong." Tsudao looked up, and her eyes had faded to their light amber, the black pupils wide and pained. "Did anyone see?" Tsudao whispered.

"Only I . . . and Tanitsu."

"Good." Tsudao nodded. "It is best that they did not." Tsudao lowered her gaze for a moment, angered that she felt embarrassed by this strange touch upon her soul. The visions rarely came to her, and they always marked some great change in the world around her. "I do not know what this portends, but I know that this vision was stronger than any of the others."

Tsudao looked at her friend, seeing only love and concern in his eyes. "Tanitsu, you cannot speak of this to anyone. The visions do not come often. If the Scorpion knew—" a long pause, and a shudder— "they would rob me of my throne."

Tanitsu drew his sword and laid it on the ground at Tsudao's feet in imitation of the sensei's gesture. "You are the daughter of the Imperial House, and I am yours to command. I swear by the soul of my cousin Toshiken, the Emerald Champion, and by the heart of my house, the Lady Doji herself. None will hear of this from me."

Kekiesu nodded solemnly, and Tsudao smiled through her brief tears.

"You spoke of a woman," Kekiesu said. "A woman and blood."

"There were images of pain and of darkness shrouded in fire. The Empire is in danger." Tsudao said with certainty. "My father will need me." She stood, gathering her equipment. "I am going to bathe, Kekiesu," Tsudao said, both embarrassed and suddenly bone-weary. "I will meet you in our chambers in a candlemark, after I have rested in the bath."

She walked away into the crowd gathered around a merchant's booth. Kekiesu and Tanitsu watched the princess as she moved through the celebration, both feeling a certain dread and foreboding in their hearts as she vanished into the throng.

"Are you certain that these dreams are true?" Doji Tanitsu questioned softly. "Could this not be some strange trick of the mind—some shugenja, testing the princess's resolve with foul magic?"

"The visions are always true, and their portents always come to pass. They are brought upon her by the Sun—Amaterasu's legacy to the world she left behind. Her spirit lives within the princess." Moshi Kekiesu stared at him levelly as if daring him to question her words.

"Yes, but . . . how do you know?" The Crane opened his hands, still confused by the revelations suddenly thrust upon him.

"She is a holy gift, a legacy to the Empire." The Centipede shugenja's words were proud, but not arrogant, sure of their message. "She is Toturi Tsudao, princess and heir to the Empire. Daughter of the Sun."

"But—"

"I am born of a minor Clan, Crane, and so perhaps you do not think my word is worthy. Then accept another. Listen to the speech of the heavens. For look, her words have already begun to come to pass. The sun does not rise in the north." Kekiesu pointed. "Yet the dawn rises through teeth of stone."

Far to the north, Tanitsu saw the sharp edges of the Dragon Mountains.

They were shrouded in red flame.

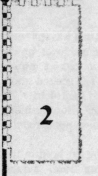

2 SERVANT OF THE EMPIRE

Four
years
later.

The Imperial Legions, their white tents ruffling slightly in the warm breeze that blew up the hillside from the sea, were camped along a ridge just outside the southern mountains of the Phoenix. To the south, bandits—vicious Yobanjin raiders—beleaguered the peaceful villages of the Centipede, and the Legions had been sent by the Emperor to bring peace.

Kitsu Dejiko rode her bay stallion at a run up the coastline, his hooves pounding against the surf. She was the commander of one of the legions, trusted as second-in-command to the young general. On the hill, the banners of command flew proudly over an open tent, and Dejiko saw the officers gathered to plan their next defense.

Dejiko slid from her horse as it slowed, unwilling to wait for it to stop. She was a tall woman, her long hair dyed golden-red in the Lion Clan style, and her unpleasant face revealed cunning and integrity rather than the soft features of beauty. She was muscular, her armor well cared for, and she walked with a faint limp from a wound that was still sore.

Within the tent, two commanders argued over broad maps, their hands making sweeping gestures across miniature mountains and tokens of each army. The general stood beside them, hand at her chin, listening to their debate. At her side, a shugenja handmaiden knelt on a soft cushion, reclining her head in meditation as the soldiers pondered the battles to come.

Dejiko knelt before the general, lowering her head in the presence of a member of the Imperial House. "Rise," said the commander, and Dejiko looked up at Toturi Tsudao with something akin to awe.

Tsudao was young for her command—just twenty years old, but few dared mention it. Black hair hung freely down her back, and her amber eyes were serious. She was beautiful enough to make courtiers write poems in honor of the curve of her cheek, but Tsudao was uninterested in their flattery. Toturi's eldest child was more proud of her victories than of her fair skin—victories that she had earned in plenty. She had not been raised to the rank of general by her father's hand but by the commendations of her superiors. Under her guidance, the Yobanjin raiders had been driven back from Crane lands, forced along the coast toward the Phoenix territories in the north, and now were effectively scissored in these mountains. They had no resources for food other than the small villages of the Centipede and could run nowhere. Blocked to the east by ocean, and to the south and west by Tsudao's forces, they could run only north—into the empty wastes of the Mountains of Regret. Soon, they would be destroyed.

"Tsudao-sama," Dejiko said, gazing up at her leader. "It is as you thought. The Yobanjin have moved to the east side of the village of Utsiku. They likely plan a raid—and if they are successful, they will gain enough grain from the Utsiku stores to keep themselves alive for months. Perhaps all winter."

Tsudao said quietly, "I had anticipated that. If the Fortunes are with us, we can end this here." She motioned for Kitsu Dejiko to stand and turned toward the table.

"Samurai," Tsudao said, her voice cutting through all argument. "We have been granted our chance to destroy these raiders. Are you with me?"

A solid, "Hai!" came from the two men at the table, and their eyes shone with interest and pride.

"As Dejiko-san has said, the Yobanjin have moved here, here, and here. We will move three units to the west of the village and drive the Yobanjin back into their own passes when they attack. Another unit will take advantage of the enemy's haste in order to position themselves here, behind them, and slip into the pass to seal it after they come through. When we drive them out of the town, they will flee the way they came, and we will have them trapped. Our rear guard will seal this pass—" she indicated the Yobanjin's entry point to the village— "and we will have our raiders at last."

The other commanders nodded in agreement, and Tsudao gestured to a man wearing the Dragon mon.

"Mirumoto Junnosuke, you will command that rear force. Take your men and maneuver up this side of the canyon. When the pass is empty, make your way into it, and prepare to halt their retreat. Kitsu Dejiko and Matsu Domotai will take the far side of the encampment. I will be with them. We have nearly two thousand men—more than a match for the Yobanjin. Only their cunning has kept them alive this long. We are about to end that. Hai?"

"Hai!" shouted the commanders.

"And Junnosuke . . ." Tsudao said, lifting her eyes to the Dragon field commander. "Our orders are to capture these Yobanjin and bring them to justice. You will remember that?"

Junnosuke was a thick-bodied samurai, his broad shoulders rippling with muscle and his hands thick with calluses. He stared sullenly at Tsudao but nodded in forced agreement. "As you wish, Toturi-sama."

Tsudao said nothing else but stared for a long moment at the Dragon. He had been reprimanded twice for brutality toward prisoners in his care, but she could not fault his effective leadership. The Dragon in the Imperial Legions followed him almost blindly, and others spoke frequently of his fine swordsmanship and cunning mind. But she could not bring herself to trust him.

"Go," she said. "In four hours, their assault will begin. Just after dark. They wish to use the night against us."

"They will fail." The soft voice belonged to Tsudao's handmaiden. She was a shugenja and bore the mon of the Centipede, whose lands the Imperial Legions now fought to defend. "The Sun will shine, though we cannot see his face."

Tsudao nodded, and gave the order to spread word throughout the legions. The time was near.

* * * * *

When darkness descended through the little valley, the shouts of bandits carried on the air. They were bold, pushed by starvation, and without care for their lives as they raced out of the pass toward the small village of Utsiku.

The horses pounded into the village, their riders whooping and screaming in fury as they set fire to the village huts. The Yobanjin, while technically Rokugani, were larger, less slanted in their eyes and burlier in appearance. Their ponies were a rugged mountain breed, strong and squat. The men were good warriors, but the last few weeks of combat against the Imperial Legions had worn them to bone and muscle covered by filthy rags.

Half of the racing bandit horde turned to the grain silos, leaping from their horses to fill bags with the rice and grain that the villagers had gathered. The other half terrorized the peasants, grabbing some of the young women and throwing them over their horses' backs. Some cut down innocents with their strangely curved swords, allowing the ponies to churn mud and bone beneath steel-shod hooves.

Then, to the west, a single clear note sounded in the darkening night.

Hoofbeats charged down the mountainside, scattering as they rushed the village from the western hilltops. The banners of the Imperial Legions were gray and pale in the moonlight, but the shouts of the Yobanjin bandits revealed that they were well aware of the danger. Tsudao saw Kitsu Dejiko turn her troops to the left, and Matsu Domotai took his to the right, as had been planned. Within a few short moments, the village would be surrounded on three sides, and the Yobanjin would be forced to retreat directly into Junnosuke's soldiers. Their only hope would be to escape into the darkness, hide, and trickle away, one by one, into the night.

"We have to force them toward the pass!" shouted Kitsu Dejiko.

Tsudao turned her steed and clung to its back as it reared in protest at the sudden stop. "Now, Kekiesu!" Tsudao shouted, raising her fan of command. "Bring the Sun!"

The shugenja tugged on her horse's reins until it stood still, then she raised her hands to the sky. She began to chant, first in a quiet voice but then gaining resonance as magic swirled around her bare arms. Small bursts of light exploded against her skin, illuminating her hands as they lifted in prayer, and Tsudao heard the Centipede call upon the power of the Immortal Heavens. Then, with a strong punch toward the sky, Moshi Kekiesu opened her hands and a rush of light exploded upward.

The flare sang toward the heavens, bursting into brilliant light a few hundred yards above the village rooftops. The blazing light of the sun shone down, illuminating the entire valley in a shower of sparks.

"*Now!*" cried Tsudao, lowering her fan.

Hooves pounded against the rocky ground as the legion charged. The Yobanjin horses were sturdier, more used to the mountain terrain, but the legion had the higher ground and the advantage of surprise. It would be a fair fight.

The small village was quickly surrounded to the north and west, and Tsudao's soldiers advanced into the twisting city streets toward the Yobanjin raiders. Men scrambled out of huts, carrying as many provisions as they could load upon their backs and leaping toward their horses. In the village, peasants screamed in fear, cowering from the barbaric Yobanjin and screaming to the Fortunes for salvation.

Tsudao's horse reared as three of the Yobanjin riders beat their steeds toward her. As the stallion rose, Tsudao swept her sword against one of the men, and blood sprayed from his wound. The bandit pounded her horse's withers with a sturdy wooden club, and her steed leaped aside—only to be penned in by another of the Yobanjin riders. Snarling, Tsudao struck again, and her sword rang from one of the Yobanjin's hastily upraised scimitars. His sword trembled for a moment under her strike, then shattered into shards of falling steel. Tearing into his horse's reins, the rider jerked away as if afraid to fight the general without his blade. Ah, the better part of valor ...

Tsudao released her war-horse's reins, trusting that the beast could find its own way through the harassing riders, and engaged in rapid swordplay with two of the Yobanjin who closed in upon her. Their thick, curved blades were far slower than her katana, and her sword wove between their weapons like a striking serpent. She cut the ropes that held one of the saddles to the horse's back, watching in amusement as the warrior fell onto the stony ground.

The other, a far cannier opponent, gripped Tsudao's hand and twisted, hoping to make her release her blade, but she was far stronger than the bandit had anticipated. With a shove and a rapid punch to the nose, Tsudao sent him flying on top of his fallen companion. She turned her steed to face another brigand, trying not to chuckle as the two behind her fled on foot. Let them flee. They would carry less of the village's possessions that way.

Another Yobanjin barbarian hurled himself from the back of his horse toward her, nearly knocking Tsudao from her own mount. She clutched his arms, and a desperate wrestling match ensued atop her rearing war-horse. Raising her foot precariously from the wooden stirrup, Tsudao placed it upon the bandit's chest and shoved. She twisted his arms, refusing to allow him to grip her armor-ties, and once more she hurled another bandit to the ground.

"I see why you Yobanjin leave your northern homes so often," she said as the bandit climbed to his feet. "You need the riding practice!"

The man growled. He crouched, his strange and dirty cloak sweeping the dusty village road. The Yobanjin wove back and forth before her horse as if seeking an opening. With a swift motion, he pulled a long, curved knife from his boot and charged. Tsudao lowered her sword to meet his thrust, deflecting the thick knife with her elegant katana. He cut beneath her guard, and Tsudao kicked his knife hand. The Yobanjin snarled and swung again, and again her katana met his parry with perfect precision. This time, however, she twisted her sword blade to raise his knife above her thigh. Tsudao moved swiftly and caught his wrist in her other hand. She twisted, pressing against the exposed tendons of his wrist, and the bandit's knife fell to the ground.

He stared up at her in fear and fury, and Tsudao introduced his gaping jaw to the steel-shod bottom of her sandal. The Yobanjin's head twisted with a jerk, and he collapsed to the ground, a small sigh escaping the man's filthy lips.

Tsudao looked out over the village rooftops, rising to stand in her stirrups as she surveyed the battle scene. The bandits had broken and were running out of the village with anything they could carry. Already, her men drove errant runners back from the north and south, pushing the entire bandit horde toward the pass. Kekiesu's spell still lit the night and provided blazing counterpoint to the dark shadows between the huts. The forest surrounding the village was darker, but a corps of Imperial archers moved among the trees and pelted fleeing Yobanjin with rock-tipped arrows—bruising but not killing their targets. Confused and harried, many of the bandits dropped the village's supplies and fled.

The Yobanjin, infuriated and unable to find any other source of retreat, charged blindly to the north. They had come through the mountain pass once, and it led back to the twisting box canyons of the Mountains of Regret. If they could make it through, they could go back into hiding and seek another source of food.

But as Tsudao watched the bandits race between the high boulders outside the Centipede village, she heard screams of surprise and battle cries from the pass. Mirumoto Junnosuke's men. Kitsu Dejiko's soldiers raced their steeds to catch up with the rear of the bandit forces, driving them onward into the pass. Tsudao ordered more men into the village, watching as they flushed more Yobanjin from huts, cutting them down if they refused to surrender, rescuing screaming villagers from the bandit's clutches.

Moshi Kekiesu called to Tsudao, "General-sama!"

Tsudao turned, urging her steed to the left until she saw Kekiesu standing at the end of an alleyway between two burning huts. At the other end of the alley were six small children and a wild-eyed Yobanjin with a thick sword in his shaking hand. Two of the children were badly injured, and a third desperately tried to staunch their wounds, but a bandit stood beside them, sword bared.

"Let me go!" he shouted in broken Rokugani, "or I destroy the children!"

Kekiesu was already injured, her arm hanging by her side in a bloody sleeve, but she held her short spear with care. "I cannot overcome him," she shouted to Tsudao. "He has the babies."

Tsudao urged her steed onward, and as it leaped past the Yobanjin, she hurled herself onto the bandit. His sword cut into her side as she wrestled him to the ground, but she ignored it. Behind her, she heard Kekiesu shouting to the children to flee. Tsudao fought to force the Yobanjin to release his sword's hilt. She slammed his hand into the ground once, twice, and then his hand gave way. The thick-bladed sword fell to the ground, and Tsudao rolled to her knees. With a fierce punch of her gauntleted hand, she drove the bandit's head into the ground, knocking him unconscious.

The imperial princess looked up to see the Centipede children, as one, bowed to the ground with their faces in the dust. Only the seriously injured girl was not kneeling, and the others had turned her so that she, too, could express her thanks. Moshi Kekiesu rushed to them, helping them to their feet. "The Daughter of the Sun has no time for your thanks, but know that she protects you. Now, go. Carry Shenko. Make for the woods to the north, away from the fighting. You will know when it is safe to return."

Quickly, the children did as Kekiesu asked, and Tsudao half-dragged the body of the unconscious Yobanjin out of the flaming alleyway. More screams and shouts came from the pass where the Yobanjin fought against Junnosuke's legions, and Tsudao cursed. She saw Kitsu Dejiku, calling her men back, away from the opening of the pass, and the commander's face was red with fury. Beyond her, Tsudao could see Junnosuke's Dragon forces, marauding through helpless opponents. Though the Yobanjin lifted their swords in surrender, still Junnosuke commanded the assault. Soon, no Yobanjin would be left alive upon the field of battle.

"Junnosuke . . ." Tsudao muttered, and Kekiesu looked toward the combat.

"He's killing them," the handmaiden whispered, aghast. "All of them."

Tsudao clenched her fist, calling for a nearby samurai to give her a steed, and she climbed upon the back of the horse. She galloped to the edge of the village as the last of the magical light faded from the valley sky.

Kitsu Dejiko turned to face Tsudao, shame and bitter anger in her eyes. "I ordered him to cease the attack!" Dejiko shouted over the sound of battle. "He would not listen!"

The screams of dying men faded as the last of the Yobanjin bandits fell from his steed onto the ground. Tsudao turned to face Junnosuke across the corpse-laden battlefield. His eyes were wide, exhilarated, and his gauntleted hands were covered in blood.

"Withdraw the troops," Tsudao shouted to Dejiko as soon as she was within hearing distance, "and bring Junnosuke to me!"

* * * * *

In the command tent outside the Centipede village, Tsudao let her anger rage. Her commanders, Kitsu Dejiko, Matsu Domotai, and Mirumoto Junnosuke knelt before her, their armor still soiled from the battle. Tsudao's amber eyes flashed, her hands balled into fists.

"The Yobanjin have been destroyed," Dejiko said, "to a man."

"Better to kill them than allow them to live on Rokugani sympathy," Junnosuke contested. "They would only have returned in the summer. If they believe us to be weak, their next force will be three times as strong, and then—"

Domotai, the third of Tsudao's commanders, interrupted. "The Yobanjin were given the order to surrender. They did not put down their swords." His words were stilted, spat out between clenched teeth. Domotai had been Junnosuke's closest companion in their youth, and it had been his honor that convinced Tsudao to give Junnosuke a final chance despite the words of the old Scorpion that decried Junnosuke for a coward and a fool.

"Yobanjin do not put down their swords," Tsudao snarled.

"They hold them above their heads when they surrender. Whether you knew that or not, Junnosuke—" she raised a fist toward the Dragon commander's kneeling form— "you were *ordered* to withhold your bloodlust!" Her anger slipped through her carefully cultured exterior. "You were *commanded* to keep yourself in check, to allow them to surrender. You disobeyed my command."

"I did what any samurai would do!" Junnosuke growled. He crouched like an animal, pointing savagely at the battleground past the thin walls of the tent. "I fought with honor."

"Honor?" Dejiko said, rising to her feet. She stood, her eyes afire. Dejiko placed her hand on the hilt of her sword, ready to draw upon Junnosuke in her anger. "There was no honor in killing starving men. No honor in butchering the helpless, nor in disobeying a general's command!" Staring into Junnosuke's face, Dejiko spat upon the ground. "You have no honor."

Junnosuke stood at her words, his hand finding the hilt of his katana. He clenched his fist against it, and the knuckles turned white from the heat of his anger. "I will not accept such words from you," he hissed. Before he could draw, Domotai leaped between the feuding pair.

"No." Domotai said, his voice quiet and level. He managed to keep his composure despite the low snarls of the two samurai at either side of his outstretched arms. When he spoke again, his voice held a tone of cajoling reason. "This is the tent of General Tsudao, daughter of the Emperor. Neither of you will dishonor her by spilling blood here. This matter is for her to decide—not us. Sit, commanders—" his voice was a lash— "and let our lady speak."

Two pairs of eyes filled with hatred stared over Domotai's shoulder as the Lion and the Dragon slowly backed down. At last, Junnosuke lowered himself to his knees before Tsudao, muttering a quick apology for his actions. Shamed by Junnosuke's humility, no matter how false, Kitsu Dejiko could only do the same.

"When your old commander," Tsudao said gravely, "the Scorpion Kitagi, threw you out of his legion, I should have listened to his word. Yogo Kitagi said that you burned an entire village of innocents just to ease your anger. I did not believe him, and it is to my shame that I now know he spoke the truth. You cannot be controlled, Junnosuke. Yet I gave you a second chance—to fight by my side—and you failed me. This is not a matter of honor. It is a matter of duty. This was the last chance for your honor to be righted. You have failed in your duty, Junnosuke—no matter how you justify it. By rights, I should have you hanged."

Hanged. The word descended upon those in the tent with the coldness of ice. To be hanged instead of given the chance to commit seppuku was the worst punishment a samurai could receive. Their honor and that of their descendants would bear the shame of it for generations.

"My lady," Domotai murmured, touching his head to the floor as he sank to his knees with the others, "on behalf of Mirumoto Junnosuke, I beg for his honor. He has been a brave general, and he has served beside me. I would place my honor with his—if you could find the Fortune's grace to show mercy. He is my oath-brother. If you have loyalty for me, I ask this as a life-boon. Release him with honor."

To the other side, Dejiko was quick to speak up. "He is a traitor. Leniency only shows weakness. Junnosuke understood your orders—and chose to disobey them. He deserves a traitor's death." She glared at the Dragon with fury, biting back the rest of her words.

For a long moment, Tsudao considered her three samurai, staring most intently at Matsu Domotai. All had served bravely in the past, and no man was without fault, but this . . .

At last, she spoke in a voice that brooked no argument. "Domotai-san. Your words have been heard. Dejiko will witness them. I grant you this life-boon, not because Junnosuke is worthy of your loyalty, but because you are worthy of mine." She sighed. "Junnosuke." The lack of honorific cut across the cold air. "Rise. Take your weapons and your men and return to the Dragon Mountains in dishonor. I forbid you to commit seppuku. I have also heard Dejiko's words, and I am in agreement with her. Samurai die with honor. You no longer have that right."

Mirumoto Junnosuke's face reddened, but he bowed his head.

"Leave me." Tsudao rose, and the others quickly stood from their cushions. Junnosuke stormed out, immediately bellowing for his legion, while the two Lion commanders followed with more somber steps.

"I will return, Lion," Junnosuke snarled just within Dejiko's hearing. "You will meet me again, and when you do, you will pay for your words." Junnosuke spat upon the ground, narrowly missing the Kitsu woman's sandal. "As will she." His eyes were narrow and hard, and Dejiko's moved for her katana when she felt Matsu Domotai's hand on her sleeve.

"Why do you sympathize with him?" Kitsu Dejiko snarled to her companion, her dislike obvious.

Matsu Domotai shrugged, his eyes troubled. "He saved my life, and I owe him." He watched as Junnosuke called for his horse. Climbing into the saddle, the samurai kicked the beast savagely, bringing blood to its lips with a brutal yank of the reins. The horse screamed, turning quickly and racing toward the Dragon tents in fear.

"It is not enough," Dejiko spat. "Not enough to justify his treason." She turned on her heel and, with another curse, marched toward her own tent.

Matsu Domotai watched in silence. A life-boon was a once-in-a lifetime promise from samurai to his master and could never be refused. But once given, that samurai could never again ask anything of his master. It was the final request and never given or asked without grave consequence.

Sighing, Domotai lowered his head. "Oath-brother," he whispered to Mirumoto Junnosuke's retreating form, "my debt is repaid."

3 | BLACK HEARTS

A quiet flame whispered through the Dragon Mountains, illuminating the tops of the high cliffs with fire and lava. For five years, the mountains had been in a constant state of eruption. Though the largest volcanoes had not yet erupted, the small tremors and faint lines of lava that trickled through the lands were ruining numerous villages and threatening some of the sanctuaries of the Mirumoto and Kitsuki, the most prosperous families of the Dragon. Soon, entire cities would be swallowed by the dark flame, burned to ash and covered with lava as a child piles sand in a sandbox. Already, the sad trail of Dragon refugees sought shelter in the lowlands—lands controlled by the Phoenix Clan. Thousands of peasants walking one after the other like long, twisting trails of ants poured into the quiet fields of the Shiba. Thousands more died before they could escape the flames. When the true eruptions began, more would burn in the infernos released upon the Dragon lands.

The Imperial Legions rode northward, over the Mountains of Regret and into the Phoenix lands. Sobered by the destruction of the Yobanjin, Tsudao had been only too happy to comply with a Phoenix request that the Emperor's Hand investigate the rumors of destruction and war within the Dragon mountains. The two clans were bordering on war because Dragon peasants had been forced out of their mountains and migrated to Phoenix lands. The position was difficult but not untenable. At least, the Imperial Legions would be in a position to rescue and not destroy.

A Phoenix banner marked a small unit of samurai that raced across the plains just below the edge of the mountains, and Tsudao held up her fist to cease the advance.

"Shiba," breathed Moshi Kekiesu, ever at Tsudao's side. "I know the mon on that banner, and I recognize the ambassador's aura. He is Shiba Yoma, called the Voice of the Masters. He speaks with the confidence of the Elemental Masters who rule the Phoenix Clan. If he speaks for peace the Masters themselves will not deny his decision." Kekiesu's brow furrowed, and she brushed a lock of her short, black hair out of her eyes. "I can only hope the Dragon are taking this as seriously."

Toturi Tsudao nodded, watching as the Phoenix horsemen galloped across a wide field of rustling grasses. From the height, she could see the width of the field, looking north to the first few dots of the Phoenix villages and the sharp peaks of the Dragon lands beyond them, to the west. "This is a good site for our negotiations. Kekiesu, tell the commanders to allow the men to dismount and prepare camp. The plateau here is wide and should be comfortable for a few nights, and the view is . . . more than acceptable."

Her handmaiden nodded. "I will tell them."

Kekiesu broke into a wide smile, her white teeth flashing. She turned her horse and trotted back to the legion commanders, disseminating the general's commands succinctly. Tsudao looked down again at the Phoenix ambassador and his men as they approached the trail that would lead them to the high plateau. They would be here in less than half a day, but the Dragon were nowhere to be seen. Their lateness could only reflect on their seriousness about these peace negotiations—and if they were too late, the Phoenix's honor would be too insulted to parlay on good terms. The Dragon emissaries were nowhere in sight, which meant they were still more than a day from the meeting place. Tsudao sighed.

And she had hoped this would be an easy negotiation.

*　*　*　*　*

Three days later, the Dragon and Phoenix were finally assembled around the negotiating table in Tsudao's open tent. A low circular table had been set in the center of the tent, with seats for all, and a higher stood for Tsudao, placed slightly to one side of the table. She was there as an arbiter, a neutral voice—but also as an imperial princess and leader of the Legion of the Emperor's Hand. It was appropriate that those around her be reminded of both her duty and her station.

The tent was open and airy, the walls rolled up in order to allow a full view of the breathtaking panorama of the Phoenix-Dragon border. The colors of the Imperial house were muted, overcome by the blue and gold of the Imperial Legion. The tent was lightly guarded, and only Tsudao's own handmaiden was there to serve the honorable guests.

Kekiesu knelt on a cushion in the center of the table's arc, ostensibly to serve water to both sides, but also because Tsudao wished the shugenja to be accepted by the Dragon and Phoenix as Tsudao's voice among them. To her right, the Dragon ambassadors sat, resplendent in golden kimono patterned in green; to her left, the Phoenix, with Shiba Yoma at their head. His two assistants both wore the personal mon of the Asako, a lesser Phoenix house, and seemed overburdened with papers, maps, and writing utensils. One spread a sheet of rice paper on the table, dating it accurately in small print, and kept a complete record of the meeting.

The Dragon, on the other hand, had arrived more than a day late for the meeting—then demanded a day's rest after their "dangerous travels." They were of the Mirumoto and Tamori families, and Tsudao recognized the hard-faced man who sat at the head position. His name was Mirumoto Ukira, once the Topaz Champion of the Empire. Although Ukira was young, he had earned high station and the respect of the Empire with his bold fighting style and command of Dragon *ni-ten*, the two-sword stroke. The Topaz Champion was an Imperial tournament held for those who had been given their gempukku during that year—and only one samurai each year could claim victory, title, and station from the tournament. Those who did so were marked by their clans as "up and coming" in the most flattering way and were often given positions of respect and responsibility very early in their lives.

At least the Dragon had sent someone of honor and station. The Phoenix could not be insulted that they weren't being given proper respect. Not that they wouldn't try.

"My lords," Tsudao said from her seat after all the ambassadors had arranged themselves on their cushions, "my honored father, Emperor of the Chrysanthemum of Rokugan, as well as the rest of his proud and noble Empire, wishes these disagreements to be ended as swiftly as possible. The instability in the southern regions of the Phoenix and Dragon lands is noted throughout the Empire, and it is not looked upon with grace." She unconsciously imitated her father's stiff and formal style of speech, ill at ease with such duties. "Speak your mind, and with the good will and blessings of the Seven Fortunes and Lord Sun, we will reach a compromise." Tsudao laid her fan of command on the mahogany tabletop as a sign that she was listening.

It took only an instant for both the Phoenix and Dragon ambassadors to begin speaking all at once.

"Honorable Dragon-san," Shiba Yoma began, "I offer greetings in the name of my Masters—"

"Enlightened Shiba-san, you will of course excuse our tardiness—"

Both emissaries fell silent, and a spark of annoyance lit in the Dragon's eye. He cleared his throat a moment, looking back at the other Dragons behind him, and began again. Again, the Phoenix spoke at precisely the same instant.

"Noble Phoenix, perhaps you would consider allowing me to speak first—"

"Mirumoto-san, your tardiness is not at issue. Surely your trip was disrupted by important matters—"

Again, they both ceased their speeches, and this time, the Dragon's ire was obvious. The Phoenix was deliberately baiting him, giving back a bit of spite in exchange for having to wait for the Dragon's arrival. Tsudao raised an eyebrow, curious, but the Dragon refused to become angry. He motioned for the Phoenix to speak first and took a sip of the water that Kekiesu offered. He would win nothing by continuing the ridiculous duel of volume.

Shiba Yoma turned to Tsudao and smiled. "My Lady Toturi-sama, I would like to thank you for hosting this meeting. I am certain that your presence will aid our Dragon cousins to see that their troubles are, of course, an internal issue, and not a matter for the Empire. The Phoenix resent being dragged into the personal difficulties of the Dragon, but we wish to help our weakened neighbors in whatever way we can."

At the mention of "an internal issue," Mirumoto Ukira stiffened. When the Phoenix reached "weakened neighbors," the Dragon's hand clenched upon the table. It was obvious that the Mirumoto agreed with him on neither issue, although he struggled to maintain a stoic face while his opponent spoke.

"The Dragon," he replied with false courtesy, "are strong. But our mountains rob us of our hard-earned harvests. My companion, Tamori Matiu, can speak to you of the villages that have been destroyed by—"

Shiba Yoma cut in, whispering loudly to his Asako behind his fan, "Oyishi, do you know of these Tamori? Are they, perhaps, a family of the Scorpion or Crane?"

Mirumoto Ukira's face turned red at such a blatant show of disrespect. "The Tamori are of the Dragon," he growled. "They were elevated to High House status as a stipulation of the treaty that ended the Wars of the Spirits. Hantei XVI granted a family name to their patriarch for his loyal service during the war."

"Emperor Hantei . . . ?" questioned Yoma again, far too loud to be a true whisper. "But our Emperor is Toturi." Tsudao reddened in annoyance at the courtier's obvious baiting.

Yoma's Asako assistant said, "It is said they earned much honor." Yoma shook his head, pretending confusion, and sighed.

Tsudao saw Mirumoto's knuckles whiten. The Tamori had followed the Hantei Emperors when they made war upon the Toturi line, but in the end, the Toturi lineage had kept the throne of Rokugan. That the Tamori had supported the losing side was not something most Dragons were proud of, but they had indeed served "their" emperor with honor and courage.

Mirumoto Ukira unclenched his jaw enough to speak in a clipped voice. "The Tamori have been a family for six years. They are well known as loyal to both Rokugan and to Emperor Toturi-sama."

"Ah, well . . . my thanks, Mirumoto-san," Yoma said. "So it has been six years since the Tamori claimed their name? Ah, the same age as my youngest son. Already, he can read and write and ride his pony—within the yard, of course." He shone a sinister yet impeccably polite smile at the comparison. "I do not visit Dragon courts of late and do not know all of the new details pertaining to their politics." He motioned to the Asako, indicating that he should write down what Ukira had said.

The Dragon and his assistant reddened, and Tsudao heard one of the fine calligraphy brushes beneath the table snap. Quickly covering the long silence, Kekiesu offered the Mirumoto water and poured until their cups were full.

Shiba Yoma spoke pleasantly with Tsudao while his opponent regained composure, a mocking smile on the Phoenix's lips. After the Dragon had a sip of his water, Yoba began once more. "My honored Dragon companion—" his voice was smooth and practiced— "although we would be interested in assisting you with these issues, I'm afraid the Phoenix clan has never been particularly prosperous with harvests. Our wealth is knowledge, and our knowledge tells us that your people should remain in their own lands, not," he added coldly, "within ours."

"The mountains disagree," Mirumoto said. "The lava they throw forth has destroyed villages, made thousands of homeless peasants who will starve when winter comes. Soon the mountains will explode, and entire cities will fall to ash. That day is coming. Our prophets and our shugenja have forseen it." Mirumoto Ukira's eyes narrowed. "We are willing to offer trade and service in exchange for land and harvest. Without it, our peasants will starve."

"Trade and service? In exchange for land that our families have worked for generations?" Yoma was unbelieving. "We have never given away territory in the past. If we were to begin doing so, the Phoenix heimin would have nowhere to live, no crops to farm. If we support you, our own peasants will die of starvation. We must think of our own before we turn a hand to help others. The burden you place on our lands kills children, destroys crops, and turns our fields into mud from the march of these refugees. You bring this war upon yourself."

"There is no other option for us. The mountains writhe in anger. The ground bursts into flame—"

"Remove your peasants." Shiba Yoma cut off the Dragon's response, each word slow and deliberate. The implied threat lay upon the table like a knife.

There was a long, pregnant pause, followed by, "We cannot," from Mirumoto Ukira.

"You will leave our lands, or there will be war," said Yoma Shiba. "It is our right, as ordained by our birth as a noble clan. We have protected our lands for centuries, Dragon. We will defend ourselves from invasion."

The Dragon half-stood, his fists clenched on the low table. "If you harm one peasant, Shiba, then we will raze your libraries with Dragon fire and see how well your Clan withstands the heat of the Fortunes."

Now, Yoma's face darkened in fury, and Tsudao quickly stepped in. "Samurai," she said formally. "This disagreement has been brought on by the will of the Fortunes, who caused the mountains to breathe fire. Surely their most dedicated supplicants can overcome it. You, Phoenix-sama—" she gestured toward Yoma— "you speak for the Masters themselves. Can you not tell us of their wisdom and willingness to compromise? And Dragon, you raise the voice that commands thousands—thousands who may starve, if you fail here." Tsudao cut to the heart of the issue without pretense. "Would you surrender their lives for your pride?"

Both men glowered at each other like great cats, circling for another attack. Tsudao exchanged concerned glances with her handmaiden.

Mirumoto Ukira scowled, his temper barely under control. "The truth, Phoenix, is that we have *nowhere else to go*."

"Then," Shiba Yoma said, standing and chopping the air with his closed fist, "you will die."

The rest of the Phoenix stood, bowing as one to Tsudao. Without further word, they left the table, maroon silks swaying in the wind of their fierce departure. The Dragon sank back onto his cushion with a low growl, and his two assistants whispered words of concern. Tsudao watched as Shiba

Yoma headed for the Phoenix tents. She placed her fan upon Ukira's shoulder.

"We can do nothing else." Mirumoto sounded defeated. "He calls our bluff. It is well within the Phoenix's right to claim war upon us. Our heimin invade their lands like a tsunami. We cannot stop the heimin from migrating. Certainly, some will throw themselves on our blades to save honor, but others . . . ? They will starve if they do not seek land and shelter. Our mountains no longer shelter our farmers. Or us." Mirumoto Ukira's eyes closed in fatigue, and his fingers pinched the bridge of his nose to ease the tension building there. "It is as if the Fortunes themselves turn away their faces." After a moment, the Dragon opened his eyes again. "I must apologize, General Tsudao-sama. My weakness shames my clan."

"On the contrary, Mirumoto-san," Tsudao said. "The care you show for your people proves your honor."

The Dragon nodded gratefully and stood. Bowing to Tsudao, he signaled for his assistants to come with him, and he walked silently from the open tent.

The general of the Imperial Legions rested her chin on her fist, staring bitterly at the valley beyond.

* * * * *

A few days later, the Imperial Legions watched as a Phoenix unit rode into their peaceful valley. Shiba Yoma, the Phoenix ambassador, gave Tsudao formal thanks for her hospitality before he rode out to meet his Clan's samurai. Further negotiations had been no more useful than the first meeting. Both sides were set upon their courses.

Tsudao looked down upon the marching legions, watching as they lifted Shiba banners in defiance. Dragon units, stationed just within their mountainous borders, raised aloft their own yellow and green flags. Both sides made camp just on the opposite edge of the border, waiting for the other to make the first move.

And still the refugees came like ants over the mountain, seeking shelter from the storm.

"A missive from the Emperor, my lady," Kekiesu handed the note to her mistress with utmost respect, bowing her head before the Emperor's seal. Tsudao took it gently, nodding to her father's mark before she opened the delicate rice paper.

Even as she skimmed the words, Tsudao knew what they said. The Emperor sent his greetings to the Firstborn Daughter and good wishes to all in her company. Winter was approaching, and the Imperial Legions were recalled to Otosan Uchi. Tsudao sighed. The time had come to withdraw.

"It will snow soon," Kekiesu said softly. "Winter will stop their fighting for some months. There will be another chance for peace when spring comes."

"I only wish we could have done more," Tsudao said. She folded the letter and placed it within her vest. "Though blood does not yet stain the field, it will, Kekiesu. One day soon . . . it will."

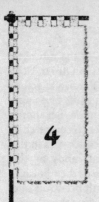

4   HER FATHER'S EYES

The high wall of Otosan Uchi poured like a river of stone against golden fields, and trees that had turned red and yellow with autumn stood half-empty of their leaves. Winter touched the ground with a kiss of frost where the sun had not yet turned his light, and the wind from the wide bay seemed colder than it ever had.

Ships flocked like white geese across the waters of the ocean, porting at Otosan Uchi's docks for the last short weeks of trade before the cold winter storms set in and the snows began. Even then, a few brave sailors would fight their way up and down the coast from the Mantis lands, ignoring the ice to the north and the hurricanes to the south in order to make just a few more koku during the lean season.

Inside the city, peasants ran merrily to and fro, readying the city for the Bon Festival, the final festival of autumn, the final day of the month of the Dog and the darkest night of the year. At the Bon Festival, the dead were given libations and asked to rise and give visions of the future to their descendants. In a few nights, the streets of Otosan Uchi would fill with representations of the Great Kami, and actors portraying ghosts and spirits would walk in white face paint through the excited crowds. As Tsudao rode her horse through the city's gates, she looked down at the eager children, already recounting the stories of their ancestors in the hopes that they would be given gifts and candy by the "spirits" to mark their dedication to the tales of their lineage.

The Bon Festival would be celebrated with fireworks and festivities, and at the end of the night, the river that flowed through Otosan Uchi would light up with thousands of floating paper lanterns. The lanterns, one of Tsudao's favorite traditions, were each marked with the name of someone who had crossed over to the land of the dead during the last year. It was a holiday filled with cheer and sorrow, both the reverence of death and the celebration of life. An appropriate time, thought Toturi Tsudao, to return home to her father and to her past.

The streets of the city were wide, some cobbled and some made of simple dirt. Streamers decorated the road, arching overhead from building to building as workers shouted beneath them. A man on a long ladder leaned against one of the houses, lifting a string of unlit lanterns into place across a wide crossroad. Tonight, the city would be lit with a thousand stars. One of the city guards, recognizing Tsudao and her handmaiden, snapped to attention with a loud *kiop* of respect. The princess nodded, accepting his reverence without drawing too much attention. Of course they knew her here. This was home.

The Forbidden City rose from the center of Otosan Uchi's gently curving streets, its four high walls shining with a faint glow even beneath the light of the morning sun. Within its gates, the nobility of the city practiced their political games, whispered secrets, and curried her father's favor. Small palaces, one for each of Rokugan's eight Great Clans, rose up above the stone walls, their roofs shining with painted tile—blue for the Crane, orange for the Lion, and violet for the Unicorn. Tsudao could see only those from this vantage. The others were hidden by the expanse of the city's inner walls. Within the gates stood the grand palace of the Hantei, now the home of the Imperial Family of the Toturi dynasty. It was an imposing, formidable building, tiled with golden eaves and shining green mosaics on the walls. The outer doors were carved in marble, still marked with a faint black stain where a great darkness had touched them during the war against Fu Leng. But that was long ago.

Tsudao and Kekiesu passed through the gates and into the Forbidden City with only cursory formality. The guard pretended to give a great deal of thought to his inspection of Tsudao's traveling papers and her badge of rank, but he knew her well. If she had tried, she could have called the Seppun guard by name.

"It's still lovely." Kekiesu smiled, her eyes shining as she took in the wide streets of the inner city. She reached to brush her fingers against the dark limb of a spreading cherry tree, now far out of season and barren of blossom, fruit, and leaf. "Even when winter claims the Emperor's City, it is still magnificent."

Tsudao's eyes never left the palace. "Otosan Uchi has stood for a thousand years. It will stand for a thousand more, and perhaps some other young Centipede will walk among its gardens and say the very same thing."

"Perhaps she already has, hundreds of years ago." Kekiesu laughed at the thought. "An eternity of stone, surrounding a city that fades and dies bit by bit as mortals pass away." After a moment, she continued:

Stone ages not
Will it remember our passing
Like a gentle crack?

Tsudao grumbled. She hated poetry games, but her mother had forced her to learn them so that she would appear cultured in the Imperial Court. She remained silent as they approached the palace, speaking only after they had given their horses to the stable hand and begun the walk up the palace stairs.

Memory is stone
Unyielding, unchanging, undying
But blind to every flaw.

Kekiesu laughed, covering her mouth with her hand. "Your Imperial Highness is getting better, but I still think you should not enter any competitions."

"Competitions—bah!" Tsudao growled good-naturedly. "Words are nothing more than blunted swords, and half as effective as a drunken drill sergeant. I'd rather seize the world than woo it."

The servants at the palace opened the huge oak doors, and they swung wide on silent hinges to allow Tsudao and Kekiesu to pass. Seppun servants formally greeted the two women. The Seppun were a noble family that served the Emperor and his family. Several handmaidens fell to their faces in the hallways as they passed. After showing the two women to Tsudao's chambers, they opened all the shutters. Tsudao felt a familiar unease as she placed her armor on its stand. A bath was next, followed by a massage and clean clothing, all efficiently handled by servants who had done the same jobs all of Tsudao's life. The palace was as smoothly running as the ocean against the shore, with servants coming and going in ceaseless waves of half-noticed motion.

"Your mother has not yet returned from her pilgrimage to the Shrine of the Fortune of Prosperity." The headwoman smoothed a black kimono in her hands, offering it to Tsudao with a polite bow. "She offers greetings to you and will return to give them herself in seven days."

"When may I see my father?" Tsudao asked. She pulled the watered silk kimono over her naked shoulders, tying it in front before allowing Kekiesu to wrap a golden belt around her waist. It was long, elegant, and moved lightly around her ankles as Tsudao sat in the chair by the gilded mirror.

"He knows that you have arrived, Highness," the stout Seppun said, kneeling to offer Tsudao a pair of ornate sandals. "He is waiting for you by the Stones."

The Stones—a place of solitude and reflection, essentially a garden within a garden. Although the magnificent gardens of Otosan Uchi were open for all visitors to visit and reflect upon the beauty of the world, the Stones were a private, walled enclave within the main gardens where only the Emperor and his family could pass. A single gardener, one who never left the circle of stones that marked the sacred territory, kept it. Once that gardener had passed through the stones, he remained there until he died, keeping the privacy and secrecy of the inner garden into his next life. For such service, he was rewarded with a single star in the heavens to mark his loyalty.

To the Emperor, the Stones were a place of ultimate solitude. That he called for Tsudao to meet him there implied that he wished to speak to her as family—a father to daughter and not emperor to princess. Tsudao nodded, and a faint smile touched her lips. It had been too long since she had heard her father's voice.

"I will go there immediately." She placed her feet within the sandals and allowed Kekiesu to twist her long black hair into a maiden's foxtail, brushing out the unruly strands with a comb made of the finest jade. Two pins were set against her scalp to hold it in place. Only the faintest makeup was applied to Tsudao's ruddy face, making it pale to better befit a lady of the Noble Court. Tsudao bore it all with dignity, feeling much like a painted portrait of herself.

At last, Kekiesu nodded. "You will do, I think," the handmaiden said good-naturedly.

"I look like a Scorpion."

"No, you don't. You have no mask."

Tsudao sighed, sticking her lip out as she stared into the reflective glass. "I wish I had a mask. I would rather have one than have this paint stinging my eyes."

Kekiesu wiped her hands as Tsudao rose to leave the room. "It will have to do. After all," she called as Tsudao entered the hallway, "it is only your father."

Only my father, Tsudao thought as she strode through Otosan Uchi, trying to force her marching pace into a courtlier mince. Only my father . . . the Emperor of Rokugan. She would always think of her father as a tall man, though she knew that some of her image was colored by her childhood. It had been almost a year since she had seen him, but no image of the present would erase her childhood hero—her father, the Emperor.

Emperor Toturi had always been a kind father, though a strict disciplinarian. The image of a rugged face, sharp-featured with dark and piercing eyes rose in Tsudao's memory. He had taught her a warrior's footwork as soon as she could walk and given Tsudao her first katana when she was three. Most samurai did not receive their katanas until they reached their gempukku, when they were prepared to become a full samurai. Tsudao was ready at three, and at three she had tried to defend her father from his enemies using only her wooden sword. He had asked her what she wished for rescuing him, and her answer had been as simple and honest as her nature. "A real sword with which to protect you, father," she'd said—and he had given it to her. She still carried the weapon by her side.

Every prideful childhood dream had been whispered in his ear, and she still remembered being carried by his strong arms when she was too tired to walk the long corridors to the Imperial Chambers at night.

There were courtiers who whispered that Emperor Toturi would tire of his daughter once his wife had borne him a son. They watched as Toturi spent long hours with Tsudao in the courtyard, teaching her *kenjutsu* and *iaijutsu* swordplay when most children were still learning the most basic *kanji* characters. She threw a tantrum when she discovered Empress Kaede had borne a boy-child, and still she remembered her father's words on that night.

"Tsudao-chan," Toturi's voice flickered in her memory like a distant candle flame. "Love is not something that can be counted or claimed. Love cannot be judged against itself. I will not love him as I love you, because he is not you. I will love him for himself, as I love you for who you are. You lose nothing. You gain a brother. A brother who will need you, Tsudao-chan, to protect him." Toturi's hand touched her cheek like a benediction. "You are my firstborn."

She remembered looking down at the peaceful face of her newborn brother for the first time and understanding what her father had meant. The baby reached to grip her finger in his hand, and she was surprised at the strength in the tiny little fist. "I will protect you," she promised, kissing his wrinkled forehead. "I will be your sword."

* * * * *

The private grounds of Otosan Uchi were shadowed, and the sun had gone behind the clouds. It was still some hours from the end of the day, but the tremendous shade trees that lined the paths of the Imperial Gardens cast shadows on the grassy earth. Tsudao waved away the servants who came to offer her music or poetry. Like peacocks, the artisans wandered the ground looking for crusts of attention from the nobility. They would get no such feast from her.

The paths to the Stones were long and cobbled with rounded stones that had been recently washed. Tsudao stepped carefully, wishing her sandals were more functional and less courtly. The white marble pillars of the Stones rose above the garden bushes, wrapped with twined ivy and still-flowering vine. They rose some nine feet from the ground in a wide circle, the space between them filled with bushes and ivy to prevent a passerby from seeing the splendor within. Each of the stones held the central image of a tree—cherry on one, oak on another, and still another with a willow carved in perfect relief on the pale marble. Around the trees were carved emblems of the Hantei dynasty and of the Fortunes of the Empire, a benediction of the past and the present.

A new block of marble had been placed to one side of the garden, widening the space within by some few feet. Although it had not been there before, the workmanship of the nearby vines and green bushes was so delicate that one would have thought it a long-standing companion to the others, but Tsudao knew better. On it was carved a sapling maple, its leaves widening as if frozen in the fullness of spring. Around it the artisans had carved the symbols of her father, the first Toturi dynasty.

"Tsudao-san?" The voice was aged and weary, but pleasant. She turned to look at the golden gate between the stones and smiled as Iuko, the old gardener, peered out. "Come inside, come inside! Your father is waiting. It has been too long since you looked at my handiwork, Eldest Daughter." The gray-haired gardener's gums flapped toothlessly, and his spotted hands bore the calluses of much work, but he moved with a spring in his ancient step.

She followed Iuko into the garden, smiling at the beautiful bushes that were scattered around the small enclave. They had been carefully pruned into remarkably lifelike birds, animals, and statues of the Kami, representative of many lifetimes of work and the sure hands of many men like Iuko. A small zen garden dominated the foreground, with three dark stones placed within the curving lines of raked white sand.

On the far side of the grass, at the edge of the sand, were two low cushions. One was empty. On the other knelt a man, staring into the patterns of the garden as if seeking enlightenment between the lines. He was garbed in simple browns and grays, but the silks were of fine cloth, and gold was stitched into his belt. Two swords, the weapons of a samurai, lay at the side of his cushion, their lacquered sheaths shining with immaculate care. A faint golden glow shimmered around him, marking him as a spirit and highlighting the aura of strength that his stature seemed to unconsciously project. The aura glowed like a small sun within his soul. He had come back from the dead to live once more among the Empire, and the purity of that land still remained with him.

Toturi.

Tsudao bowed low, waiting until the Emperor lowered his head in response to her homage. After he did, he gestured to the heavy cushion at his side, and Tsudao moved to rest beside him. They sat in silence, contemplating the faint shadows on the sand and the tall dark rocks that stood out against the whiteness around their base.

At last, Toturi spoke. "You are well, I see. The troubles to the north have not injured you?"

"No, father. Though the Dragon and the Phoenix refuse all offers of peace, they have not yet drawn sword on the issue. To put it in the more poetic words of my handmaiden, 'The winter snows will be white, but spring will bloom in blood.'"

Toturi sighed, nodding. "An adequate summary."

"And you?"

The Emperor's face became grave, and it was a moment before he spoke. "Your mother says I will live the lifetimes of seven Dragons, but she is wrong. I am old, Tsudao. Old and weary. I have seen many things in my lifetime—I watched as gods rose and fell, and I faced the Nameless Kami and tore down his darkness. This sword—my father's sword and the sword of his father—has seen enough of war to end an Empire."

Toturi picked up the katana in its brown scabbard that lay on the ground by his side. It was a magnificent weapon, its ancient blade allied with a *tsuba* and hilt of solid ivory, strengthened with steel. The hilt was wrapped in black silk shot with gold thread, and the form of the pommel was that of a ferocious storm-lion, mane and tail ruffled by an unseen wind. The creature roared from the tsuba guard, as well, circling the blade protectively as if keeping the entire world at bay.

"When you were a child, you asked me if you would carry this sword someday."

Tsudao smiled. "I remember."

"And do you also remember what I told you then, Tsudao-chan?"

The familiar pet name filled her with memories of warm summer days long ago. "You told me I would not wield the sword, but one day, if I proved my honor . . . the sword would wield me."

Toturi held the weapon in a steady hand, refusing to allow his body to shiver with age. Though he was far older than he appeared, he had never missed a day of *kenjutsu* practice. Even now, his *sensei* swore that Toturi could just as easily teach him as the other way around.

"It is true, you know, daughter," he murmured as if speaking to the blade. "We who are samurai, we live and we die by the blade. It is the one purity that binds us to this world and gives us our place. If we are lucky—" Toturi slid an inch of the fine steel from the scabbard, and the blade glimmered faintly in the light of the winter sun— "then we die by the sword, as well. My soul has been bought and sold with the wages of death, and armies have fought at my command. I have seen enough. More than enough." Toturi looked at his daughter as if seeing her for the first time. "It is time I began to put my affairs in order."

Tsudao felt her skin turn cold, and her heart sank. Her father . . . an old man? It could not be. Yet as she looked into his weary eyes, the fire there burned more dimly than she remembered. His hands, still strong and dexterous, had soft spots of brown upon their backs, and his face was creased with wrinkles that she had never noticed before. Yet Toturi had not yet proclaimed an heir to the throne. He could not be so certain of his own end. Although she was the firstborn, it was not certain that the Clans would accept a ruling Empress. Without Toturi's hand upon her shoulder, she was no more the heir than any of her brothers, and the Empire could dissolve into open warfare. The Steel Throne would be in jeopardy. Tsudao remembered the maple sapling, frozen in marble at the gate to the private garden. Without an acknowledged heir, the newborn dynasty would find only cold winter . . . and death.

Toturi lowered the ancient sword, placing it once more at his side, and continued. "The Empire has many guardians, and I know that I leave my tasks in good hands, but my wife and my children must be cared for. You are my legacy."

"I am your heir."

"No." The word was a slap. As Tsudao's face flushed with confusion, Toturi looked back at the gardens with sorrow. "No, Tsudao . . . that has not yet been decided. I have spoken with my councilors, and they tell me tales of your courage and leadership. You would make a good Empress. But I cannot offer you the throne . . . not yet. Your mother is heir until I make a formal decision."

Tsudao's head spun with a hundred possibilities. Did he wish for her to marry? To prove herself in open war with the Dragon and Phoenix? Was he concerned about her ability to guide the Empire? Had she somehow disappointed him? She opened her mouth to speak, but Toturi laid his hand upon hers, shocking her with the touch of his warm palm.

"I know that you have never sought the throne. You would not. You have too much honor, too much courage to be so filled with pride." Toturi's words lost the commanding tone of the Emperor and became simply her father's voice as Tsudao's eyes were brushed with tears. He held her hand quietly.

"I would not fail you," she said quietly.

"I know that, Tsudao. You, of all my children, have never disappointed me. In any way." Toturi's smile was gentle. "But before I look into the future, I must tie back the strands of my past."

"I do not understand."

"No. No, I do not expect that you will." Releasing her hand, Toturi reached for a small ivory *netsuke*—a small carving—that hung from his belt. "I am about to go on a journey, Tsudao-chan. When I return we will discuss the future of the Steel Throne, and you will have your answers. Until then, keep this." He opened her hand with his, placing the ivory statuette inside and folding Tsudao's palm around the carving. "It has been mine since I was a boy and has guided me well. Now, it is yours. One day, Tsudao, you will have my sword as well . . . and perhaps my throne." His voice was a soft rumble. "But not today."

"Where are you going? Winter is coming soon. It is not best that the Emperor travel in the snows of the harsh season."

"I am going south to the Scorpion Lands."

"Scorpion . . . ?" Tsudao lifted her head. "You will need an escort. I will go with you."

"No."

"Father. You enter into danger."

"I have Seppun guards, Otomo courtiers, the finest swordsmen, trained for my personal defense by the masters of the Crane." Toturi smiled, deepening the wrinkles at the corners of his dark brown eyes. "There is no danger. I will return before Winter Court." He patted her hand. "Take care of your mother, little sword. Again, it falls upon you to keep them all safe." Toturi let go of Tsudao's arm and reached to place the ancient katana within his belt before he stood. "No matter what you hear, no matter what rumors reach you, Tsudao, know this." The Emperor stood before her, the golden glow surrounding his features softening into a halo of sanctity that shone like the sun. "I will always love you, daughter."

The sunlit glow around Toturi deepened, and Tsudao's vision blurred. She saw a flicker of movement—a sword and a strange beast, rising up from the ground, encircled by flame. *Eight swords rise in the Shadowlands, led by a single master . . . darkness takes the Emperor . . .*

Toturi touched her cheek, and somewhere within his motion, Tsudao beheld the dark shadow of death. Tsudao shook away the vision, clinging to the sight of her father's eyes.

"Do not go, Father," she whispered, suddenly ten years old again and terribly afraid.

"I must." With that, Toturi left her, striding from the garden. The bells of Otosan Uchi were ringing, and the city raised its voices in shouts as the sun touched the horizon.

The Bon Festival, the celebration of the dead, had begun, and the city would soon be plunged into the longest night of the year. It would begin with fireworks and end with a river of lights that flowed out into an empty sea. The vision was no more than her own fears, playing against her mind. Toturi was the Emperor. He was revered and respected throughout the Empire. He would—he *must* return safely. Tsudao opened her hand and looked down at the small ivory *netsuke*. It was a perfect rendition of a storm lion, mane and tail curled like puffs of clouds and lightning flashing in its wide eyes—identical to the one carved on the hilt of the Toturi family katana. It crouched almost playfully in her hand, haunches raised and front legs spread wide, baring tiny, perfect claws.

Tsudao furrowed her brow, seeking answers in the fading shadows of the sand.

* * * * *

A soft giggle in the courtyard, and the black braids of a sorceress shivered in the cold wind. Iuchi Shahai leaned against the white marble of the garden, listening to the discussion within, completely unafraid that any guard would see through the shadow of her invisibility. She did not exist within their realm, and they could not find her.

"So you see, grandfather," Shahai whispered to the skull that hovered in the air at her shoulder. "Toturi wishes to stretch his old wings one last time. To make amends with his past—" her smile was soft, seductive and deadly—"a memory for old times' sake. And I know just where to whisper this that it will do the most harm"

Her laugh echoed through the portals of the shadowy half-realm as she vanished. Where she had stood, a dark shadow stained the white marble of the Stone.

5 | DEATH'S WHITE HAND

Akodo Kaneka had not been to Ryoko Owari for many years, but the City of Green Walls still seemed the same as the day he left. Its high hills and sloping valleys were the same, and shrouded secrets still clung like moss to its walls. He had served as a bodyguard for the Scorpion nobles within the city until the War of the Spirits. After that . . . well, life had its way of twisting even the simplest truths.

Kaneka was a tall man, nearly six feet in height, but thin and wiry with the muscle tone of a solid oak tree. His skin was weathered and brown beyond his thirty years, but his face was clear and unlined. Dark black eyes shone above his hawklike nose and his thin lips were pressed into a somber frown.

- His hair was tied back into a traditional samurai top-knot, more to keep it out of the way of his eyes than out of respect for tradition. When he was young, he had been a ronin—and he had even less regard for tradition these days. Running a rough hand over his unshaven face, he stared at Ryoko Owari with the piercing gaze of a trained killer. He would not go back.

Kaneka reached into his belt and drew out the Emperor's summons once more, creasing the paper roughly.

It is time for the things of the past to be given voice. Meet with me at Ryoko Owari on the seventeenth day of the Boar, and we shall honor your mother's memory.
— Toturi I, Master of the Steel Throne,
Emperor of Rokugan

Kaneka's face twisted, and he shoved the letter back into his belt.

Toturi knew nothing about honoring her memory. Had it not been Toturi's actions that forced her to her death? Her name had been Hatsuko—a beautiful woman, more beautiful than all the noble women of the Empire, but she was only a simple geisha in Otosan Uchi's high sector. Yet even from so small a position, she had captured the heart of the Champion of the Lion. Their affair had been the whisper of the Imperial Court until his dalliances with her caused the Lion Champion to be exiled and cast out of the courts of Rokugan as a ronin. He had been with her instead of on guard while the Emperor was attacked, and for his failure both of them had been punished.

Hatsuko had leaped from a waterfall's height into the dark rocks below, hurling herself away from a world that would not accept her love for this powerful man. Some said it was love, but Kaneka believed that his mother would not allow her presence to further stain the Lion Champion's honor. She had been used against him, drawn him away from the court when he was most needed . . . and to pay for that crime, she had offered her life.

There lay the greatest shame of all. Hatsuko had not been allowed to die.

The Water Dragon, a powerful creature older than all of mankind, rose up from the waters and swallowed her in its great jaws. It carried Hatsuko for days in gentle slumber, disgorging her at the steps of a monastery deep within Lion lands. The geisha never spoke again, preferring a life of silence to a word of shame, but her belly swelled with the Lion Champion's son.

Her son. Kaneka.

For years, he had been simply another ronin, living the life of a wandering swordsman. It was a hard, cruel existence, but it taught Kaneka more about swordsmanship and about the Empire than he could have ever learned as a samurai. Few could match him. None could defeat him.

When the Lion Clan learned of his existence, Kaneka was brought before his father. Yet Hatsuko's lover looked upon Kaneka with shock . . . and did not give honor to the mother of his child. There was nothing between them—not even love for the woman that stood between them both. Kaneka's father stared at him with empty eyes, and not a word passed his lips.

Kaneka left and never returned. He was offered a place within the Lion armies and eventually accepted—not out of duty or reverence to his blood, but because the Lion respected Kaneka for his own merit. They needed his sword, not his heritage. So he joined them and swore the oath that made him Akodo.

He had never spoken to his father again, not even to tell him that Hatsuko's ashes had been burned and spread across the river where the Dragon carried her from Otosan Uchi. Now the Emperor wished to give honor to Kaneka's mother? It was ludicrous, insulting, and far too small an offering to erase the suffering of their past. Hatsuko deserved more.

Kaneka urged his stout pony onward, away from the city of Ryoko Owari. It held too many bad memories for him, too many thoughts of poverty and compromise—and Kaneka liked neither. If Emperor Toturi wished to meet with Akodo

Kaneka, it would be done outside the City of Green Walls. It would be done on the plains, without the bustle and intrusion of the Scorpion surrounding them. It was better to remember Hatsuko the woman and the mother, not Hatsuko the geisha who had traded her honor for the empty promises of love.

The hills curved away from the city, jolting upward sharply then descending into sharp gulleys and valleys. The Scorpion lands were much like their masters, holding hidden dangers and tricky footing. Kaneka's surefooted pony moved slowly through the territory, and he allowed it to have its head. If it bolted, it would likely break a leg. Even ponies knew better than that. They were close to the Shinomen Forest. Too close. Kaneka felt a shiver pass through his spine as he looked over the hills to the south and saw the green shadow of an ancient forest. That place was filled with demons and curses, magic gone awry and ancient creatures that knew nothing of honor or bushido. Most samurai avoided it like the plague. It was an evil forest, no matter what the legends whispered—evil and filled with forbidden dreams.

It was appropriate, then, that Ryoko Owari was placed so near to the forest—the City of Green Walls was known for destroying dreams and for shattering hopes. Perhaps the deep whispers of the Shinomen affected even those who lived within the city's walls, luring them to their doom upon Scorpion knives. It was gentler that way, Kaneka thought, than to pass within the forest's green and leafy gates.

So why was he here? For the Emperor? For his mother? Kaneka sighed and growled a faint curse. There was no reason. He would tell the Emperor that there would be no peace between them. Not today. Not ever.

A shrill scream echoed along the valley walls, and the rocky outcroppings of the rough terrain reverberated with the sound of battle. Akodo Kaneka sat straight in his saddle, attempting to pinpoint the direction of the attack. When he found it, he urged his pony forward, making for the top of a nearby outcropping.

Beyond the crest, the road from the north led down toward the Shinomen Forest then curved west toward the City of Green Walls. The lowest curve of the path hung just a stone's throw from the Shinomen itself, and there, at the edge of the shadowy forest, Kaneka saw a vision of pure nightmare.

The caravan of the Emperor was surrounded by corpses, and soldiers fought desperately to drive back a terrible enemy—a beast that defied imagination. A small army of twisted creatures fought beside it, but it was the great beast itself that captured Kaneka's attention. It stood three times taller than most men, but its body was sheathed in scarlet scales that mocked the armor of a true samurai. Four red eyes glared from behind the helm that was its armored skull, and it grinned with the teeth of an iron shark. In one hand, the oni—for that was the name for such a monstrous demon—held aloft the broken pieces of one of the Emperor's guardsmen, blood pouring down its wrist. One of the other hands held aloft a curved sword that trickled dark steam in its passage. The oni laughed, the earth beneath its clawed feet shook, and a flaying whip held in another strong hand lashed the ground and tore apart the rocks. A thin cut cracked the armor down the side of the creature's inhuman face, seeping acid that pitted the ground.

The golden palanquin of the Imperial dynasty had been tossed aside like a child's toy and the peasant carriers scattered and shredded into bloody pulp by the minions of the beast. More than thirty guards lay about the ground, swords broken and bodies crushed or torn by the oni's attack. Courtiers, like withered flowers, lay in pools of spreading blood, their fans still held tightly in their cold hands. Nothing of their beauty remained to withstand the fury of the assault. The ground was muddied with the remains of a terrible battle, but now only a few stood to hold back the demon's wrath. Its companions tore among the dead, shredding limbs and bathing in the blood of the conquered, or screaming insults and roaring defiance at the last of the Emperor's men to stand against them—a small, stalwart group that remained defiant against the oni's attack.

Three guardsmen stood between the oni and the Emperor, holding their swords with the cold grip of those who knew they were about to die. The beast swayed, trying to find advantage, but the guards shifted not an inch. Although they were still several hundred feet away from Kaneka, the guards' stance told him that two of them were wounded.

The Emperor stood behind his men, shouting fearlessly at the enemy. His sword was stained with black blood. Obviously, it had been his blow that wounded the beast. He seemed unafraid, calm and in control, despite the danger surrounding him. His sheer will held the guardsmen at his side, and a golden glow radiated out from Toturi's shoulders like the dying light of a setting sun. Even with his courage to hold the line, the Emperor would not last long once the beast decided to strike.

Kaneka shouted a battle cry, thrusting his heels mercilessly into his pony's sides. Better to die at the side of the Emperor than to live and watch the destruction of an Empire. His mount reared, then raced down the long hillside, its eyes wide and panicked at the smell of so much blood.

Before Kaneka could arrive, the great oni struck. Toturi and his guards tightened their formation, trying to hold the line against the terrible beast, but its claws tore into the leg of one of the Seppun guards, shattering bone and tearing muscle from flesh. The sword curved down, slicing through the bone of the man's shoulder and almost removing the samurai's left arm. The man did not scream but plunged his blade into the demon's shoulder, twisting the katana between the armor plates until it broke inside the demon's flesh. The creature screamed, and the sound was like the roar of a thousand betrayed souls. Another claw shot forth, and the offending guardsman's head was no longer attached to his mutilated body.

The second guard, seizing his opportunity, thrust his spear at the creature's blood-red eyes. As he moved, the oni's flail lashed out and tore apart his face, clawing the skin with thousands of small hooks. From Kaneka's distance, it looked as if the man's face had simply exploded into shards of bone and fragments of muscle. Still swinging blindly, the Seppun launched another attack at his opponent, but it was of no use. Turning its attention from the first man, the oni simply swung its dark blade at the Seppun guard, severing the torso completely. The guard's body fell to the ground in pieces, and the smaller oni screamed and roared in appreciation of their Master's prowess.

The oni laughed then, a sick burbling in the back of its throat, as it faced Toturi and the final soldier at his side. Kaneka could do nothing but watch, his panicked steed steadily closing the distance. The two men nodded in acceptance of their destiny, then charged the beast as one.

Toturi's strike was first, his elegant silver sword flashing in the sunlight. It speared one of the oni's eyes, causing the beast to rear back and howl as the guardsman's sword cut into its stomach. The cut was true, but the creature's armored scarlet plates rang like steel, and the guardsman's sword ricocheted harmlessly away from the beast's flesh.

With a heavy swipe of its clawed fist, the oni drove Emperor Toturi to the ground. It raised its other arm to spear him on the black blade, but with a scream, the last guardsman leaped in front of the blow. The dead man's body was pinned to the ground as Toturi rolled aside. The oni screamed in frustration.

Kaneka's horse fell to the ground, and he heard the creature's leg snap with the force of its fall. He leaped from the saddle, rolling against the ground. The pony screamed in terror and pain. Kaneka rolled to his feet only a few dozen yards from the Emperor and drew his sword in a single swift motion, but it was already too late.

The oni stood over the broken guardsmen and grinned

with shining iron teeth. Toturi blocked the creature's claws with cunning blows as he backed slowly away. The Emperor's face showed no fear, only remorse and courage as he confronted the terrible demon alone. Strike after strike rained down upon him, four savage arms against the Emperor's single blade, but still Toturi stood stalwart against his foe.

The oni's lashing flail cut Toturi's feet from beneath him, and the Emperor fell. He rolled swiftly to avoid the powerful fist that caved in the ground where he had been standing.

Kaneka's steps became leaden as he charged, and he felt as if the weight of ages fell upon his shoulders. The smaller oni scattered before him, and he cut through them as if they were paper. Fearful of his fury and taken by surprise at Kaneka's power and savage intent, they scuttled away from his flashing blade, but they were many, and his progress was slow. Kaneka saw Toturi stand once more, turning to block another vicious lash of the massive beast's barbed flail, and then the oni's claws struck through an opening that the Emperor could not guard. The oni's sword rose high above its head, the blade drinking in the sunlight and casting shadows ten times its length upon the ground. The oni's free hand drove steel talons into Toturi's flesh.

This time, the Emperor had no defense. The sharp claws of the beast's tremendous fist cut through bone, cracking rib and tearing muscle, and blood sprayed in an arc across the ground. Still, Toturi refused to fall, cutting once more at the beast's head and scoring a cruel wound that opened up still more of the creature's skull to the sunlight. Again, the beast screamed, but it did not let go.

With a savage, victorious grin, the oni closed its fist around Toturi's ribcage, crushing the life out of the Emperor of Rokugan. Toturi drew a last shuddering breath—just enough to spit upon the face of the massive beast. The demon roared, swinging its massive sword, and the head of the Emperor fell to the ground at the creature's feet. Toturi's body slumped to the ground. Slowly, the golden glow around the Emperor's shoulders dimmed and died, vanishing into twilight.

Kaneka screamed in fury, and the oni turned toward him. Its torn face was lit by a savage grin as it opened its hands wide and raised its weapons, the steel talons spreading in anticipation of another battle.

Then the massive oni roared in pain. Rearing up to its full height, the beast seemed to fight against some unknown leash, stepping back on shaking feet. Slowly, it stepped into the dark shadow of the Shinomen Forest, and the mists of the grove beyond gathered as if in expectation. The others fled, and Kaneka heard the clarion call of trumpets—battle horns. He looked beyond the dark mass of his enemies and saw a Scorpion legion to the north, charging toward them on night-black steeds. Too late. They had come too late.

Kaneka ignored the smaller oni, turning toward the creature that had fought Toturi.

"Fight me!" roared Kaneka as he swung at the creature's leg. His katana connected and black fluid sprayed across his kimono, searing his flesh where it touched him. The beast did not fight back but roared once more in resigned anger. It took another step backward, and the darkness beneath the overhanging trees of the Shinomen enveloped the creature fully. Before Kaneka's very eyes, the beast's form dissipated into the mist, swirling into the fog that rose within the depths of the ancient forest. The oni roared in anguish and regret, snapping its wide jaw once more toward Kaneka before the mystic leash pulled again, jerking the demon-beast upright as the mist closed about its body.

Kaneka drew back to strike for the oni's heart, but the beast was gone.

* * * * *

The Scorpion troops attacked, their shining blades cutting through the lesser oni as their trumpets sounded again. Yet amid the battle, Kaneka felt incredibly alone. He stood on the fields outside the Scorpion city, staring down at the Emperor's corpse. Akodo Kaneka sheathed his sword, wiping it on his hakima pants instinctively before pressing it into the enameled scabbard. He fell to his knees beside the Emperor's crumpled form, unwilling to accept the truth that lay before him on the bloodstained earth.

"Emperor Toturi-sama," Kaneka gasped. "Toturi-sama?" Kaneka's voice was hoarse with barely restrained emotion, and tears threatened to fall upon his cheeks for the first time since childhood.

The Emperor's body was cold and gray. His blood spilled upon the rocks, as red as a summer sunset over the bay of Otosan Uchi. Beside him lay a magnificent sword, a snarling storm-lion curled about the hilt, still pure despite the touch of the demon's blood. It was not the Emperor's own sword but one he had taken from his guardsmen. Nevertheless, the ancient blade shimmered with dimming fire in Toturi's hand. The weapon clung to him like an old friend that would not leave his side. Its ancient blade glimmered in the sunlight like pure water—or the gentle shimmer of a maiden's tears.

Nothing remained of the man Toturi had once been, save the flesh that had held him. Toturi I had crossed into the Land of the Dead for the final time.

"Father . . ." Kaneka whispered, hiding his tears from the wind, "forgive me."

6   THE STEEL THRONE

It was the end of the month of the Boar, and snow fell softly upon the northern plains of Rokugan. Soft white frost glittered on the cobblestone streets of Otosan Uchi, but the low, thick clouds had not yet released their bounty upon the city. The Phoenix and Dragon were snowed within their mountain passes. To the south, even the stalwart Crab complained of the oncoming cold.

The Winter Court assembled, the courtiers of every clan moved within the Imperial Palace, but the gates had not yet closed for the season. The Emperor had not yet returned. Some whispered that he had deliberately gone to Ryoko Owari to spend a quiet winter among the Scorpion Clan, and others murmured of secret loves in the Crane lands. Both were equally ludicrous.

Toturi Tsudao stood in the burnished hallway of the Imperial Chambers, listening to her mother prepare for the day's court. She smiled, looking out the window into the gray sky. Empress Kaede softly hummed the ancient chords of a lullaby, and Tsudao remembered being put to sleep by the sound of her mother's voice.

Kaede, unlike her husband, hardly seemed to have aged. Many years had passed since their wedding, but still her face was unlined, her eyes clear, and her hair as black as the sand of the Mantis Islands. Tsudao looked at her with a quiet smile, wondering if her mother's youth was a sign of her happiness or if it was some gift of her station as the Hand of the Dragon. Kaede was more than the Emperor's wife. She was the Oracle of the Void, a powerful shugenja and the servant of the Void Dragon, that mysterious and enigmatic being that lived within the stars. Tsudao did not remember a time when her mother seemed sorrowful or ill content, although her responsibilities were almost as great as those of her husband.

"The comb, please, Tsudao-chan," Kaede's voice held strange echoes of night and the warmth of summer breezes. Tsudao reached for a golden comb that lay beside her mother's kimono and handed it to her. Toturi had given it to her before he left for the southern lands, promising to return before the first winter snow touched Otosan Uchi's palace walls.

Where was her father? He should have returned. It had been more than a month since he left—plenty of time to make the journey. Tsudao's brow wrinkled, and she reached to the hilt of the sword at her side. The small ivory amulet that her father had given her swung from her scabbard, held aloft by a golden cord. She could feel the snarl of the carved lion as it growled in her palm, and Tsudao ran her hand over its elaborately curled mane.

"Do not fear for your father." Kaede smiled, knowing her daughter's thought. "He has the Fortunes themselves with him." The Empress twisted her long, thick hair into a braid and allowed her handmaiden to coil the braid around her head. "Go, Tsudao. I have no need of you. Court will begin soon, and it is better that you arrive before I make my entry.

Your brothers will be there soon, and you will be missed."

"Yes, mother," Tsudao bowed very low. Her mother knew that she hated court. There was only one reason to send Tsudao ahead—to greet an old companion who would be attending the court this year.

Doji Tanitsu.

Tsudao swept her kimono into the hallway, hating the thick coil of dark silk that clung to her knees. It was difficult to walk in such garments, but court demanded no less. At least she was allowed to keep her swords by her side, tucked carefully into the golden belt—a gift from the Centipede Clan. She would not have left her room without the swords, nor would she have been expected to. She was a samurai and general of the Imperial Legions, no matter what other duties she was forced to entertain at Winter's Court.

The hallways of Otosan Uchi were wide and beautiful, the dark wood contrasting with white rice-paper walls and delicate black calligraphy hung from colored frames. Small tables holding barren flower arrangements, their dark branches and soft cattails marking the gifts of winter, marked the corners of major intersections within the palace. Tsudao ignored them. Unless the servants began to hang swords and axes on the walls, she wasn't likely to give much thought to the decoration.

"Her Imperial Highness, Daughter of the Sun, Sword of the Empire, and General of the Imperial Legions—"

Just her luck, to have been noticed by the heralds as she made her way toward the room where the court gathered. Sighing, Tsudao gave up her hopes of a quiet entrance.

"Toturi Tsudao-sama!" The herald stepped back from the door, his fat face beaming as he swept his arm aside to allow her entrance. She stepped into the hall and was unable to find her brothers' faces among the crowd. She was the first of the Imperial family to arrive.

The courtiers bowed as Tsudao stepped into the chamber. Kimonos ranging from the ice blue of the Crane to the dark scarlet of the Scorpion wavered like flowers in some great wind, and the rustling of fans marked whispers too low for Tsudao to catch. The Imperial throne room was wide, capable of holding hundreds of courtiers. Cushions were spread out in small clusters, and there were even a few Unicorn chairs for the comfort of that barbaric clan. A high dais commanded the view as Tsudao entered, and she bowed to honor tradition as she passed before the tall Steel Throne.

Oh, but the wolves were out tonight. In force. Three Scorpion tried to catch Tsudao's eye as she strode through the crowd to the courtiers in blue. A Crab tried—unsuccessfully—to get her attention by clearing his throat loudly, but she ignored them all. This wasn't her battlefield—best not to play on their terms.

She saw Tanitsu, the same irrepressible grin marking his features. He was taller, his hair still dark, and his eyes laughing. Instead of the traditional ice blue of his family, he wore gray and red, with a black belt that held his twin swords by his side.

"Have you married a Scorpion, Tanitsu-san?" Tsudao teased good-naturedly as he bowed. "You look like a Bayushi dressed you."

Tanitsu chuckled, spreading his arms so Tsudao could see the careful painting that covered the sleeves of his fine garment. "No. But my sister has. She insisted that I display her art at Winter Court in the hopes of getting the artisans to favor to her husband."

"Who is her husband?" Tsudao whispered loudly, winking her eye. The nearby Cranes giggled behind their fans at the imperial princess's frankness. Tanitsu held up one sleeve and pointed behind it, indicating a tall, thin Scorpion courtier. The man looked like a reed, sticking up a head above his fellows, and half as thin. Magnificent paintings covered his kimono, but he was so thin that the kimono hardly had any room to show the talent of the artist.

Tsudao whistled softly, understanding his point. Tanitsu grinned again and shrugged.

"Who is he?" she asked. It felt as if they had never been apart. Tanitsu's smile, his laugh, and his open friendship had always put Tsudao at ease. They had partnered together often during their training at the Lion dojo and still enjoyed sparring outside the ring of swords.

"Bayushi Kuisi. His brother, Bayushi Paneki, is a close friend of mine."

"High praise."

"I'm surprised you think so, given the way *you* abandoned me." His eyes sparkled, and his tone was teasing.

Tsudao rolled her eyes, remembering the pattern of their conversations as if it had been just yesterday. "If you call a promotion and advancement within the political stations of your clan 'abandonment,' then perhaps I should speak to the Crane Champion about how he treats his underlings."

"I am certain the Crane Champion would be fascinated to hear such a perspective," a quiet voice behind them said with a laugh. "Particularly as his younger brother is still unwed."

The courtiers quietly applauded with their fans, smiling at the newcomer to the conversation.

Tsudao turned to see her brother, the second eldest of Toturi and Kaede's three children. Sezaru was far paler than his siblings. His skin was the color of rice paper, and white hair—natural, not dyed in the fashion of the Crane—flowed down one shoulder, caught up in a braid that encircled his neck like a serpent. It was marked to either side by long black strands at each temple, a sign of his wisdom and a mark of great spirituality. His eyes were a fragile blue, and he had grown a small, sharp goatee to help hide his perpetually sarcastic smile. Instead of a kimono, he wore the raiment of a sanctified priest of the Kami—a spellcaster and servant of the divine. Sezaru held one thin finger to his lips as Tsudao opened her mouth to greet him.

"Ssh, sister." He laughed softly. "I am not here." He indicated the Imperial Herald at the door, and Tsudao realized belatedly that there had been no announcement of her brother's entry.

"Not here, Sezaru-sama?" Doji Tanitsu chuckled. "As you and other priests of the Kami have often said, none of us are where we believe ourselves to be."

The imperial prince smiled at the Crane's recitation of the sacred Tao, nodding.

"Sezaru and I," said Tanitsu, "have a long history of being nowhere together."

"My honorable and revered brother Sezaru-san," Tsudao replied soberly, looking at her brother's priestly vestments, "is very good at such things."

"Sister, may I introduce Bayushi Paneki-san?" Sezaru said, his voice still no louder than a soft whisper, yet easily heard above the murmurings of even such a large room.

"I have heard your name, Paneki-san," Tsudao said formally, bowing slightly in return to the Scorpion courtier's low obeisance.

"May I have the honor of a word with you, Toturi-sama?" The Bayushi was a pleasant-looking man, his formal golden mask hanging gently over even features. His lips were smiling, and his deep brown eyes seemed to hold secrets.

Tsudao felt her hand reach for the hilt of her sword, but she stopped the instinctive gesture before it became obvious. Glancing at her brother and friend, she bowed slightly to the Scorpion courtier.

"Of course."

They walked slowly across the great hall, and Tsudao could tell that the Scorpion was very skillful at avoiding anyone who would steal Tsudao's attention from his words. Although she disliked being manipulated, the Scorpion's pleasant voice and intriguing manner made Tsudao curious.

"There is news that you must hear, Tsudao-sama. My informants in Ryoko Owari brought it to me this morning. I have told your brother, but there is no time to be spared. This news must be taken to your mother at once. And you, as the eldest child, must be prepared for—"

Before he could continue, the Imperial Herald raised his voice above the crowd and cried, "All hail and honor give to Her Imperial Majesty Toturi Kaede, Oracle of the Void, Keeper of the Truth, and Mistress of Rokugan!"

Again, everyone in the hall bowed as one, and Tsudao started forward to greet her mother. She was shocked when the Scorpion gripped her elbow, preventing the movement.

"You must trust me," he hissed into her ear. "There is no time to spare. Kill me later, if you must, but for the sake of the Sun himself, you must *listen*."

Tsudao froze, her hand on her sword hilt. Something in Paneki's voice chilled her to the bone. She froze in place.

He continued to speak as Kaede crossed the floor toward the Steel Throne, her orange and gold kimono flowing out behind her as four Seppun guardsmen escorted her to the dais. Tsudao watched her mother walk slowly and gracefully through the parting throng, all the while listening intently to the Scorpion who had dared to touch her.

"Your father's palanquin was attacked. There was an oni— a demon of the Shadowlands, sent by an enemy we do not yet know." Tsudao's face drained of color, but she managed to keep even the faintest emotion from coloring her features. Paneki continued, "The oni destroyed his retainers, cut through his guardsmen . . ." The Scorpion's voice fell to the faintest of whispers, and his hand tightened about her shoulder. "Your father . . . is dead."

As Kaede turned to greet the audience of the Winter Court, she raised her hand for silence. Standing before the Steel Throne, her mother seemed small and fragile, and Tsudao felt her eyes burn with unshed tears. Before Kaede could speak, the Imperial Herald choked back a shout, and the crowd at the entrance to the great hall scattered back from the opening in ungraceful haste. The Seppun turned, shocked at such an interruption to the Empress's words, and saw a single man standing in the doorway.

To either side, a Lion samurai knelt in obeisance, and the

man in the center bowed slowly and reverently. His clothing was simple, and both his gi shirt and hakama pants were clean, but torn. The well-cared-for swords of a samurai hung from his belt.

"Your Imperial Majesty," he said in the gravest tones, "I regret to interrupt the festivities in such a way, but I bear terrible news."

Kaede looked at the samurai as if recognizing his sharp features, and her voice was no more than a low whisper as she responded, "Speak."

"My name is Akodo Kaneka," the Lion said as he straightened to address the Steel Throne and the tiny woman who stood beside it. "I have just returned from the city of Ryoko Owari. Your husband—" His voice faltered but gained again as he controlled himself. "The Emperor is dead."

The court stood in silent shock, their faces registering the words. One of the Phoenix fell to the ground in a dead faint. She was quickly lifted by her companions and carried from the scene. It was considered shameful to show emotion in public, but to show remorse and shock over the death of an Emperor would be seen as the highest virtue. Tsudao frowned.

"Tell us . . . how he died." Kaede said evenly, resting her hand on the arm of her husband's throne.

"He was attacked by a demon. An oni." Kaneka raised his chin defiantly, as if daring anyone in the room to challenge his next words. "He fought bravely, was sorely wounded, and he died with honor."

A rustle spread through the room, the parting fans of the courtiers. Tsudao heard Paneki whisper in her ear, "Princess . . . you must not move. I was not swift enough to prevent this, but I can stop it from going further or causing more bloodshed. Whatever happens now, you must be still and accept. Now is not the time." His voice was bitter, and his head lowered in sober contemplation of the court around them.

The words held no meaning for Tsudao in the wake of the pain she felt. She saw Sezaru lower his eyes, still watching the courtroom while others turned their heads toward the Steel Throne. He stared at Tsudao with a strange curiosity in his eyes, a curiosity that grew when the Empress spoke once more.

"Akodo Kaneka, son of Akodo Toturi," said the Empress, and another chill spread through the assembly at this revelation, "we are given great sorrow by your words. If the Emperor is dead, then the Empire bleeds with his loss." Kaede looked once toward Tsudao, then stepped before the throne. "We believe your tale, for no samurai could dare come before this throne and stain his honor with such a lie."

Kaede's voice betrayed a great sadness, a terrible emptiness that Tsudao feared would never leave her mother's eyes.

"My husband . . . left no formal heir. Until a ruler can be determined from among Toturi-sama's children—" Tsudao was not alone in noting the absence of the word *legitimate*— "then I adopt his throne for the good of the Empire. May the Kami shine their mercy upon us all."

Tsudao started forward, her face flushing with anger. She was the firstborn. She was Toturi's heir, his eldest child by the Empress. To be denied her right to stand before the throne was an insult to her honor.

Again, Paneki's hand on her elbow held her back, and she felt his breath warm against her neck. "If you step forward and challenge for the throne as rightful eldest, then the Lion can challenge as well. He is the first son of Toturi. The court knows it, and the Empress has said as much without actually offering him legitimacy. What she has done, she has done to stop a civil war. Would you step forward now and begin one?"

Tsudao's hand shook in anger, her eyes narrowing and her jaw tightening with the Scorpion's words. Yet, with a warrior's control, she forced herself to study the situation as if it were tactics on a battlefield. The Scorpion was right. With a single deft maneuver, Kaede had prevented the brash Lion from claiming his "birthright" and challenging the throne, but in doing so, she had also blocked Tsudao's rightful petition. A necessary move to prevent civil war.

"Enough," Tsudao hissed, drawing her elbow from the Scorpion's touch. "I see your point, Bayushi, but this decision cannot stop the Fortune's will—or that of my father, wherever his soul rests."

"No, my lady," Paneki whispered again as the audience of the vast court chamber bowed slowly and formally to the Empress seated upon her throne. "It cannot. But for now—" he lowered his head and joined in the reverence as it swept through the chamber— "it can stop the destruction of the Empire."

Tsudao watched as the Champions of the Seven Clans lowered to join the homage, one by one as the wave swept slowly through the crowd. At last, there was no one left standing save herself, Sezaru, and the Lion at the door. Sezaru narrowed his eyes in contemplation for a flickering moment before lowering his torso slightly toward the Steel Throne, but Tsudao's eyes locked with those of Akodo Kaneka. Above the backs of the gathered courtiers of Rokugan, the cruel-eyed Lion and the Princess fought a silent battle of wills that ended in both bowing toward the other, but it was not the humble bow of a courtier, symbol of homage to the Steel Throne.

It was watchful bow of opponents, preparing for a duel.

7　BLACK ICE AND DARK WINDS

Shahai's voice ebbed and flowed like the river she walked beside, echoing lightly from the waves that splashed toward the sea. Her long, black hair swayed in braids and loose strands around her lithe form, the thin kimono pressed against her body by the cold wind that heralded a new-fallen snow. Her feet, bare and white, pressed against the carpet of ice that covered the ground, and she smiled an angel's smile.

She was the most powerful sorceress in the Empire, made so by the fury and darkness of blood-magic. Where others would fear walking so close to the Emperor's own city, Shahai did not care. They could not harm her, and their shugenja were weak and useless. She had walked the tops of the Dragon Mountains while they erupted. The spells that guarded Ototsan Uchi meant nothing to her.

Otosan Uchi was dark with mourning, its gates covered in black crepe and lanterns burning low in every house.

Such a beautiful sight . . . a city of death. Such a waste that it would pass.

"I had so hoped for a duel," she said softly, her lower lip curling in a pout.

The skull that hovered at her shoulder cackled, floating away as the wind lifted it high. "Tsudao and her brother?"

"Or her mother . . . or any of them, really." She sighed. "Little troubles, too easily overcome. We must think greater than this, Grandfather. Greater than all of them. The Empire's foundation is made of stone . . . but that stone is built on sand."

"Enough water," cackled the ghost, "and the sand will wash away!"

Shahai smiled, brushing the icy water with one slim foot. "The wave is not yet ready. The Dark Oracles are not prepared." She sighed again. "You cannot hurry the elements. I wish you could. They are so ponderous, so long-winded. That's why I could never be a spirit. I have too much to do and so little time."

Her laughter swelled again, and a touch of scarlet drifted down the river as she lifted her foot from its current. Her grandfather knew what her answer would be before she said it, yet he always asked. He knew why she had turned her back on the Unicorn clan and sought the power of blood. Even her house, with its horses and swift winds were far too slow for her. Power was everything.

"You were always meant for better things, granddaughter," the skull crooned.

"Yes," said Shahai. "I was."

She walked farther down the river, away from the Emperor's city. Ahead of her, the ocean crashed against the shore, tearing its fingers on the sharp cliffs and rocks.

"I have readied the world for darkness, maneuvered the Emperor into a position where he could be taken advantage of, and allowed others to claim credit for his death. A pity that we had to give Toturi up. Imperial blood could have been such an advantage to our cause."

"Still time. There is always time!"

"Yes. I suppose there is." She looked up at the cliffside, where a small fire burned. "Ah, look," she whispered. "They are ready."

Shahai left the icy river behind, walking up a thin and shadowed path into the cliffs to the north of the imperial city. The ground was dark with stone and rich soil that clung to her bare feet. The cold did not bother her. No pain could reach the Queen of the Bloodspeakers. She reveled in the caress of the icy earth, the touch of the grave beneath her step. From this height, she could see out over the Bay of Otosan Uchi, where a winter's storm blew snow and frost upon an uncaring sea. The wind tore through her braids with fingers of ice, turning her hair into a dark cloak around her slight form. When Shahai reached the top of the cliff, four men dressed in black robes lowered their heads to the ground, kneeling before her as a servant to an Empress.

The fire burned with a strange reddish flame, and an altar of mahogany shone in the light it cast. A woman—semiconscious, dressed only in thin silk robes, her hair unbound and loose, her hands tied behind her back—lay on the ground before the altar.

"Your will is our will," the sorcerers murmured in greeting.

Shahai watched as they bowed before her, their faces pressed to the cold earth. "Yes," Shahai murmured as she walked among them. "Yes, it is." She ran her fingers into one man's hair in a strange caress, twisting it cruelly as she stepped away. He did not move or flinch, and she was pleased.

Shahai walked with slow steps around the ritual area, feeling power in the presence of the woman's fear. She was young, her eyes red from crying, and the ropes on her wrists had chewed the flesh, leaving raw red marks. Tears stained her porcelain face, and dirt smudged her white robes as she writhed against the cold ground. The robe was marked with the symbol of the Asako—a peaceful, scholarly Phoenix family with close ties to the imperial Throne. The girl's station drew no pity from the dark sorceress who glided toward her.

"All is ready?" Shahai asked as her fingers brushed a black-handled knife on the low table.

"We wait only for your command."

Shahai's face was cold but not joyless. A light sparked in her eyes like stars in the black heavens, and she drew the thin-bladed knife from the table with delicate slowness. Gently, as if kissing a lover, Shahai drew her tongue along the edge of the blade to test the sharpness. A single drop of blood traced her lips, staining them as red as those of a geisha. Shahai smiled.

"We are the Bloodspeakers," she said, and the men surrounding the altar rose to encircle her. They spread their arms, thick sleeves of dark silk fluttering in folds against the sea breeze as they began to chant softly. Shahai adored the smell of fear that drifted from the now-silent girl at her feet. "Before you die, little Asako, you must bear our message into Jigoku, that Toturi will know his enemy lives on even after his death: We are the followers of Iuchiban the Black. Through sorcery, he seized the Throne of Rokugan in his bloody fist but was denied by the power of the Kami. He has not been forgotten. We hear his blood speak to us, through us, and we listen. Those who hold the Empire in their grasp are so concerned with their own whispers and ideals that they no longer hear the call of blood within their veins, the beating of their nearly dead hearts. Turn your back on emotion, little Asako, turn your face away from the call of darkness and the passion of the body, but we will not.

"Before the Kami came, before the Great Clans rose and threw the people of the land into slavery, we stood on the earth that was Rokugan, and we have sworn to destroy those who have turned our world into a place of waste, whispers, and frozen flesh." Shahai touched the dagger to the woman's arm, drawing forth a thin line of blood while the Asako keened in pain. "We will never forget. The most powerful magic does not come from the elements. It comes from pain."

Shahai's fingers spread above the wound, and black arcs of lightning flowed from her palm down into the woman's bleeding arm. The skin around the wound burst into dark flame, and the howls of demons screamed within the woman's sobs. Something ancient and old moved in the shadows of the blood that stained the ground, and Shahai's eyes glowed with power and glee.

"I call upon Iuchiban the Old, thrice chained and twice freed. Hear me!"

Lightning roared out at sea, and the frozen storm that had drawn closer seemed to gather over the ocean like a predator. Another cut, this time upon the woman's cheek, and before the blood swelled Shahai saw the icy whiteness of bone.

"I call upon blood, upon the dark *maho* sorcery of our ancestors in the time before time began. To the power of pain and agony that has been forgotten but not destroyed."

The blood turned black and dark upon the Asako's face, staining the shoulders of her white robe as she kicked and screamed in the bonds.

"Hear me!" Shahai screamed.

The storm howled, its winds racing toward the high cliff's edge, bringing with them the stench of the far south. In the ice and snow, black flakes fell upon the frozen ground. Where they touched, the earth seemed to wither and grow thick, and the four cultists shivered. Shahai felt the Taint upon the wind, a dark force that corrupted flesh and withered the soul. It was the power of the Shadowlands to touch and taint those who worshiped it, but the Taint did more than simply mark them—it gave them strength, heightened their abilities, and promised more . . . much more. Still, the sorceress did not pause, did not question, and the skull hovered above them all, laughing in maddened glee.

A third cut, opening the woman's belly, and more blood

REE SOESBEE

stained her torn white robes. "I call upon Fu Leng!" Shahai cried into the wind, her arms raised as black lightning poured down upon her. "Father of Darkness, Master of Lies! I call to your successor who rules upon this earth. I stir up that blood that is your own and call you forth! Hear me!"

The black-robed men chanted and knelt as the storm burst upon them in full force. They pressed their palms together as Shahai spread her arms open to the wind, and another bolt of black lightning crashed down only a few feet from their ritual circle.

"Show me your vision, brother of blood!" Shahai screamed, letting the fury of the storm take her. "Show me my path, and I will bring the Empire to its knees!"

The clouds over the ocean broiled and twisted as though stirred by the blade of some dark knife, and then they filled with a dark vision that only Shahai could see. Mountains rose above shattered terrain, and blood trailed down the sides of high peaks like rivers of lava. Shahai laughed. She had seen this place before. It was deep within the Shadowlands, where the very ground mocked the life that rose to the north and where the oni roamed as masters of the earth and sky.

But then the view changed, torn from the mountains with awful force. Shahai felt as though her perspective was hurled a thousand miles from that site, and stone and earth flew past her mind with a ferocious roar. At last, it slowed, and she stared down upon another site, though still watching from the view of a high mountain cliff.

"I see the path, granddaughter!" The skull laughed, dancing madly in the air, then its voice changed, twisted, and became deeper. *"Beneath the ruins of the Iron Citadel lies a sleeping beast. There, when the warm winds blow, my son will come to greet you. Go to him, and he will show you the Way."*

Shahai laughed again. It did not matter if the words were born of Iuchiban, Fu Leng, or born of her own madness. The Dark Lord had assigned her a task, and she would not falter.

A son to rule the world—one to claim the throne once Shahai had destroyed their enemies. The line of Toturi would fall. The line of Iuchiban, of the dark god, would rise once more.

Shahai stepped back from the scene, relaxing her control as the storm began to swirl independently of her will. Too much and she would lose command. She would need its strength in a moment, but it had already grown too powerful to command fully. Better to allow some of its energy to fade, not take too much, than risk unleashing things that could not be controlled.

"We must go, and soon," Shahai murmured. "It will take us all winter and more to find the place within that vision, and yet I cannot leave the imperial court to play its games without me. Who knows what they might do?"

Twisting the dagger upon her own cheek, Shahai pondered her options as she watched the snow around her grow thick and dark. The storm might have unleashed its burden, but it remained high above Otosan Uchi's bay, covering the land and the sea with a thick layer of gray snow. Such a fountain might bring its own dangers, but the sorceress was not satisfied.

Shahai held the knife loosely in her hand, ignoring the half-dead woman at her feet and the crouching black-robed sorcerers. Once more, she closed her eyes and let her power flow.

"Come to me, dark ones, crafted desire and false honor. Come and hear my bidding." She called forth energy from the woman's blood once more, watching as the power sprang up toward her from the darkly stained ground. "Rise from the shadows and hear me."

Something deep within the ground shuddered and rose, detaching from stone and earth, sliding up within the pools of scarlet that swelled beneath the writhing Asako's cheek and bloody arm. It lapped hesitantly at the blood and turned its head to listen. The oni was of the type known as Pekkle, a small spirit that enjoyed deception and vindictiveness. It would be pleased with its new task.

"Go forth," Shahai whispered to the twisted spirit, "to the far south, and return with something . . . extraordinary. Something small. Something subtle. Offer them blood, sacrifice . . . and the amusement of a winter's season. I already have an ally within the imperial court. He will aid you. He will make certain that you can pass within the court and get close to our enemies." Shahai purred, catlike emotion crossing her delicate face. "Very close, indeed."

The creature bowed, sinking back into the earth as if melting from within. Its half-formed arms twisted and shriveled, and its gaping face seemed to run as though made of bloody wax. Within moments it was gone.

Shahai raised the steel blade to the storm once more, reaching for the power of blood one final time. She felt her hair rise with energy, and her eyes watered with blood as it cascaded only a few feet from her body.

The circle of blood burst into flame. Shahai pointed again, and the bodies of the Bloodspeakers within the fire exploded, one by one. High overhead, her grandfather's skull cawed in glee. At last, the flames drew inward, guided by the lightning and the movement of Shahai's dagger. The woman's corpse charred to ash. The Asako had not even had time to scream.

"My grandfather taught me to be a good girl." The dark sorceress smiled and released the storm. She would need it no more. Nor would she need the Bloodspeakers. "Always clean up when the work is finished."

Shahai turned her back on the flames that engulfed the high cliff, ignoring the scent of roasted flesh and the strangeness of cold snow beneath her feet as the fire scorched her fingertips. She walked back to the river, leaving nothing behind save blood and ashes.

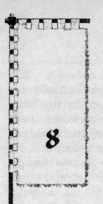

8   WINTER COURT

It was cold, far colder than Tsudao remembered. The court had moved to Kyuden Miya to finish the last snowy months of the year. Other winters, she had havened inside the Imperial palace, playing *go* beside wide fireplaces and listening to music by the artisans of the clans. This year, she had hardly been inside at all. The cold, with its chill and ice, suited her far better than the warmth of companionship. Only her handmaiden, Moshi Kekiesu, could make Tsudao come inside at all—although Doji Tanitsu had done his best to stay beside her in the gardens. He could not stay long without his fingers turning as blue as his robes.

Cranes. They withered too easily in the chill.

Tsudao sat beside the open door of the court chamber, ignoring the courtiers who shivered on the distant side of the room. None would dare tell her to close the door, and she could not care less for their delicate constitutions. Let them freeze. Let the entire Empire freeze for what it had done to Toturi.

Kaede had given Tsudao her father's blade, and now it lay darkly against the frozen snow. When he had held it, it had been a blade of honor and strength, its brown and gold saya shining in his hand. The sword was made by the finest smiths in the Empire, forged to ultimate perfection. Even today, no other blade was its equal. Not even the swords of the Celestial Heavens could match its perfect edge.

Now, the sword seemed empty of purpose. Without a hand to wield it, the katana was nothing but a piece of metal, straining to fill the shape that had been its life. It had been in Toturi's hand when he died. He had fought well, but this one perfect blade had not been enough.

Father . . . Tsudao's eyes were cold, but her heart ached with loss. I failed you. I was not there. . . .

On the far side of the room, the courtiers laughed at some meaningless tale, and Tsudao grimaced. "Tsudao-sama," a smooth voice said, "join us. I think you will find this discussion . . . of interest." It was not a voice she could easily ignore.

She turned from her view of the snowy landscape to stare at her youngest brother. Hantei Naseru extended his hand in invitation, but his stance was that of a trained warrior. Unlike Sezaru, Naseru was a soldier like Tsudao, although he fought both with the words of law and the steel of his sword. Today, he wore a long green and yellow kimono, thickly embroidered with the symbol of the Emerald Champion, and the golden laurel crown of the Emperor's Magistrates—the highest order of legal guard in all of Rokugan. Although he was not a magistrate, he wore the trappings of one to remind others of his station as a creator of law. His long, black hair was tied into a queue, and his narrow chin seemed even longer by the thin beard and moustache he wore.

Naseru smiled, very obviously manufacturing the motion.

Tsudao sighed and moved her black kimono aside so she could stand in a single, fluid gesture.

The Steel Throne sat empty, Empress Kaede having long since retired to her chambers. Several courtiers gathered around it, murmuring and smiling like porcelain dolls. Tsudao frowned as she followed Naseru to the gathering, realizing that she was the last to be invited.

Already, Sezaru and Kaneka, Tsudao's other brothers, stood to either side of the high dais, speaking to the courtiers as they approached. Tsudao grimaced, realizing that Kaneka was no more relaxed than she felt. The former ronin's shoulders were square, his answers too blunt for a courtier's taste, and already two Scorpion stood behind him, waiting for the opportunity to carry all his secrets home.

Sezaru, far more used to the game of the court, gently fielded all of his questions to Kaneka, smiling enigmatically when the older man stumbled in his answers. Naseru moved behind them as gracefully as a stalking leopard and entered the conversation. He gave an amused smile to Tsudao.

"Our sister has come to join us." Naseru smiled again, a bit less mechanically. For a moment, Tsudao thought her manipulative little brother had almost gained a human emotion. Then the smile faded, and the ice returned to his eyes.

Naseru had been raised by the last of the Hantei Emperors, the dying dynasty that had proceeded Toturi's reign. He had learned the cruelty that was the handiwork of the sixteenth Hantei, as well as his greed for the throne. Only a few years ago, the Hantei had tried to seize Rokugan once more—nearly destroying the very Empire they had sought to gain. Only by offering them his youngest son in tutelage had Toturi been able to end the war, and as far as Tsudao was concerned, Naseru was the last scar of that bloody era. If he had not been her brother, she would have challenged him long ago.

She did not know the courtier who stood beside Naseru, though the man's robes proclaimed him to be of the Miya family. The Miya had stood at the side of the old Hantei emperors but now claimed to be loyal to the new masters of the Imperial Crown. Tsudao tried to offer everyone a fair chance to earn her trust, but the Miya had never done much to impress her. They were heralds and couriers for the Emperor, and she knew little of them outside of their histories. One was speaking as Tsudao entered the ring of courtiers.

"Shinsei once said that even a mighty avalanche begins with a single pebble." His words were smooth and trained. "How are we to know that on this day, we might begin the changes that will unify the Empire?"

"Gensaiken-san," Sezaru said quietly, "I think you over-simplify the issue."

The young herald frowned. "Do I?" His eyes flickered over the Imperial four, noting the differences in their stances— and their followers. "The divisions between the four children of Toturi are already painfully clear. You are the four winds of change, each blown by fortune. The Great Clans struggle to curry the winds' favor, even as the winds themselves struggled with one another to prove their worth."

Many of the courtiers nodded and grinned behind their fans. Tsudao felt her hand creep toward the hilt of her sword and stilled the gesture. She couldn't help feeling as if the assembly were laughing at her behind their painted smiles and fluttering fans.

"An astute determination," a Scorpion's voice poisoned the tale, "but not very useful to your political career." There was scattered laughter at this, and Miya Gensaiken's face flushed. "Tell me, Miya, do you know who these samurai are, or do you only know their histories?"

Mocking laughter followed the Scorpion's words, and the herald blushed.

"I know them well," Miya Gensaiken replied. "This is Toturi Tsudao, the Sword of the Empire, called such by Toturi-sama's chief advisor after her defeat of the Yobanjin barbarians at the head of an Imperial Legion." Gensaiken moved to the left, facing the youngest of Toturi's children. "Hantei Naseru, the Anvil upon which law is made. Already, your judgments are legendary, and your wisdom is known throughout the Empire. You take your name from the man who trained you—the last Hantei to stand upon this world."

Some scattered murmuring greeted Gensaiken's appraisal, and the ronin stepped forward with a dark threat in his voice. "And me?"

"Akodo Kaneka. The Bastard." The Miya did not blush or stammer but stared directly into Kaneka's eyes as if testing him. "My apologies if that title does not suit you, Kaneka-sama."

"I know my place," the ronin said, amused at the young herald's forthrightness. "For now."

"And Toturi's oldest son, Toturi Sezaru," Miya Gensaiken bowed before the priest. "Honored with the title Wolf, I believe."

"Some call me that—" Sezaru smiled— "but others, who are wary, call me nothing at all." There was no threat in his tone, but the courtiers waved their fans in polite appreciation of Sezaru's point.

The Miya bowed meekly and moved away.

"But come, sister," Sezaru extended a hand to Tsudao. "Let us leave this game and see who else has attended the Winter Court. We already know our family. Let us become better acquainted with the Empire."

Tsudao felt a wash of relief but was careful not to let it show. Anything to be out of the eye of the court. She nodded brusquely and followed Sezaru. The assembled emissaries watched, practiced eyes unreadable. Tsudao knew only two of the gathered courtiers personally, but she knew the others by their reputations. Bayushi Paneki and Doji Tanitsu whispered behind their fans, and Tanitsu winked roguishly at Tsudao when no one else was watching.

A few representatives of the Minor Clans were present as well, including Usagi Fuyuko, a newcomer to the court. Gensaiken was watching the young Hare curiously. Her wit and charm had surprised the assembly since her arrival only days ago. Even the dour Crab who muttered impolitely in the corner had quickly warmed to the clever and inquisitive Hare. She had become a favorite of the court, and even now her beauty and grace turned the room to her whim. She stood close beside Toturi Naseru, and Tsudao wondered if the girl had placed her favor in his hands. For some reason, the notion sickened her, and Tsudao looked away.

"My Lords, my Lady," Fuyuko said, bowing deeply to the Steel Throne as she spoke, standing by Naseru's right arm. "I know that your time is precious and I am but an undeserving vassal of the Empire, but perhaps you would do me the great honor of indulging me. We have heard much talk of what virtues each clan finds most important in an Emperor, but what are your thoughts? Excusing my impertinence, it may be enlightening to find what traits the heirs themselves value most in a ruler."

Tsudao spoke first. "Compassion," she said. "Certainly we can all agree upon the need for peace."

"Tsudao, please," Naseru said with a dry chuckle. "Let us attempt to be realistic. Peace is an admirable dream, but it is only that—a dream." Seeing Tsudao bristle, her younger brother raised his fan in an elegant motion. "Peace is a commodity that men of action cannot afford. The reality is that men and women will always fight one another. A true Emperor must recognize that there will always be war and that hiding from reality simply leaves one unprepared. A true Emperor uses the fortunes of war to bring prosperity and strength."

"War as a tool to strengthen the Empire?" Tsudao sneered, suddenly angry with her brother, his argument, and his careless treatment of the lives of others. "You relish the death of innocents, brother?"

"Innocents? You misunderstand me, sister. I conserve my pity for the truly innocent and have collected it in great quantities. To be sure—" Naseru's eyes flickered over his audience— "I have not yet met a man or woman who is truly innocent."

Tsudao's face reddened in anger. Akodo Kaneka bristled,

and Sezaru raised an eyebrow.

"Present company excluded, of course," Naseru said, and a light chuckle echoed through the court.

Usagi Fuyuko arched an eyebrow and turned toward Kaneka.

"Naseru has a point, Tsudao," Akodo Kaneka said. "Samurai are warriors. To pretend otherwise defies the Celestial Order. Everything has a purpose. We have ours. An Emperor's strongest virtue is courage."

"I understand your lust for battle, Kaneka, for your life has given you nothing else." Tsudao clenched her teeth, fighting back the same unreasonable anger that she could see in her half-brother's eyes. "I do not understand Naseru. His talk of war seems bold for one who has never seen battle."

"I have never seen the Fortunes or the Kami either, my sister," Naseru returned with a calm smile. "Have you heard them? Have you seen them?"

Tsudao regarded her brother with stony silence, refusing to fall into his trap.

"As I thought," he said. "So by your own logic, surely you must deny their existence. It must be difficult to lead one's life without faith. Do you not agree, brother Sezaru-san?"

Sezaru glanced up, eyes narrowing in surprise. He looked away again quickly, his face masked in disinterest. "These games are worthless," he said. "I thought you were seeking peace. You do nothing but snipe at one another."

Kaneka's brow furrowed as his hand strayed toward his sword. Sezaru turned and looked back at his brother calmly, with the patience of a coiled snake. Tsudao and Naseru held themselves taut, their eyes locked across the dais that held the Steel Throne.

One false word, one false move, and Rokugan's hopes for peace would be destroyed, perhaps taking the life of a Wind with them. Tsudao could feel the pressure in the room building. Something else was egging them on, but what? Naseru's face was drawn and cold, but this clawed frankness wasn't like him. Sezaru—peaceful Sezaru!—seemed almost ready to call down magic upon the bastard ronin.

"My lords," Miya Gensaiken said quickly. Clever man, Tsudao thought. He was risking the Winds' wrath turning toward him just to get them to turn away from one another. "For such a complex issue, my lords and lady, you should consult the wisdom of those who have served the Empire since the war against Fu Leng."

His oratory was smooth and cultured, but Tsudao could sense fear in him. Gensaiken had served as a herald, but this kind of bristling attention was not his normal ground.

The nervous courtier stepped forward hesitantly. Bowing deeply, he said, "The Miya are brokers of peace. We are diplomats and builders. While all the noble Winds speak truly, it is with Sezaru that we must agree. Courage, compassion, and wisdom are fine things, but they are nothing without faith. Only faith can move a mountain."

Gensaiken turned to Usagi Fuyuko. "Would your honorable father not agree, Usagi-san?"

Turning her face toward him, Fuyuko replied, "Oh yes, Gensaiken-san. He would indeed."

The courtiers around the Steel Throne nodded, and Naseru favored her with one of his half-real smiles.

Gensaiken's eyes narrowed, and Tsudao could see that he was not quite so taken. Through the mounting anger and annoyance, she could sense something sinister lurking just beneath the surface of the maiden's pleasant countenance and easy charm. It was so difficult to tear her hand away from the hilt of her sword, to release the anger and turn away from the challenge in Naseru's eyes.

"Interesting," said Miya Gensaiken. "The Usagi Fuyuko recorded in our heraldic registries is the child of a dishonored mother and an unknown father. She would not respond in such a manner, for to do so would bring even greater shame upon her father's name and the name of the Miya. Who might you truly be then, I wonder? Or—" Gensaiken

lowered his fan to point at Furiko as she recoiled in shock—
"did I not mention that the Miya are historians, as well as
heralds?"

A hateful snarl distorted Fuyuko's features. The girl's white
hand sprouted a full set of blackened claws and darted forth
to rip at Gensaiken's throat.

Tsudao moved with incredible swiftness, but her half-
brother was closer. A blur of movement from the dais and
Akodo Kaneka stood between the Miya and his snarling
opponent. Kaneka's blade flashed toward the woman's neck,
but she dodged aside. Still, it was not quick enough to avoid
all injury, and Fuyuko shrieked as her severed hand fell to the
floor. Her other hand lashed out and ripped at Kaneka's cer-
emonial armor, sending him sprawling to the floor.

Tsudao moved between the beast and Gensaiken, drawing
him back with her hand on his shoulder. He flinched at the
touch, but it was easy to remove him and step in the way of
any new danger. Toturi Tsudao blocked the creature's hissing
strike, her sword deflecting the claw just as Naseru twisted
his metal fan open above his head. He shouted in a clarion
voice, ordering the dazed emissaries to flee as Tsudao faced
the growling demon-creature. Even as he did so, the soft
whispers of Sezaru could be heard above Tsudao and Kaneka
readying their steel.

Two burly Imperial Guards charged the beast from either
side, but Fuyuko ducked below one's strike while catching
the other's blade in her remaining hand. A smooth flick of
one hand sent both men across the room, impaled upon
their own blades. Even as it turned from the carnage to
attack again, a look of fear flickered in the creature's eyes. As
it faced Tsudao, the imperial princess heard another warrior
step up beside her. Out of the corner of her eye, she recognized the gray hakima and perfect stance. Akodo Kaneka.

The Sword and the Bastard. Each of the seasoned warriors
avoided the creature's clumsy defenses. Kaneka's blow sliced
the oni across its midriff while Tsudao buried her own

katana in the thing's skull. The corpse disappeared, belching forth a thick cloud of darkness that permeated the room, burning the eyes and nostrils of those present.

With a whisper and a gesture, Sezaru's Void magic dispelled all traces of the stench, and the court stood in shocked silence.

"Well done," Naseru called out suddenly, no trace of concern in his voice. His calm tone did much to pacify the panicked assembly, and many of the courtiers burst into speech all at once. Tsudao slid her sword against a cushion, watching as the oni's blood stained the pale silk. She lowered her sword into its saya with a faint click, turning away from the courtiers. They whispered at Tsudao's coolness, wondering if she would speak out against her brothers once more.

There would be no more show for the Empire's tiny voices. Let them see only ice in her eyes.

"The court is secure," Naseru told them, lowering his fan. "You are in no danger here."

"Do not be so eager, little brother," remarked Sezaru coldly. "Those were the machinations of a Pekkle, a trickster oni. They are beasts of corruption and deception, sent by our enemies to tear us apart. Even now, the Shadowlands watch." Sezaru's eyes narrowed, and he turned his back on the proceedings, stepping toward Tsudao. "There is no way to know if that beast accomplished its purpose. The true ramifications of this encounter are not yet known."

"This is pathetic." Kaneka spat on the floor. "We stand within the imperial court itself, yet we cannot keep one oni from our presence? I'll have no more to do with these foolish negotiations. Brothers, sister, contact me again once you have something to discuss. Until then, I'll be in my chambers, meditating on the safety—" Kaneka's voice was venomous and cruel—"of the Empire." With that, Akodo Kaneka turned on his heel and stormed out of the room.

Hantei Naseru closed his tessen with a deft snap. "My brother is not known for his patience. Nor am I known for my forgiveness." He turned toward Sezaru and Tsudao. "This session has been closed, I see."

With a bow, he turned and summoned his guards. Within moments, he had departed as well, trailing three swordsmen in the colors of the Emerald Champion.

"And with that, goes all hope of a simple agreement where the Steel Throne is concerned, my brother," Tsudao said to Sezaru.

"This meeting was not my idea, sister," Sezaru replied. "I do not feel that the throne is best served with speech."

His meaning was clear, and Tsudao was grateful for it. Action was needed to save the Empire. Action alone would prove Toturi's true heir. No amount of political maneuvering by Naseru would change that. Tsudao scowled in the direction her youngest brother had gone, wishing that his ambition burned less fiercely. Even with his devious ways, Naseru was still her brother.

"Sister, walk with me." Sezaru gestured to the gardens, his sleeve moving faintly with cold wind from the open door. She nodded, and Sezaru walked away from the still-whispering courtiers, hiding his face from their open stares.

With small and precise steps, he led her out onto the wide porch of the Miya palace. The snow outside seemed even colder than before, and a chill wind howled softly from the ocean. Tsudao listened to the dying noises of the court inside, listening as the story of the oni's visit was passed down from courtier to courtier and into the history books.

"Tsudao-san," Sezaru said, "when the spring comes, I intend to make a journey to the north."

"North? To the shrines of the Ki-rin, perhaps?"

"No," Sezaru said quietly, keeping his voice below the wind. "To the mountains of the Phoenix and the Dragon. There is . . . a call that guides me there. I must listen, and I must find its source."

Tsudao frowned. Sezaru was the only one of her brothers whom she didn't want to choke right now, and to hear that he intended to journey into danger only made her feel more protective.

"What do you expect to find? More information for your priestly studies on oni?" The comment was a joke, but Sezaru did not smile.

Her brother looked up into the whirling whiteness that blanketed the roof and windowsills of the great palace. He sighed, dark eyes enigmatic. "I don't know, but I believe that if I search for her, the Oracle of the Wind will hear me and give me some insight on what has happened to our father. First, I must go to the mountains of the Phoenix to find the Master of Air, Isawa Nakamuro, who will tell me how to find the Oracle of Wind. Then I will seek her out and she will give me truth."

"If the Oracles will hear you, do you think they will know the truth of what has occurred?"

"They may. They will certainly know more than most."

"But our mother . . . the Empress Kaede is an Oracle. Surely she does not know more than she says?"

"Kaede is the Oracle of the Void, the element that looks beyond this world. The mysteries of Rokugan are not important to her, nor to the Dragon she serves. No." Sezaru shook his head. "It is to the Oracle of Wind that I must go, for all whispers and truths are eventually spoken . . . breathed into her domain."

Tsudao looked at her brother's troubled face for a long moment, watching as his long fingers brushed the snow out of the air and cupped it into his palm. Sezaru had always been somewhat of a mystic. He was one of the most powerful shugenja in the Empire and a dedicated priest of the Kami. None could question his integrity or his passion for the spiritual. It had been his inheritance from their mother, his gift from the Fortunes themselves upon the day of his birth. Once, when they were very little, Tsudao had seen him carried in their mother's eyes, tears of blood running down his childish face. It was then that she suspected she had visions very similar to his own—but far, far darker.

"You cannot go alone," she said finally, making up her mind. "But you also cannot travel with only a palanquin of guards, lest the same trap that caught our father be placed for you. The Imperial Legions must make their way to Dragon lands when the snows thaw to stop the war between the Shiba and the Mirumoto. Will you travel with me, brother?"

Sezaru looked at Tsudao, the snow melting slowly in his pale, cold hand. "Shinsei once wrote that a wise man can find allies even in times of great betrayal." He looked back at the courtroom, where a stain had begun to spread across the dais upon which the Steel Throne stood. "The oni we have seen is not the last of their minions. There are more—here and elsewhere. The forces of the Shadowlands gather. They have tainted the Throne, killed our father, and broken our spirit. If we are to succeed, Tsudao, then we must overcome everything that stands in our way." He looked at her, his dark eyes piercing her pale amber ones. "One of the things that stands against us . . . is ourselves."

There was a long silence, broken only by the soft cries of the wind and the sound of falling snow on hushed pines. After a long moment, Tsudao turned toward Sezaru and held out an open palm.

Sezaru smiled and slowly took her hand. "Good," he said quietly. "So it will be."

* * * * *

After Tsudao had retired, Sezaru returned to the throne room. He walked through the chamber where once a hundred courtiers had swirled. The snow on his clothing melted away as if it had never been, and Sezaru lifted dark eyes to the Steel throne. Humble servants scrubbed futilely at the stain on the dais, unable to change the darkness that frosted the pale wood. The pekkle oni had done its job well. Its master would be pleased. To one side of the room Miya Gensaiken stood quietly before the fire. His fan was pressed to his breast as if in deep thought, but the herald's eyes were deeply troubled.

Although he was loath to disturb the herald's well-earned moment of silence, Sezaru stepped to the edge of the fire and stood in the golden light of the flame.

"Miya Gensaiken-san," Sezaru's voice was soft and smooth, "your insight may have saved the Empire."

"You honor me," the herald replied, bowing low to the imperial prince.

"I am not a man who is well used to courtly intrigue. I could make good use of an attendant such as you, especially against the underhanded schemes of my brother, Naseru. Will you join my retinue?" The offer was a serious one, something that most courtiers would live a lifetime and never see. To serve the imperial prince directly was a great sign of respect—and a great trust.

"I would be honored, Sezaru-sama," Gensaiken answered with a deep breath. He bowed deeply, lowering his fan.

"Then follow me," Sezaru said. "I wish to depart this place at once. I have a mission to fulfill, and this farce of a court has been a drain upon the little time that I have left." Toturi Sezaru folded his hands into the wide sleeves of his silk robe, lowering his voice once more. "If the dark sorcerers managed to dispatch one minion into this palace, it is likely there are others. Someone must be working with them to allow such a creature to make it this deeply within the imperial court." Sezaru's face darkened. "Remember this, Gensaiken. The Horde is never alone."

Sezaru turned away from the fire, the shadows highlighting the severe angles of his face.

"Meet me in the morning within the Miya libraries," said Sezaru. "There are histories that I must see before the end of the winter comes."

With a faint nod of dismissal, Sezaru stepped away from

the fire and crossed the courtroom without a backward glance, leaving Gensaiken alone.

The courtier paused, turned, and looked back at the Steel Throne. A black smear now stained the Steel Throne, the only remnant of the oni's passing.

Gensaiken smiled at the sight. Pausing, he looked down at his hand. During the struggle, he had been cut upon his arm. Now a thin stream of clumped black blood trickled down his fingers. He pulled his sleeve over his hand so that his new master would not see and followed in the wake of Toturi Sezaru.

"You are right about one thing, my lord." Gensaiken chuckled. "Creatures of the Shadowlands never come alone."

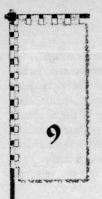

9 | NASERU

Inside the Miya Palace, the youngest of the Four Winds stalked the hallways like a tiger, his green and gold robes snapping behind him. His one eye glowed with anger, the black patch shadowing the features of his right side. It gave him a sinister visage, and servants scattered before him in fear of the imperial prince's brooding wrath.

The gambit had not gone as planned. Despite his careful attention to detail, none of the Winds had dishonored themselves nor blackened their chances at the throne. Although his plans had nearly come to fruition, in the end, the court had simply faded away like snow in the light of the sun. And the oni . . .

Naseru scowled, clenching his fist. The oni. He had given the Scorpion Clan full endorsement to search the castle and interrogate any of the guests whom they believed to be involved. The clan would no doubt find many secrets—but none involved with the oni. The Scorpion owed him for this opportunity to test their strengths, but he knew already that they would not find what they truly sought.

The servants outside his personal chambers bowed low as their master approached. They slid open the ricepaper doors before Naseru even slowed his pace. Inside the chamber, a man waited. He was a member of the Seppun family, a guardsman in plain robes, yet he was Naseru's most trusted ally and his personal guardsman. Isei was an older man, his face badly scarred by a long-ago sword strike.

"Your will, Master?" the Seppun said quietly, sensing Naseru's ill mood.

"Already the stories of the court spread. The rumors grow." Naseru flexed his fist again, running his fingers through his short beard. "We must initiate, Isei-san. We must remain at the forefront of the contest or the throne will be lost."

Seppun Isei nodded gravely as his Master spoke. "The tales of the oni's presence will likely overwhelm your own movements."

"Yes," growled Naseru. "The one thing we can thank the little wretch for." Naseru fell silent for a moment to assess his position. He walked across the room, sparsely furnished in the traditional style. A simple wardrobe held the rolled futons for sleeping, and another stood to the side and contained Naseru's robes. A low, round table with small sake cups dominated the center of the room, and the only other furniture was a *go* stand, where the game had been laid out. In progress. Naseru paused beside the board, lifting one black stone into his hand.

"Kaneka—" he snarled the name— "has no claim to the throne. His lineage is weak, unrecognized. He has little political support and no grasp of the powers he dares to claim. He is no threat to me so long as I keep my current alliances strong. One day, Isei, we will see him spitted upon his own sword, and he will die in dishonor . . . just like his mother." Naseru's voice was cold. "I will be certain of that.

"My true brother, Sezaru, is a priest. He is not a leader of men, nor will he ever be. Although his ties to the Kami are strong, he was not born to be a leader. He is extremely powerful in magic, and he has a strong will, but he, too, cannot rule. And more—" Naseru smiled— "I have made sure that Sezaru will be well taken care of. Very soon, he will find that the water in which he stands has begun to rise above his head. Sezaru will have no time to spend thinking of the Steel Throne. His claim will be removed as well.

"But Tsudao . . . Tsudao, my honorable sister. Always so certain of herself, she has avoided every trap I have set for her. She kept the Phoenix and Dragon from the war I so carefully planned for them, and she has managed once again to slip past the dangers of the court. Of them all, only Tsudao is worthy of contesting with me for the throne. She is the one I must destroy.

"Rokugan is an empire with a long and glorious history. More than any other, I, the chosen of the Hantei, know its past, and I was born to be the anvil upon which its future is forged. A future that I will control." Naseru dropped the black stone upon the *go* board, shattering the pattern of black and white that had dominated the glassy board. "I will not be denied."

"Tsudao's weakness is her loyalty," Seppun Isei said quietly.

Naseru's eye widened with agreement. "We must turn it against her. I have played gently with my sister up to now, hoping that I might bend her without shattering the Sword. I can no longer afford to be so—" Naseru's lips thinned into a sinister smile— "kind."

Naseru sat before the *go* board, stealing the stones with a quick gesture and lining them up by color at the side of the board. Isei turned to watch him, aware that Naseru's cunning mind was already creating a plan.

"My lord?"

"Yes, Isei?"

"I bear some news that may be of use to you."

"Speak," Naseru said, not looking up from the stones.

The Seppun bowed his head and withdrew a scroll from his inner sleeve. "The Phoenix and Dragon have engaged at the Shrine of the Ki-Rin. The battle was light but brutal, and three thousand Phoenix lie dead on the snow of the Ki-Rin's mountaintop."

"A winter battle?" Naseru raised an eyebrow, suddenly interested. "Some would have considered that a suicide mission, especially at the height of the Ki-Rin's shrine. Who initiated it?"

"The Dragon, and they were clearly victorious. They now control the Ki-Rin's shrine and command all of the surrounding territories." Isei paused, knowing that the news would have a hundred complex significances. "It will be a blow to the Phoenix when the spring comes. Their generals had planned to use it as a main stronghold in their offensive. The strike will not seal the war, however. It will only bring the Dragon threat to the eyes of the Phoenix Masters, and they will no longer sue for peace. A dangerous risk, but better than the Dragon Clan's other option. If they cannot steal the land from the Phoenix, then they will have to tread south rather than east. And to the south are their most dangerous enemies . . . the Lion Clan. The Lion," Isei said gravely, his aged face somber, "are Tsudao's greatest allies. She trained with them, led their troops to victory in her early years with the Imperial Legions, and she still has many loyal Lion among her personal guard."

Naseru nodded. "Continue."

"The Dragon offensive was led by one of their strongest generals. You may recognize the name." Isei did not need to check the message from Naseru's spies. He knew the man as well as his master did. "Mirumoto Junnosuke."

The imperial prince's face lightened, and he leaned back on his cushion. Turning away from the *go* board, Naseru steepled his fingers before his face and considered the implications of this news. "Excellent. His temper has served us well in the past, and his dislike of my dear sister is legendary.

I hope the Scorpion that we sent to aid him were . . . useful."

"He could not have won the battle without their aid, my lord," Isei said without inflection. "The Phoenix are fortifying their cities, but the Dragon have command of the westernmost lands. Still, the volcanoes have not ceased their eruption. The Mirumoto will have to find another source of land, for their refugees will rapidly outgrow even the territories they have seized. When they do, the Dragon will have two options: continue the fight against the Phoenix, or combat the Lion."

"As we have sealed the continuing treaty between the Lion and Phoenix at this Winter Court, to attack one will serve only to anger the other." Naseru eyes shone. "Plans within plans. Our foresight has served us well." He rose from the table to walk across the boards once more. "Tsudao's orders will be to take the Imperial Legions north after the winter to stop the Dragon and Phoenix from their war. She may not know that it is too late, but we will help our gentle sister. The Dragon will not fight the Phoenix." Naseru spread apart his hands in a gesture of generosity, then his smile turned cruel. "They will fight both Phoenix and Lion, and Tsudao will ride to the defense of the Matsu—and find an old friend there, waiting for her."

"Lord," Isei said, careful not to question, "Junnosuke will have no mercy when he faces Tsudao and her Lion troops."

Naseru nodded. "I see three options, Isei-san. First, it is possible that the Kami will lend Mirumoto Junnosuke all the strength of Osano-wo, Fortune of Storms. They may grant him the courage that he does not possess, and they may even offer him a sword made of the heavens to make up for his regrettable lack of skill." Naseru's voice was filled with pleasant sarcasm, his lips twisted in mild humor. "If this happens, then Junnosuke will kill Tsudao on the field of battle. Her death will be honorable, in combat, and her spirit will ascend to the heavens." His wry words came from a face that seemed as innocent as a child's. "It is an unlikely and regrettable occurrence that will nonetheless remove a rival to the throne. That would be the swiftest end to our current difficulties."

Walking to the go board, Naseru placed a black stone in the center between two lines.

"The second possibility is less short-term. If the Dragon, Lion, and Phoenix go to war, it could last years. Tsudao's sense of loyalty and her misguided alliances within the Lion will force her to stay with her troops. She will be seen to have chosen sides against the Dragon, and there are many who will take offense at Tsudao's choice. Her support within the Empire will shrink, and with the exception of the Lion the other clans will no longer trust her decisions." Naseru shook his head in mock regret. "The situation will rapidly become politically disastrous and physically dangerous. An errant strike on the battlefield could end it all, but more likely she will waste valuable time while I secure my hold on the throne. When I negotiate a peaceful end to the war in a few years, all the glory will be mine. Tsudao will appear as a failure in the eyes of her former allies. A pity."

He placed a white stone beside the black one, running his finger over the cool smoothness of the go pebble.

"The most likely outcome is less fortunate for us but still advantageous if properly managed. Tsudao may well defeat Junnosuke. Her skill as a general is renowned, but still, she must do so without angering the Dragon Clan, for Junnosuke's victory at the Ki-Rin shrine has made him somewhat of a favorite." Naseru touched both stones with his fingertips, brooding once more. "If she is clever, she may succeed, and gain even more support than she has now. If she unifies the three clans and maintains her own popular support, she may yet best us and claim the position she was born into."

Isei frowned, lowering his head. "Tsudao as heir to the Throne?"

"Yes." Naseru overturned the stones. "Of all my siblings, only Tsudao is worthy to contest me. That also means only she is worthy to beat me. But do not plan on it, Isei-san. I will not settle for defeat so easily."

"Where do we step now, Master?"

The imperial prince looked up from the *go* board. "We speak to the Dragon emissaries here at court. Arrange for Junnosuke to be placed in total command, then we send word to Junnosuke that we are . . . well pleased with him." Naseru considered for a moment longer. "We must put Junnosuke's vengeance to good use. He does not need to be indebted to us. Never allow him to know who moved him into his new, prestigious position, but we do wish to ensure that he has enough samurai to give my sister a challenge and to drag him away from the Phoenix front." Naseru steepled his fingers once more, eyes narrowing. "We shall send a letter to the Phoenix ambassador . . . one that deeply regrets the assaults on the Ki-Rin's shrine. And one that reveals the Dragon troop movements into the western mountains and away from the southern border. Once the Phoenix realize where the Dragon forces are weak, they will find a way to strike. The Dragonfly lands, perhaps."

"The Dragonfly?" Isei asked.

"South of the Dragon are the Dragonfly—a small clan who have held enmity with both Lion and Phoenix for many generations. The Scorpion owe us. It will not be difficult to arrange a small altercation between the Dragonfly and the enemies of the Dragon. From such simple movements, entire wars have begun." With a flick of his wrist, Naseru scattered the stones upon the board, removing the pattern entirely. "With the fall of the Dragonfly, we shall see a new season, Isei. A season of war."

10 A SLENDER THREAD

A lark sang in the bare branches of the cherry trees outside Miya palace. White patches of snow shrank in protest at the sun's touch, and small buds of green were brushed upon the trees and bushes like an artist's first strokes at the canvas. Already, the Imperial Legions had begun to gather, taking advantage of the early snowmelts to precipitate their movement through the southern roads. Tsudao marched through the corridors of the palace, glad to feel the wind blow through the open windows and wide doors. The palace had been opened to enjoy the first breezes of spring, and it was a blessed relief to feel the warmth of a dawning sun.

Crumpling the missives of her men in one fist, Tsudao allowed herself an eager grin. Soon, she would leave the Miya enclosures to meet with the legions to the north of Otosan Uchi. From there, they would head toward the Ki-Rin's shrine and the Dragon Mountains.

Tsudao reached her chambers in the palace, pausing to

allow the servants to draw aside the doors. "Kekiesu?" she called out to her handmaiden. "We need to pack, imme—"

Her voice froze when she saw the three samurai, all lined up in a precise row and kneeling upon the ground. They were dressed in a jewel-toned rainbow of color—the colors of the Dragonfly Clan. As one, they bowed their faces to the floor, but not before Tsudao saw the smeared mark of tears upon one woman's heavily made-up face.

To the side, Kekiesu also bowed, although hers was less low. "The Dragonfly, my Lady, seek audience with the general of the Imperial Legions."

The young handmaiden spoke carefully, her eyes lowered but her face pale. Tsudao immediately sobered, her brows knitting into a thin line. Kekiesu continued with the formalities, flickering her eyes to her lady's to relay a message of intense concern. When she was done, Tsudao lifted her hand from her side in a gesture to the Dragonfly, and the courtiers raised their heads from the hardwood floor.

"Great Toturi-sama," the older woman, obviously in charge of the delegation, spoke first. Despite the marks of tears upon her face, the Dragonfly's voice was calm and composed. "I would not trouble you if I did not believe that throwing ourselves on your honor would be the only means of saving lives." She gestured to Kekiesu and declared, "The Moshi speak of the Daughter of the Sun with admiration and many noble words. Your sense of duty to the Empire is well known." The others nodded solemnly. "I ask you now to turn your eye to our cause, General Toturi-sama."

"The General-sama has received your request and will consider it," Kekiesu said, and she lifted the paper in her hand to Tsudao. The imperial princess took it without a word. "You may go."

Without another word, the Dragonfly ambassadors bowed, their hands open in supplication. They rose as one, their jewel-toned robes shining with green highlights in the bright light of the spring morning, and filed out of Tsudao's chamber.

Tsudao turned to Kekiesu, and the handmaiden bowed once more. The servants closed the door with a *shh* that sounded like a mother's comforting, but it did not reassure Tsudao.

"What has occurred?"

"The Dragonfly have been attacked at Gentle Visage Pass. The roads from the Dragonfly to the Dragon Clan lands have been sealed by the Phoenix, and there are Lion troops marching to the north. The watchtowers of Gentle Visage— and their villages—have been burned. Three hundred Dragonfly lie dead, and the Phoenix will not accept a suit for peace." Kekiesu's words rang like the tones of a deadened bell.

"And the Lion . . . ?"

"Have not made their intentions known." Kekiesu's hands fell into her lap. "Tsudao-sama, this war is wrong." She looked up at her mistress with tears in her eyes. "The Minor Clans have done nothing wrong, yet we are being used as tools to anger the Great Houses. The Dragonfly cannot defend themselves against the Phoenix—much less the Lion. The Dragon will come to defend them, but too late. A war on Dragonfly territory will destroy them as easily as the death of their samurai. Their lands will be ravaged by the march of legions and their villages burned."

"All this," murmured Tsudao as she unfolded the formal request letter of the Dragonfly, "because the mountains burn."

"*The Lesser Houses shall fall . . .*" Kekiesu whispered. "The Sun has foreseen this, and you are his daughter. Your vision must guide us. We must ask the Sun—"

"No," Tsudao said harshly, crumpling the delicate paper in a careless hand. "Those visions are part of my childhood. We speak no more of them."

"No, Tsudao-sama," Kekiesu raised her chin in stubbornness. "*You* speak no more of them, but to the Moshi, they are words of truth. There is no fear in it. You must realize your place and accept the Sun's blessing. The Fortunes themselves were not so gifted, and to turn your back on it is to deny the Empire its heir."

Tsudao's fist slammed down on a low table, and the wood creaked under the harsh blow. "Speak no more of this, Kekiesu-san. These . . . *visions*—" Tsudao snarled— "are no part of being a samurai. They are behind me. There shall be no more."

"Tsudao-sama." Kekiesu lowered her head to the floor, then raised it again. "If you deny these visions, then you deny your very soul."

Tsudao said nothing, her eyes dark with conflict and suppressed anger. "Pack our things, Kekiesu. We leave to meet the legions in an hour."

Without answering Kekiesu's challenge, she turned her back.

* * * * *

"Hold!" Tsudao shouted, raising her hand to the sky. The horses of the Imperial Legion plowed through muddy ground, their hooves churning the soil along the northern road. At last, after weeks of travel, the Dragon Mountains loomed high above the sticky earth, rising like boulders upon the shoulders of a giant. Beside Tsudao, Sezaru shielded his eyes from the sun and peered at a flock of buzzards circling one of the highest peaks.

"There," Sezaru breathed. "Just above the peaks. There is a palace in the clouds. That is the temple of the Master of Air—and for me, the beginning of my path to the Oracle's wisdom."

Tsudao stared into the clouds, but the brilliance of the sun burned her eyes, and she was forced to look away. "I wish I could go with you, brother."

The last two weeks of travel had brought Tsudao a greater understanding of her solitary brother and his strange ways. Sezaru saw more than Tsudao realized—about the court, the

Empire, and life itself. There was one more thing they had in common—an intense distrust of Naseru.

"The clouds will take me, sister, and all will be well. The truth of our father's death rests somewhere, and I will find it."

She darkened, staring into Sezaru's face. "I would give up my command to go with you."

"I know you would." Sezaru's voice held no sense of condemnation. "But you have a duty, my sister. Defend the Empire. Without an Emperor to command their respect, the Clans will wage war." He lowered his eyes and stared into hers, his blue eyes peculiar and distant. "If one of us is to seize the Steel Throne, then we must be sure there is an Empire to rule."

Sezaru spoke of such things with a peaceful tone, but Tsudao knew that the steel in her soul was echoed in that of her brother. "The throne must be safe," she agreed. "If I must place my honor before it, I will keep the Empire whole."

"I know you will, Tsudao-san." Sezaru smiled. The two children of Toturi rested for a moment in silence, the wind of the high mountains ruffling the manes of their mounts. Neither chose to speak or to fill the goodbye with useless words. For men like Naseru, words were a shield that covered the true meaning of his actions. For Tsudao and Sezaru, they were no more than a waste of breath.

At last, Tsudao tugged on her horse's reins and turned back toward the legions that awaited her command. "Find our father's murderers," she said, "and I will destroy them." With that, she raised the fan of command once more into the sunlight, and the armies turned west, toward the Dragonfly lands.

She did not look back to see Sezaru nod his agreement. She did not need to know his mind.

Somehow, some way . . . they both knew Toturi would be avenged.

It was in their blood.

* * * * *

The Dragonfly lands were wide and rolling, with small hills and wide rivers dotting the gentle landscape. To the north, the Teeth of the Serpent mountain range tore open the sky above the Dragon lands, and to the south, the Lion plains opened into fields of shining gold. The last time Tsudao had seen these lands, they had been prosperous and welcoming. Today, they were in flames.

Dragonfly Palace rose above the hillocks, its jeweled sides shining in the afternoon sun and reflecting the light of the flames like two towers of wrought crystal. Around it, units of Dragon Clan samurai fought beside the men of the Minor Clan as Lion soldiers screamed battle-*kiops*. In the air, three groups of Phoenix shugenja hurled spells down upon the Dragonfly, igniting the fields with explosions of flame.

"Damn," Tsudao cursed as her scouts raced back into formation. She lifted her hand into the air, shouting at the commanders of the Imperial Legion. "Matsu Domotai-san, take two forces toward the Phoenix troops and command them to cease fire. Moshi Kekiesu-san, you will go with him. Use your magic to halt their spells. Kitsu Dejiko-san—" Tsudao spun on her horse, facing the two Lions who listened to her orders—"take three, and ride to the Lion. They know you. They will hear your words. Command them to stand down. If you are fired upon defend yourselves, but do not raise your blades first. I will meet with the Dragon myself."

The two commanders bowed, aware that they were being sent into danger. Dejiko's face shone with fierce exhilaration, while Domotai's was dark and brooding. He disliked Tsudao's entering combat, but he understood the necessity. The raging armies of the Dragon would listen to no one other than the imperial princess and General of the Legions. They might not even listen to her.

The Imperial Legions raced down into the valley before the Dragonfly Palace, their banners streaming in the wind of their passage. As they approached the crux of the combat, two legions turned south toward the Phoenix conclave, and three more separated from the main force, heading toward the Lion troops.

Four thousand men raced at her back, and Tsudao led them into the flames that surrounded the palace. Blades struck around her, and both Lion and Dragon screamed battle cries, too overwhelmed by the smoke to recognize their true enemy. Tsudao's pony leaped aside to avoid a lowered pike, but it was too late. The sturdy horse shuddered and fell, hurling the imperial princess into the fray.

Tsudao rolled onto the ground, trying to escape without serious injury as she heard her horse's death scream. Behind her, Imperial troops swirled into the thick smoke of the battlefield, raising their standards and screaming out the names of their legions to try to keep some form of order. Overhead, another roar of flame, and a massive explosion shook the earth. Fire rained down, and the imperial princess covered her head to avoid the blistering sparks.

After a moment, the rain ended. Tsudao rose to her feet with effort, testing her legs and arms as she drew her blade. Save a few burns on her arms and calves, she was uninjured. The Fortunes themselves had spared her. Only their intervention had killed the pony and thrown her out of the range of the blast. The Phoenix shugenja were still chanting, their voices calling down strokes of lightning just outside the doors of the Dragonfly palace, and the Dragonfly shugenja's spells of protection had begun to buckle.

Out of the flame, a Dragon samurai staggered, smoke and flame burning his eyes. Hardly recognizing Tsudao as anything more than another samurai, he raised his blade and charged. To his side, three more Dragon answered his yell, racing into the smoke to assist their companion.

Tsudao set her feet, waiting for his first strike. Despite her anger at the wrongful attack, she knew that the smoke had all but blinded the men. They did not understand what they did, and she would not kill them for their confusion. Though afterward, the samurai might well wish she had.

The first man roared, his blade cutting toward Tsudao's shoulder. She parried easily, turning the katana aside and raising the hilt of her sword to punch the Dragon samurai dead in the center of his face. There was a disturbing crunch, and he howled in pain. The second used Tsudao's distraction to aim a cut at her thigh, but she was ready. Grabbing the man's arm, she twisted his elbow until the joint popped loudly, and then struck his knee with a perfect snap-kick to the side. He fell beside his wounded opponent, but the third and fourth attacked together as Tsudao was engaged with the others.

Tsudao lifted the second man and hurled him into his two charging companions. He fell into them, but it only slowed their rush. The first chopped downward in a perfect overhand cut, while the second launched his sword toward Tsudao's helm. She avoided the first blow, and blocked the second on the hilt of her katana, praising the craftsman that had made the hilt of her blade. It held despite the force of the Dragon's strike, and Tsudao kept her hand.

From the side, a Lion battle cry attracted the attention of the two Mirumoto samurai, and they paused. Tsudao blessed whatever Matsu had just cried out and used the fragment of a second to drive her foot into the belly of one of the Dragons. His enameled armor snapped from the force of the blow, and the breastplate caved in beneath Tsudao's iron-shod sandal. The second realized that his friend was in danger and cut at Tsudao again, forcing her to drop to the ground to escape his blow.

Rolling, she swept her leg against the man's knees, hurling him into the mud. He fell with a gasp but quickly rolled away to try to regain his footing. Before he could stand, Tsudao was upon him, her fist cracking against his temple with the power of a tiger's claw. His eyes rolled up into his head, and he slumped to the earth, mud covering the side of his slack-jawed face. That would certainly leave a bruise.

Tsudao looked up, watching a troop of Lion soldiers race

past her. They had seen her in combat with the Dragon and assumed she was one of their soldiers. Tsudao shook her head, climbing to her feet and raising the horn that hung from her belt. With three sharp notes, she called to her soldiers to reform upon her position. The high towers of the Dragonfly Palace loomed ahead through the smoke, and Tsudao heard her men shouting as they gathered around her. Many of them seemed injured, though not badly. They were, after all, the best legions in the Empire.

Another horn sounded, and Tsudao peered upward to see Moshi Kekiesu in the air above them, summoning the wind spirits to part the clouds. The Phoenix shugenja were nowhere to be seen, and as the smoke cleared, Tsudao recognized the Lion banners moving away from the main battlefield.

"Toturi-sama!" one of the lesser commanders yelled. "The Dragon have broken the main Lion force. With the Phoenix holding from our orders, the Dragon are driving the Lion back from the field."

Tsudao growled. Although it would bring an end to the fighting—at least for the day—it was not good news. If the Dragon believed themselves victorious, they would not appreciate the aid of the Imperial Legions.

"Where stands the Dragon commander?" she cried.

"To the north, at the gates. He wishes to speak with you."

No doubt. Tsudao sheathed her sword. As the smoke cleared, no more samurai would mistake the Imperial banner for that of their enemy. Signaling to her men to flank her, Tsudao followed the road that led up the slight incline toward the Dragon gate. As she exited the battlefield, Kekiesu drifted down beside her, landing effortlessly to the right of the imperial princess.

At the top of the hill, the Dragon forces had assembled. Their faces were blackened with soot, and their armor was covered in blood. The injured—mostly Dragonfly—had been drawn to the side where the shugenjas tended their wounds. They were brave samurai, and few cries could be heard from the hillside.

Tsudao's men marched up the muddy road to the gates of the palace, and the princess tried to ignore the blood that stained the ground and turned it to mush. Despite Kekiesu's spell, smoke still broiled from the fires on the battlefields, but the towers themselves were spotless, completely undamaged. The shugenja of the Dragonfly had managed to hold the line, but all that remained of their clan and their lands were two jeweled towers, standing in the center of devastation.

In the center of the gates, a command of Dragon samurai stood at attention. Their golden armor was lightly stained, and their hands were on their sword hilts, though the weapons were sheathed at their sides. From the rear came their commander, walking stiffly through his men and shoving them out of his way. As the Dragon general approached, Tsudao felt her heart turn cold and angry. She knew this man.

Mirumoto Junnosuke.

"How pleasant that the Imperial Legionnaires have decided to come and watch as the Lion and Phoenix destroy us all," Junnosuke said from the top of the hill as Tsudao and her men halted. Tsudao could feel blistering hatred radiating outward from the Mirumoto and his men.

"By the order of the Steel Throne, we have been sent to bring an end to this war."

"How convenient that you step in just after the Lion have been routed." Junnosuke snarled. "Were the roads too muddy for speed, or did you stop in one of the Lion villages for dinner?"

Tsudao refused to allow the Mirumoto's words to anger her, and she chopped her hand through the air.

"There will be no more fighting until after the ambassadors have met."

"Now that the Dragonfly armies have been completely destroyed, their fields ruined, and their peasants have suffered countless murders—now there will be no war? No, Imperial Princess. You are wrong." He stepped forward and threw a scroll marked with the seal of the Dragonfly. It landed at Tsudao's feet. "Our honorable allies in the Dragonfly have turned over their autonomy to the Dragon. They bow beneath our feet and have invoked our protection against their invaders. By Imperial Law," he sneered, "that makes this little war a matter of honor, and the Dragon are its arbiters. The Dragon Clan respect the Imperial Legions," he said in a voice that denied his words, "but we have been asked to be the arbiters here. Not you. The attack on the Dragonfly is an insult to their honor, and according to law, all matters of honor must be settled the same way. In blood."

Behind Tsudao, Kitsu Dejiko stepped forward with her hand on her sword hilt. "I beg you, General, let me answer this man's words with steel."

"Yes, Dejiko! Come and fight me." Junnosuke pointed at her, his hand curling into a fist as he all but cast her threat aside. "You stand on lands that the Dragon guard. You cannot hide behind your princess. If you challenge me, we will stand astride the Dragon's coils, outside the domain of Imperial Law, and you, girl—" he spat at Dejiko's feet— "you will die."

Dejiko leaped forward, but Tsudao's hand caught her elbow and forced the Lion back. "He is right, Dejiko—like it or not." Tsudao scowled. "These lands are held by the Dragonfly. If they have asked the Dragon to be their arbiter, if they have turned over their autonomy and demanded that honor be appeased, then he is right. There must be blood." Tsudao turned toward Junnosuke, ice in her eyes. "If we remain, then we break the very law that we are sworn to guard. So long as the fight continues on Dragon land, it is their right to refuse us arbitration and take matters into their own hands. This battle," she said soberly, "is his."

Dejiko stiffened but moved no further.

"If the Dragonfly are no more, than hear this, Mirumoto."

Tsudao moved past Dejiko with the grace of a stalking tiger, her long dark hair flowing out behind her helm. She walked to Junnosuke, pausing only when she stood mere inches from his face. In a hiss, she spoke. "The Imperial forces shall withdraw with the armies of the Matsu into Lion lands. When the Dragon decide to make good their threats about this debt of honor, they will have to invade into Lion territory . . . and I doubt the Lion will see things the same way that you do. They will ask for no arbitration, and your armies will be on their lands. Within the bounds of Imperial Law."

"They have destroyed the Dragonfly."

"And the Dragon have adeptly taken their place." Tsudao glared into the Mirumoto's eyes without flinching. "Whatever else your courtiers tell you to say, Dragon, remember this: You will not be able to retreat and ignore this 'debt of honor' you crow about so loudly. It had best be answered, and swiftly." Tsudao pointed at the horizon, where the moon had begun to peer over the thick trails of smoke. "When the month of the Hare ends, this matter will become an unanswered rivalry. Under Imperial Law, unanswered rivalries— even causes of honor—are a matter for the Imperial Magistrates." She was so close to Junnosuke that she could smell the man's foul breath, but Tsudao refused to back away. "If that happens, I will step in, and no amount of politic will halt the fury that I will rain upon your head."

The sheer force of Tsudao's presence was like a physical blow, and Junnosuke took an unwilling step backward. A faint flicker of doubt grew in the Dragon's eyes, and Tsudao stepped away.

"Run back to your Lions, Tsudao-sama." Junnosuke shouted as she gave the command for the Imperial Legions to turn back. "Guard them. Guard them well. Soon they will die, and then you will follow!" He laughed then, but it was the false pride of a desperate man.

Kitsu Dejiko offered the general her own pony and stood beside Tsudao as she mounted.

"Why did we not simply kill him where he stands?" The Lion commander's stance was guarded, and she did not take her eyes from Junnosuke's rigid form.

"Kill him?" Tsudao questioned. "And ensure that the Dragon have even more allies in this war? No, Dejiko. He has discovered a fine line within the law, and we must step back. The law is everything. It must guide us all. But do not fear. The thinner the thread, the more likely it is to snap. Even with the Dragonfly lands under their control, the Dragon cannot feed their peasants. This acquisition will only make them hungry for more. No, Dejiko . . ." Tsudao looked back at the palace of the Dragonfly as her troops marched south. "Today, he has won. But tomorrow . . . tomorrow, we shall wait in Lion lands, and we shall catch the Dragon when he falls."

11 | A MATTER OF HONOR

The wind rose around him, drifting through his tent in quiet passing. A woman's scent hung upon it, the scent of faded blossoms, and then . . . she was there. The dream was as real as breath. Each movement of her body shifting beneath silk drew his eyes to her. Delicate braids swung within the long cloak of her unbound hair, and her radiant eyes shone with all the fever of the brightest stars. She was beautiful, her alabaster skin shining in the last rays of moonlight, and the robes that flowed about her slim form were black and violet—the colors of night. He wondered for a moment why she was there, but his question was forgotten in the first kiss of her soft, red lips.

"Your strength," the woman murmured, the long soft hair shifting about her shoulders and falling gently into his face, "is in your sword. She cannot best you." Her hands brushed his cheeks, and with twin kisses, she closed his eyes. "Cut off the head, and the serpent will die."

Her whisper faded, and Junnosuke awoke to the first brilliant ray of dawn.

* * * * *

Tsudao gazed over the encampment, pleased with the efficiency and cleanliness of her soldiers. Ten days had passed while the Lion forces stood guard at the border of their northern lands. The fires within the Dragonfly lands had faded and died, but the anger within Lion hearts had not yet dimmed. Phoenix shugenja met with Lion battle-commanders, readying strategy for the next assault. The Phoenix had found a ready ally in their war with the Dragon. The Lion still cursed the day the Dragonfly seized their autonomy as a minor clan, and in doing so, stole a Lion's bride. Though such events were long in the past—the bride had died more than five hundred years ago, by Tsudao's best estimate—the Lion had long memories. They had never reconciled with the Dragonfly, and this recent battle only allowed them a place to vent the most recent hostilities between the two clans.

Although the imperial forces camped apart from the Lion and Phoenix battalions, Tsudao had ordered her right hand, Kitsu Dejiko, to maintain contact with the Matsu forces. The princess refused to meet with the Lion directly, knowing that to show them such favor would only increase the gossip and lies that fed the courtiers and politicians. Already, they spread rumors that she had moved the Imperial Legions here to aid her own allies, not to serve the Empire. Foolish lies, but dangerous ones.

As Tsudao practiced her morning exercises, moving the wooden practice sword in slow, precise forms with the control of a master swordsman, she became aware of someone kneeling patiently just outside her view. Tsudao finished the forms and lowered her weapon, sweat touching her forehead.

"Yes?" she said without looking.

"My Lady," the voice was Moshi Kekiesu's. Since their falling-out at the Imperial Palace, Kekietsu had said hardly three words to Tsudao unless they were directly related to her duty, and Tsudao's heart ached to hear the formality in her voice even now. "There is a small band of emissaries moving from the east. They are headed for the Dragonfly palace."

"Whose emissaries?"

"The Scorpion," Kekiesu said. "They have a treaty with the Dragon, and no doubt seek to lend their aid."

Tsudao snorted. "Scorpion are poor fighters."

"But excellent negotiators . . . and twisters of truth."

Nodding, Tsudao opened her eyes and looked at her hand-maiden. "Kekiesu-san—" Tsudao frowned, reaching for words that were difficult to say— "I do not wish to insult your family's beliefs, but this notion that I am the chosen heir of the Sun Goddess . . . your clan is mistaken."

"With respect, Tsudao-sama—" Kekiesu lowered her head— "we are not."

To think that the Empress had once called Tsudao stubborn . . .

"Kekiesu, listen to me. I am mortal, as are you. As are all who have descended from the Kami. I am no more than this."

"You foresaw all of this—the fires in the mountains, the refugees, and the wars. How can you say that you will not also prophesy peace?"

"There is no peace," Tsudao stood, placing her practice sword among the others at the edge of the field. "There never will be, until the Steel Throne is secure."

Kekiesu looked directly at Tsudao, her brow furrowing in relentless devotion to her ideals. "Have you seen the light once more, then? Has the Sun shone through your eyes to tell you this? Because I think that it has not. I think you do not know when there will be peace, and you fear it as much as you fear these visions."

Tsudao turned, anger flashing in her eyes. It was the first time anyone had ever said such a thing to her without standing for a duel. Controlling herself with great effort, Tsudao rumbled, "I fear nothing."

"Then do not fear my devotion—or the desire of the Empire. You sit and ponder how the Empire was when your father lived.

Open your eyes, and see it as it has become." Kekiesu knew that she walked along the edge of a fine blade, but she did not falter. "You have only known battle. Your honor is untarnished, through courage and through your sense of duty, but your eyes know fear. What if fighting is not enough to save Rokugan?"

Tsudao started to speak, but her handmaiden lowered her head again and continued. "The Sun Goddess, Amaterasu, is dead. Her place in the heavens has been usurped, and you are all of her that remains to us. Look into the light of the Sun and tell me it is not so. Your father believed it enough that he gave me into your service as a child. He knew that one day you would be forced to fight something that could not be assaulted with the blade—and that you would falter. Tell me you do not fear the day your sword will not be enough. Show me you truly have no hesitation, and I will commit seppuku in payment for my rash words. But before you send me to my death, Tsudao-sama—" Kekiesu lifted her head and her dark eyes contained a challenge— "tell me truthfully that there is no doubt within your soul."

Tsudao stared into her companion's eyes, trying to maintain her anger in the face of such a raw confrontation. Yet as she searched her own heart, she knew that Kekiesu's words held truth, and she said nothing at all.

"You have turned away everything you could not define by your sword, Tsudao-sama, but you will not drive me off that easily." Kekiesu's words were soft, but their barb was sharp.

Tsudao reddened, and Doji Tanitsu's face surfaced in her mind. Serenely stoic, the little Centipede shugenja raised herself from the ground. She sat back on her heels for a long moment and considered.

"If I cannot make you believe in my truths, Tsudao, then at least allow me to help you find your own. I have used my magic to spy upon these Scorpion emissaries, and they are far too heavily armed to be mere diplomats. Further, I recognize one of them as a companion of your brother, and I believe that bodes ill for any hope of peace."

"One of Sezaru's men?"

Kekiesu shook her head. "A servant of Hantei Naseru."

Tsudao nodded, uneasy. "What would Naseru wish with this war? What would serve his goals?"

There was only a faint pause, and then Kekiesu whispered, "Your death, my Lady."

Her eyes haunted with some inner demon, Tsudao shook her head. "No. He would not wish me dead."

"You are his rival."

"I am his sister."

"As you wish." The Moshi shugenja lowered her head again, allowing Tsudao a moment to consider. "But if we cannot turn the Scorpion from the Dragon's side, we will have gained another enemy. The Empire is changing, Princess. We must change with it."

"How?" Tsudao murmured, looking to her friend for guidance. Kekiesu was her handmaiden, but she was also a shugenja, and as she had already proven, a true friend.

"The Lion-Phoenix alliance cannot continue to fight the Dragon. We must find another way, and it must be done without angering the Scorpion. Junnosuke must break his own ties, or we will be bound in them.

Tsudao pantomimed severing a thread. "The spider does not become entangled in his own web, but you are correct, Kekiesu-san. We must let the Scorpion pass . . . and deal with the repercussions as they rise. Perhaps the Fortunes will show us a way through that we have not yet discovered."

"Amaterasu will guide us, my Lady," Kekiesu said firmly, no doubt in her eyes.

"I hope so, Kekiesu. I hope so."

* * * * *

Four days later, the Dragon armies marched. They raised their gold and green banners, and beneath the standards hung the jewel-tone symbol of the Dragonfly. As one, they advanced through the gates of the Dragonfly Palace, through the twisting hills and valleys of the central Dragonfly land, and to the border of Lion lands. There, the armies ceased their march, mere yards from the campground of the Lion and Phoenix.

As soon as the Dragon had moved, the Lion and Phoenix horns sounded, and a battalion of allied forces faced their enemies across the invisible border of the territorial divide. The golden grasses of the Plain of Ten Stones waved in a faint breeze as the armies paused both to the north and to the south. Tsudao's own Imperial Legions, less than half the size of the gathered Dragon troops, stood to the east. There they would wait until this matter was decided—or until the Dragon set foot on Lion land.

On the east flank of the Dragon lines, a small group of Scorpion stood just apart from the main line, their banner of scarlet and black contrasting sharply with those around them. Tsudao rested upon her horse and watched the Scorpion. Wherever this battle was fought, it would be the uneasy alliance of Scorpion and Dragon that would turn the tide. Although they had few men upon the field, the Scorpion did not need more. They would not fight with swords.

From the forefront of the Dragon lines, Mirumoto Junnosuke rode forward with his two commanders. Seeing this as an offer of treaty, the Lion and Phoenix also sent their unit captains, and Tsudao signaled to Kitsu Dejiko and Matsu Domotai. The three pressed their heels to their steeds and galloped onto the wide field, headed for the gathering in the center of the Plain of Ten Stones. A lone Scorpion followed, his steed loping across the field.

As she slowed her pony beside the sturdy steed of Akodo Ijiasu, the Lion general, she could see fury building in the man's face. Beside him, Shiba Yoma clenched his fist upon his thigh; the Phoenix's steed shied to the side as it felt its rider's tension increase.

"You would not dare say such things if General Toturi-sama stood before you," Akodo Ijiasu snarled.

"She is here." Junnosuke sneered, regarding Tsudao with contempt.

"Say what you will, Junnosuke." The Phoenix's lack of the honorific was not lost on the Mirumoto. "The Empire is listening."

Tsudao stared at Junnosuke, her eyes narrowed. The Dragon lifted his chin as if to signal his complete lack of fear. He laughed once, a short bark, and his commanders glanced at each other in concern.

"I do not see the Empire." Junnosuke turned a cold eye on Tsudao, then looked away. "I see only a cur squabbling for her father's scraps, and two clans who hide behind her like children."

The other commanders met this remark with silent amazement, and Dejiko's mouth actually dropped open. Domotai reached for his sword, uncertain and angry. Tsudao's face reddened, but she forced her rage to obey her will. Junnosuke was deliberately trying to provoke a duel with the Lion commander. If Junnosuke could provoke them into a duel, then he could use its outcome to back the Dragon's claim that this was a matter of honor and not a war. To do so would keep the Imperial forces at bay even longer— perhaps indefinitely. By the red flush that crept over Akodo Ijiasu's face, Junnosuke's gambit was working.

"So, Junnosuke, you think it is so easy to ignore that your clan invades our lands," Shiba Yoma interjected, trying to turn the Dragon's barbs away from the Lion, "destroys our sacred shrines?"

"That has no purpose here." Junnosuke stared at the other commanders. "The only matter to be contested is that the Lion defamed Dragonfly lands for no purpose and destroyed the honor of their house."

"Which we did," snapped the Akodo, "only after your peasants flooded through the Dragonfly lands and into our villages. We drove them back—"

"No!" Junnosuke cut him off. "You slaughtered them."

"As you slaughtered the Yobanjin at the Mountains of Regret?" Dejiko's level voice was accusing, and Tsudao stared at her for a moment. She hadn't realized how much anger the Lion held within until she spoke.

"Stop this." Tsudao raised her voice, cutting the argument off. Her pony half-reared in tension, but she clamped her legs upon its sides and forced it to remain still. "The Imperial Dictates command that wars between the clans will be resolved by Imperial arbitration. Your claim that the Dragonfly have had their honor smeared by the Lion attack is all that keeps our forces from your door, Junnosuke-san. Within days, this will all be moot, and the Imperial Dictates will allow me to step in formally. Forcing a duel with the Akodo will not help you. Nothing will help you." Tsudao's voice was low with rage, her hands clenched on her horse's reins.

"There are no Imperial Dictates here," the Mirumoto snarled. "Only a matter of duty and common respect. A matter which you––" he pointed an accusatory finger at Tsudao—"insult and deface at every opportunity. You tread on the Dragon's honor, and we will stand for it no more."

The Scorpion ambassador's pony reined in at the edge of the group, and Tsudao was surprised to recognize the man who rode upon its wide back—Bayushi Paneki, the same man who had aided her at Winter Court when the news of her father's death was announced to the Empire. He nodded at Tsudao and inclined his head to the other ambassadors with a faint smile.

"I see the negotiations go as well as I had thought," Paneki said as he took in the reddened and furious faces of the Lion and Phoenix commanders.

"There are no negotiations," Junnosuke snapped. "I do not negotiate with dogs."

With a strangled roar, Akodo Ijiasu reached for his sword, but Tsudao's words cut him off. "Very well, Junnosuke. You have what you came for. I challenge you to defend yourself.

If you stand so firmly on Dragon honor, then prove to me that your footing is secure."

Junnosuke laughed, and it rang of victory. "I accept! When I am finished, whelp, I will send your head back to your brothers and beseech the Imperial family to breed a better class of heir."

"Very well, then, honored samurai," Bayushi Paneki cut in smoothly. "If you will please call your lieutenants to remove the steeds, we can clear this section of ground for the contest. Tsudao-sama, I assume that the young woman by your side will be your second? And Junnosuke-san, your lieutenant will be yours?"

Junnosuke suddenly looked at the Scorpion as if the man had lost his mind. "This is not suitable ground for such a duel."

"Ah," the Scorpion countered pleasantly, "Dragon soil is not stable enough for you? I had hoped that the mountains would not erupt today. . . ."

Reddening, Junnosuke threw himself from his horse and drew his swords from the beast's saddle. "I will fight here. There is no better place to prove my honor than on my family's territory. Come, Princess, and see if you are worthy to bleed upon my blades."

Domotai stepped to his lady's side to help her dismount. Tsudao lowered herself from her pony slowly, already regretting her hasty words. She had been trying to prevent the Lion and the Dragon from just such a duel—and in doing so, had placed herself in the very trap that Junnosuke had set for the Lion. One of the lieutenants of the Imperial Legion rushed forward at Dejiko's signal and dragged their horses away from the killing ground. Dejiko smoldered at Tsudao's side, obviously wishing that it were her blade preparing to cut through Junnosuke.

"If I should die—" Tsudao said quietly, as an aside to Dejiko.

Her Lion second barely concealed her barked laughter in

the surrounding commotion of all the other commanders stepping off their steeds. "You think *he* can hurt you?"

Tsudao leveled a steady gaze at her impulsive follower. "Anything can happen when we put our fates in the hands of the Fortunes, Dejiko-san."

Domotai glanced over at the Dragon commanders, where Junnosuke was stretching his legs in preparation. "Junnosuke was a commander of the Imperial Legion for a reason. He will not fall easily to any blade. I taught him to fight against the Lion stance, and I regret that. He is my Oathbrother, but he has failed me. Still, for all that, I believe there is good in him. He can be redeemed. I beg you, Tsudao . . . bear that in mind."

"You have already asked me for his life once, Domotai," Tsudao said. "You have no right to ask again." Domotai grew somber, and Tsudao continued. "Take the Legion to the south. Request the aid of the Crane as arbiters. Doji Tanitsu—" the name fell heavily from Tsudao's lips— "will know what to do. He will avenge my death. And tell Kekiesu . . . tell her . . . she was right."

"I will," Dejiko agreed.

"Are you ready, your Highness?" Paneki called from the center of the makeshift dueling circle. Around the edges, the Phoenix, Dragon, and Lion commanders had gathered in tight circles, their faces grim. Tsudao nodded once and removed her helm and gauntlets. She handed them to Dejiko and stepped onto the field.

Junnosuke entered the circle only a few seconds after Tsudao, a sword in each of his hands. Bayushi Paneki began to speak, but Junnosuke cut him off. "Say what you will, Scorpion!" Junnosuke snapped. "This is Dragon territory. I will fight with the style of my family and the blade of my ancestors."

Two swords was the traditional style of the Mirumoto family, and Junnosuke had the right to demand that he be allowed to use them, given that this was not the formal iaijutsu duel of the court, but a kenjutsu duel upon the field of battle.

Paneki turned to Tsudao. "Do you wish a second weapon?" he asked.

She shook her head. "I need no other blade."

The Scorpion nodded and stepped to the side, watching as the competitors lowered their blades. For a moment, Tsudao was reminded of her trial match, and she could almost hear her Lion sensei's voice whispering in her mind. *Approach with grace; strike without mercy. Do not rely on your strengths. Rely on your opponent's failure. You will always have your strengths, but the opening he will give you will be the only one you need.*

Paneki raised his hand, a long white sash fluttering in the breeze. "Ready?" His voice was firm, controlled. Both opponents nodded, taking their fighting stance. Tsudao watched Junnosuke's katana and wakizashi begin to spin slowly, sunlight flashing from their long steel blades.

Never stand still. Lead your opponent onto unfamiliar ground. Release your thoughts and allow the sword to move you.

"Ki-i-i-i!" Paneki cried, the flag in his hand dropping to his side.

Tsudao was in motion before even she realized it. Her sword, released from its scabbard, leaped toward her opponent but slid away from his upraised defense. Junnosuke's second sword curved toward her legs, only to be deflected by the tip of Tsudao's katana as she stepped away. Junnosuke's other hand rose, searching for a weakness in Tsudao's stance. She twisted, rolling behind him, providing no opening for him.

Tsudao's return strike was brutal, slicing through Junnosuke's pants with a sharp, tearing sound. He moved at the last moment, throwing himself to the ground to avoid her steel, and her sword caught only fabric. Using Junnosuke's momentary distraction, Tsudao launched a kick to his wakizashi and was rewarded by the sound of snapping fingers. His second blade fell to the ground, and she spun to recover her stance.

Junnosuke backed away, his features blackened by ferocious rage. He shook his left hand cautiously, trying to flex his fingers but with no luck.

"Your ancestors do not favor you, Junnosuke," Tsudao taunted, "or they would not have taken away their swo—"

Junnosuke roared, hurling himself at her before Tsudao could finish the taunt. She parried his strike and slid beneath his blade to thrust her elbow into his ribs. There was a sharp cracking sound, but Junnosuke continued to push forward against her—and Tsudao felt the cold touch of steel at her side.

He had drawn a concealed dagger from his belt and held it lightly between the thumb and forefinger of his broken hand, his wrist turning purple from the effort. The shattered bones in his hand significantly weakened his thrust, which saved Tsudao's life. Though pain burst through her torso, she still breathed.

Tsudao reached for Junnosuke's injured hand before he could stab again, twisting against the broken bone and hearing Junnosuke scream in agony. The dagger dropped to their feet, and Tsudao slammed her fist into Junnosuke's face. The Dragon staggered back, blood pouring from his nose. He held his katana between them as if to ward Tsudao away, but her fury could not be contained.

A massive blow and his sword wavered. Junnosuke fell to one knee, trying to regain his footing as the earth beneath his feet was churned to mud. She struck again, her eyes as gold as the sun burning down upon the field. Junnosuke's katana shook, dipping heavily to the side before returning to attempt another deflection of Tsudao's blows. But Junnosuke could not parry the third strike, and Tsudao's katana cut through his blade with the clear ring of a bell. His sword shattered, raining fragments of steel upon the ground, and the Mirumoto fell onto his back beneath his opponent's rage.

Tsudao raised her sword again, readying for the final strike that would rid Junnosuke of his life, but the throbbing pain in her side drew the strength from her arm. Sunlight flashed in Tsudao's eyes, and she heard another sound enter her mind. It was not the relentless teachings of her Lion sensei, but the soft, clear sound of her handmaiden's voice.

What if your blade cannot carve away these wars?

Junnosuke stared up at her, hatred and disgrace written upon his features. Around the golden field, the commanders of the four armies strained at the edge of the circle, desperate to see what Tsudao would do next. Tsudao lifted her sword again, her mind filling with rage.

Tell me that there is no doubt within your soul.

Tsudao knew that she could kill Junnosuke here and now, stealing his life with the keen edge of her blade, but something in Kekiesu's words stopped her. If she killed Junnosuke, the Dragon would turn against her. He was a hero to them, the hero of the Ki-Rin's shrine. He had fought for the peasants, and he had dared to stand against the Imperial Legions, the Lion, and the Phoenix in defense of his clan. If she butchered him, he would rise again as a martyr, and the Empire would never be free of his war.

Tsudao slowly withdrew her sword, aware of all the eyes upon her from around the field.

"Do it," Junnosuke hissed, baring his neck to her blade.

"No," whispered Domotai at the edge of the field. His knuckles turned white, hands clenched into fists. "Oath-brother . . ."

With no emotion on her expressive face, Tsudao lowered her sword and stepped away. This was not a time for death. It was the time to bring peace, and peace could not be given rest on a bed of blood.

"No!" screamed the Dragon commander, crawling to his knees and reaching for her sword. "You will kill me!" His cry was bleak and hovered on the border of madness. For the first time, Tsudao looked at Junnosuke with something akin to pity. This disgrace was too much for him, and it threatened to unhinge his mind. "You will not leave me this way!" he howled.

"Mirumoto Junnosuke," Tsudao's words were as cold as winter snows. "You have violated Phoenix ground, and you have challenged the honor of the Lion, the Phoenix, and the Imperial House. You have been proven false by the will of the Fortunes in honorable combat, and your authority ends here. You will not lead the Dragon any longer—not because you are not Mirumoto, but because you are no longer samurai."

"You cannot do this," Junnosuke shook with anger. "Bayushi Paneki-san, our clans have been allied for a generation, and I call upon that treaty now. Lift your sword and kill me with honor. Let me die without this shame. I will not have it—not from her." Junnosuke seethed, venom and hatred burning in every syllable.

"You are wrong, Junnosuke." Tsudao's eyes were hard as stone. "You will, and you must."

"If you do not stand with me, you break the treaty!" Sweat flew from the Dragon commander's face as he screamed at Bayushi Paneki.

"You have already broken the treaty—and proven that you have no honor, Junnosuke," Paneki said. "You drew another weapon within the duel. I had already allowed you two swords. No dagger was granted to your use, yet you drew, and you attacked. Despite your treachery, Tsudao still bested you, but you dishonored yourself and me, as the arbiter of your duel." Bayushi Paneki clenched his fist, then opened his hand with a motion like falling cherry blossoms. "The treaty of honor between our two clans is ended, and my family will no longer place arms beside your own. May the Fortunes take mercy on your soul."

"You stand with this honorless spawn of a cur?" Junnosuke pointed at Tsudao.

"I stand with the Imperial Legion." Paneki's smile was pleasant. Tsudao felt rooted to the ground at the Scorpion's words. Paneki—*the Scorpion*—siding with her? The Dragon-Scorpion alliance ... *dissolved?*

Junnosuke roared, gripping the dagger on the ground and rushing to his feet as if to end Tsudao's life. Tsudao leaped back, raising her katana, but Junnosuke's strike was stopped by a silk scarf that wrapped around the Dragon's good wrist. With a quick twist, Bayushi Paneki snapped Junnosuke's arm back, and the Dragon shrieked in anguish. The dagger fell uselessly to Junnosuke's feet, a good handspan from Tsudao.

"Enough!" One of the other Dragon stepped forward. He was a burly man, and his swords hung out from his hip like the awkward legs of a newborn calf. "I am Mirumoto Shizare, son of Mirumoto Uso. I claim the command of the Dragon forces here, and I say that this will go on no longer."

Junnosuke glared at Paneki and backed away as the Dragon commander lifted the sword of his ancestors from the ground.

"Junnosuke," Mirumoto Shizare rumbled, "this day, you promised your armies honor, but you brought them only shame. You are cast out of the Dragon Clan, and your name shall be taken from the records of our families. Take back the sword of your father and go"

Junnosuke tore the sword from the Dragon's hands, placing its blade against a rock that lay on the ground. "If even my brothers turn against me, then I have no family at all." Raising his foot, Junnosuke lowered it upon the short sword, snapping the blade of the wakizashi in two.

Junnosuke marched back to the horses, grabbing one of the beasts by its reins and dragging himself onto the steed. "You will hear of me again, Tsudao." His snarl was discordant and strained, madness following closely upon its heels. "I swear it."

Jerking the horse's reins so fiercely that the poor beast screamed, Junnosuke dug his heels into its sides and rode away.

"Praise the Sun," Shiba Yoma murmured, making the sign of the holy deity before his eyes.

"Honorable Phoenix and Dragon—" Shizare bowed to the commanders— "although I cannot promise peace, I can at least allow your negotiators to meet with the courtiers of the Dragon to see what can be done. This war is not yet over, but we need shed no more blood upon these plains." He bowed and spun on his heel with a gesture to the other Dragon.

Tsudao nodded to the commanders of the Phoenix and Lion legions, grateful that the issue had ended with at least some small chance for peace.

"What will he do now?" Matsu Domotai murmured to Tsudao as the Imperial commanders rode from the field.

"Junnosuke?" Tsudao said. "His fate is unclear. With no allies and no honor . . ."

Dejiko's eyes followed the dark speck on the horizon as it vanished into the mountains to the north. "If he dies, then I suppose he can count himself fortunate."

"No, Dejiko," Tsudao replied. "If he dies, *we* will be the fortunate ones."

12 | WITHIN THE DARKNESS

The mountains rose like watchful guardians, sentinels of law above a shifting realm of chaos. Below, dark lava poured over the valleys, carving new riverbeds of stone. Twin rivers, black and choked with foul waters, twisted through the rugged terrain. They merged briefly, like crooked fingers twined together, then broke apart and opened fists of stone toward the sky. The mountains here were not the gentle northern peaks, but brutal teeth and claws, shredding the earth in jagged lumps and leaving behind tall shards of gray stone, the bones of the earth, opened for the sky to see.

Winds howled through the valleys, chasing one another with blasphemous laughter. The air was fetid, greenish, and thick. It burned in places where the Taint grew too heavy for the wind to hurl, searing into the ground with greenish fire. Twisted, blackened plants clung to the ground, struggling to choke their neighbors.

These were the Shadowlands, the black wastes to the

south of the Rokugani Empire. They were bordered to the north by Carpenter Wall, the towering home of the Crab, where thousands died each year to keep the evils outside Imperial lands. To the west, thick deserts prevented the Taint from expanding, and to the east, the oceans boiled with pollution and filth. Farther south, the land itself twisted and rebelled, throwing off the shackles of reality and twisting its very form to suit its perverted nature. Blood flowed down the southern mountains, pouring slime and corruption into blackened seas.

Darkness reigned, and the Taint provided all the nourishment the oni and other fiends required. Even the sun and moon did not shine here, turning away their divine faces as if afraid of the horrors they might see.

It did not matter. She did not need light to find her way. Fu Leng's voice still whispered in her ear. *Beneath the ruins of the Iron Citadel lies a sleeping beast. There, when the warm winds blow, my son will come to greet you. Go to him, and he will show you the way.*

Shahai's feet were bare, and her black and violet robes flowed in the sickly wind. Long braids writhed like snakes through the cloak of her hair, and her hands were spread in a gesture of loving acceptance. These lands were a second home to her. Twisted creatures scattered at her passing, afraid of the power that clung to her like the scent of rain. Even the powerful oni had not stopped her, though she walked through their territory. The ease in her eyes made them wary, and a single gesture of the Bloodspeaker's hand compelled them to submit. In this land of horror and despair, she was entirely unafraid.

From the high side of one river valley, she saw a great crater. The edges of the crater stood hundreds of miles apart—big enough to house an entire city. Like a wound in the earth's crust, it oozed green trails of pus as wide as a villager's hut. The crater was older than Shahai's grandfather, older than the Carpenter Wall, older even than the Empire itself, and was said to have been formed when the last of the Kami fell from the heavens because of his divine brother's treachery. The wound had never healed, boiling out Taint and corruption across all the lands of the south and twisting the Shadowlands. It was the open grave of a dead god, the anvil of despair, a place called the Festering Pit of Fu Leng by peasants who spoke in shuddering whispers, afraid of attracting the attention of the Dark Lord. To Shahai, it was holy ground.

She reached the edge of the crater as night fell and true darkness descended. The howls of oni echoed across the marshy plain, and the faint scent of blood filled the night. The demons had caught some hapless beast or man and were making sport of it. Shahai smiled. Let the fiends play. They so relished the few times they found interlopers within their domain, and the blood and torture would add to the power of this place.

Stepping gingerly, Shahai worked her way down into the pit, feeling shards of black obsidian tear at the bottoms of her feet. Within moments, they would be torn apart as if she had thrust them into a basket of daggers, but the pain soothed her. The Pit was testing her strength.

Deep within the crater, the darkness was broken only by a faint glow of power as scarlet as the blood that seeped from Iuchi Shahai's wounded feet. It might have taken hours to descend this far beneath the surface of the ground, or it might have been days. With no point of reference, it was hard to tell the difference. Already, Shahai's breath hung on the air like fetid condensation, glowing a faint blue against the red stones that shimmered in the walls of the massive crater.

The bottom of the crater was only slightly less wide than the opening far above. A thick lake of blood oozed and curdled, far thicker than any normal liquid. It seemed almost to have a life of its own, and the waves crashed and flowed into each other with no sense of current or direction. It was like a great mass of horrid flesh, rotted and wet, writhing against the shore of the crater that contained it. In the center of that vile lake stood the ruins of a palace forged of solid iron. It rose from the depths of the lake in a steel pillar, the sides of the iron citadel covered with rust but still solid despite the constant clawing of the waves.

Once the citadel's sides had gleamed with power, but then Toturi had come and killed the dark god, destroying the power of the Shadowlands and opening the way for shadows and spirits of blasphemy to run rampant across Rokugan's golden fields. Shahai wished that she had been able to see the true power of this place before the fall of Fu Leng. She closed her eyes and imagined tall, twisted spires covered in blood, and screams that echoed from high walls of steel and bone. Iron gates like the jaws of a giant monster clamped upon a wide bridge from the edge of the lake into the heart of the palace. The dream brought a smile to Shahai's face, and she opened her eyes to face the reality of the Dark Lord's hall.

It was fallen, the iron rotted and broken in columns of half-burned steel. The bridge itself hung just above the lake of blood and flesh, its columns rising from the thick water like a dead man's fingers reaching out of a tainted grave. The citadel's wide base was surrounded by fragments of the tall towers that had once graced it, and curving roofs, delicately mocking the elegant Rokugani style, hung in shards from the broken center of the crumbled building. Something shuddered deep beneath the base of the ruin, sending protesting waves through the lake around the citadel. As the drifting wave crashed upon the shore at Shahai's feet, she felt the blood of the lake cover her torn feet. A touch of madness gleamed for a moment, and a faint light shone deep beneath the rolling, fleshy waters. Shahai laughed, the sound drifting back upon the waves with envious richness.

There was still power here.

Silencing her laughter, Shahai slowly drew on the power within the pit. She pieced together fragments of bloodsong, torn remnants of earth power and corrupted winds, and fused them against her skin with words of arcane lore. The fabric of reality tore, and Shahai could sense another layer beyond the physical realm. Someone had overlapped power upon power, dream upon reality, and forged a presence greater even than the will of Fu Leng. She smiled, drinking in the shreds of energy and bleeding palms of the physical world, and willed herself to cross over. Power opened for her, allowed her in, and when she opened her eyes, the entire palace glowed with magic such as Shahai had never seen.

"Magnificent," she breathed, her eyes lighting with eagerness and desire. She completed her spell upon both worlds, the real and the profane, drawing upon the powers that lay half-dormant around the Iron Citadel.

When she was done, her body shone with energy, and waves radiated out from her presence more strongly than at any other point in the lake. When she was ready, Shahai opened glowing violet eyes and stepped out upon the lake of corruption. The fierce wind rocked against the ruin, carrying the scent of rotting meat from the lands far above. Where her bare and bloody foot touched the water, the blood caught fire, sparking out across small ripples and igniting beneath the pressure of her delicate flesh.

The waves scorched and sparked, but the water held her weight. Shahai extended her other foot out onto the surface of the rippling pool. The iron citadel loomed before her, and she would not be denied.

With each step, fire spread from her feet, circling her steps in small ignitions of pale flame. Shahai took her time with each movement, slowly forcing the lake to solidify enough to bear her above the waves. The waters protested and shivered, and something deep beneath the surface groaned with the weight of her slight form. The waters rocked and plunged, but where Shahai stood, no wave could crash. Her path remained stable, fire spreading outward in small ripples across the violent surface of the lake.

As the citadel loomed closer, Shahai felt the lake tremble as if a great creature moved somewhere in the depths. She did not pause or slow her steps but continued the slow march across. Waves splashed, sending fountains of thick, corrupted blood into the air, but she did not turn her eyes from her goal. The iron walls of the fallen palace arched over the water in collapsed spires, and Shahai walked toward them, ignoring the whispers and faint screams that churned up from the deep beneath her feet.

Only a few more steps and she would be at the broken gates. The lake around her howled and churned, roaring against the shore. The fire had spread across most of the lake, and the pit itself seemed a crucible of blood and flame. In the center of the lake, a great shadow rose, larger even than the palace itself, but Shahai did not turn. Sweat beaded upon her forehead, and the wind tossed her long dark hair, but she reached out one bloodstained foot and touched the rock upon which the gate had been placed—the last span of a fallen bridge.

As she touched it, a wail went up from the lake, and the fire went out. The crater was plunged into surreal night, made all the darker by the sudden absence of the flames. Shahai turned, her feet firmly upon the stone foundation of the ruined citadel, and saw a shadow ten times the size of a man slowly descend into the depths of the bloody water. Whatever the demon had been—and in this place, she was not willing to believe it could be other than a tremendously powerful oni—it was gone. She had beaten it. A smile curved her rich lips, and the sorceress turned back toward the heavy iron gates.

The gates moved as Shahai reached for them, tilting inward with a shriek of metallic protest. The sorceress drew back her hand, a strange innocence touching her features as the gate opened without her touch. She peered through the open gate with the delicacy of a child on a holiday morning and stepped within.

The front gardens of the citadel were formed of shaped

bone and broken glass, and scattered remnants of stained crystal were scattered across the gardens. The floor was a single tile of shaped iron and steel, the forged lines weaving around statues of bone and crystal and trees of iron with twisted limbs. Cautiously, Shahai made her way across the garden, her bloody feet leaving small prints along the rippling path. The large doors to the inner chambers of the palace were closed. They stood on a steel frame made like a typical Rokugani shoji screen, but the squares of rice paper had been replaced with stretched skin. Tattoos writhed on the skin as if seeking escape, held fast by the pins that kept the door against the building.

Shahai touched the doorframe, and it slid aside with a soft *sssh* like a serpent's hiss.

The chamber within was massive. A ceiling arched overhead, held aloft on tall pillars of iron, and diffused light poured from a tremendous scarlet stone placed within the top curve of the roof. The wreckage scattered across the outside of the iron citadel could not be seen here. Though rust stained the walls and blood pooled at the bottom of the eight huge pillars, the room was stable and magnificent.

"So," a woman's voice hissed from the distant edge of the chamber, "you have come."

Shahai walked lightly into the room, her bare feet making no sound on the cold metal floor. Her gaze searched into the room, uncertain where the sound had come from.

"You are not the one I seek," she said.

"You are so certain?" A shadow detached itself from the wall, walking into the scarlet light of the stone. It was a woman, her face smooth and beautiful. She wore gold silk robes, and her lips were wide and thick. The robes were nearly transparent, and beneath them shimmered the form of a body to tempt any man. But Shahai was not a man.

"You are not he." Shahai looked away, seeking another door out of the chamber. "Take me to him."

The woman snarled, furious at the dismissal, and her features shifted into that of the Empress herself. Her robes changed, turned into the gold and mauve of the Phoenix clan. "I am Kaede, Oracle of the Void and Empress of Rokugan. Bow before me, and be judged." A subtle lash of power struck out at Shahai's mind, erasing the improbabilities of the woman's words and her appearance. Perhaps this was Kaede. . . ? Shahai felt an overwhelming urge to kneel, but she shook her head to clear the fog from her mind.

Shahai glanced back at the woman. "No."

A faint whisper, and the woman's features changed once more. Now her robes turned scarlet and black, fitted tightly to an ample bosom. A black mask ornamented her features, drawing the eye to her magnificent, sultry smile. "You are correct. Well done. I am Bayushi Kachiko, once wife to the last Hantei, and Empress . . ." Again, the spell attempted to seize Shahai's mind, twisting her reality to accept this explanation.

With an annoyed flicker of her fingers, Shahai tore away the threads of magic that attempted to bind her thoughts. "You are not."

The creature roared in frustration, her ploys worthless. As Shahai watched, the creature's face turned black, then porcelain white, red tears of blood trickling down from the corners of her delicately upturned eyes. Her hands turned into sharpened claws of glass, and her robes swirled into misted chains. Almost before she could react, the woman clawed at Shahai's eyes, trying to tear them from their sockets, but the sorceress leaped back, and the claws passed a hair's breadth from her face.

Lifting a hand, the strangely beautiful beast began to chant, and power flowed from the scarlet stone at the top of the chamber. Shahai shouted a word of power, calling forth the disruptive energies of the void, and the stone's light flickered.

The porcelain face hissed, still strangely emotionless, and her black eyes widened in anger. She leveled her hands toward Shahai, and a black mist poured out of her ebony claws.

The sorceress's lips curled up in pleasure. She had seen this spell before and knew how to counter it easily. Although powerful, the spell was guided by sight, and vision could be deceived. The creature would not be expecting her to simply—

Vanish.

The black mist swirled in confusion. Shahai no longer stood where she had been, nor was she apparently anywhere within the iron chamber. Desperate to control the spell, the porcelain woman screamed, and the mist coalesced around one of the iron pillars. With a wrenching sound, the mist formed into bands of thick obsidian, squeezing the pillar until its shaft began to sink then twist in the magic's grasp. The porcelain creature howled, trying to loose the spell before the pillar fell, but she was no longer in control. The iron shriveled together beneath the crushing pressure of the magical bonds, and the pillar cracked.

The porcelain figure quickly cast a spell of ending, her attention focused on the tilting iron pillar and the flickering stone in the ceiling. Within moments, the black and mist-made bonds around the pillar dissolved, and the heavy iron ceiling stopped its perilous shaking.

While the other woman was preoccupied, Shahai appeared to the side of the chamber, casting a spell of her own. Her teeth flashed in a cruel grimace as she drew together the strength of blood that surrounded the ruined palace, tinged the floors, and tainted the steel walls. Never before had Shahai felt so much power, and she reveled in the pure essence of it.

"*O tesotsu suru! Mahai!*" she cried out, pointing a slim finger at the porcelain woman and drawing a dagger from her sleeve.

The woman's spell snapped, and her body jerked across the floor as though ropes had wrapped themselves around her wrists. Struggling, she attempted to free herself, but it was no use. Whatever magic held her in place had begun to tear her arms from their sockets, and she could do nothing but howl. She shrieked in fear and pain and stared in awe as her arms bled. Shahai laughed aloud, drawing the knife through the air and watching as the woman's body was wracked in agony. Her screams echoed through the iron palace, blending discordantly with Shahai's chants.

"Where is he?" Shahai said, twisting the woman's arms in the air as she danced like a puppet across the steel floor. Blood rained down from the creature's arms, spattering the iron columns. "Where is the son of darkness?"

The woman screamed, her face twisting in a grimace of hatred and defiance. Shahai closed her hand, slashing the air once more with her dagger. The puppet strings tightened, pulling the woman in two separate directions. There was a sickening tearing sound, and the creature roared.

"Where?" whispered Shahai, her voice soft and patient.

Agony lanced through the creature once more, and her back arched in torment. Shahai drew her dagger through the air above the woman's imaginary threads, and whispered, *"Mehai, oshumi shometsu . . ."*

The woman could not draw enough breath to scream. Blood trickled through her parted white lips. Shahai jerked her hand once more, and the porcelain of the creature's face cracked. The woman moaned, staring at Shahai with broken black eyes. Shahai squeezed again, and this time, the woman's emotionless face crumbled to dust, and the beast fell to ashes upon the floor.

Shahai sighed, releasing her fingers as dust sprinkled from her hand to the ground. "What a waste," she murmured.

"Not at all," a deep baritone countered. "On the contrary . . . a most excellent display."

He paced out of the shadows at the far end of the room, skin shining with transparent paleness beneath the light of the scarlet stone. The man's movements were gentle yet powerful, like the muscles of a great panther beneath its velvet fur. His aura shone with an inherent power like no other that Shahai had seen, rising from within his soul with the black fire of the Shadowlands.

"I am glad you have come, Shahai-san," he purred. He looked at her, a black mask covering his face. She could not see who wore the black robes, but she knew from the power that surrounded him that he was the one she sought.

"You are the son of Fu Leng," Shahai whispered. It was not a question. He could be no one else.

"And you are the Queen of the Bloodspeakers, the most powerful *maho* cult in the Empire. But I am more than you believe me to be, for I am also the son of the Emperor." Shahai's sudden intake of breath seemed to amuse him, and the masked figure smiled. "Do not be so amazed, Shahai-san. Are there not many who would give themselves freely to the Dark One in exchange for that which is rightfully theirs?" There was power within his movements, and his hands seemed capable of shattering stone, yet he held one out to her in the gesture of a lover, beckoning her to his side. "Come to me."

"Where are we?" She took his hand and slid toward him with the grace of a wave upon the ocean. "This is not the Citadel of the past but another, fused within two worlds."

"We are in the Iron Citadel, and we are somewhere else." She could hear the laughing smile in his voice as he drew her close. "Somewhere beyond the physical, and I will teach you to walk these realms as well as those of the Empire."

"I dreamed of this power," Shahai rasped. "I dreamed of you."

He slid his hands down her pale arms, and his dark mask betrayed nothing. "Here, where my father is strongest, you may call me Daigotsu."

Shahai's eyes widened. She had heard the name before among the blood sorcerers. He was among the most secretive and hidden members of their cult—and one of the most powerful. He had hidden for many years, gathering his strength. As she gazed upon his sleek form, she purred with satisfaction. He was even more powerful than anyone had known . . . and he would ally with her.

"I am Fu Leng's son—" his warm breath hot in her ear— "and you will be his daughter, Shahai, for you are the child of darkness as well. Let me show you the gifts he has already brought to us." The man's voice melded with the steel surrounding them, and a faint light gathered in the rear of the room. "Your servants blessed it with the Taint, and now it has come home to its true Master."

Shahai saw where the man had been sitting, where he had watched the entire combat between Shahai and the demon woman. She guessed that her battle had been a test to prove she was worthy to stand at his side. A smile danced across her features, and her bloodstained steps were light. She had proven herself. She was the daughter of blood.

But the greatest smile of all came when Shahai realized that the man had been seated not upon a cushion of flesh nor a chair of bone, but upon the Steel Throne itself, now twisted by the Taint that spread from the touch of an oni at the Winter's Court.

"I have done this . . ." she murmured, brushing her fingers where the steel turned black and red with rust.

"*We* have done this, Shahai," her companion breathed, wrapping his arms in an embrace about her delicate form, "and we shall do more. There are many we can corrupt, and many within the imperial court who are already in our debt, though they do not yet know the cost of our assistance. I am closer to the Throne of Rokugan than they suspect, and I know their every movement. Within a short time, my brothers will see that I am Rokugan's future, and they will step aside before me. Already, in their own ways, each of them has served me. The Winds of Toturi's line stand in my way, and you have already crossed blades with Tsudao. I will destroy them one by one, and we will rule the Empire."

"Tsudao is more powerful than you believe," Shahai said, not bothering to hide her hatred for the woman's name. "She is the heir to the Sun."

"The Sun died once before. So it shall again. Tsudao's honor demands she claim the throne. We must crush that honor and destroy her faith. One by one, the others will fall to us. I know their weaknesses; we will prey upon them."

"I will enjoy breaking Tsudao's spirit." Shahai's eyes closed with delight. "Her friends will turn to enemies, and in the end she will not be able to stand between them . . . and nightmare."

"She will have no choice. An army gathers of my loyal followers—those who fell and have lived in the haven of the Shadowlands for generations." The Dark Son's voice was touched with contempt. "Together with the oni, we will destroy these who stand in my way, beginning with Tsudao." He whispered into Shahai's ear, and his breath smelled of desire and ambition. "We shall send our armies like the wind, and they will bring an end to the Empire. Behold, my love, as Rokugan's future begins."

13 | STOLEN PAST

Tsudao awakened in a sweat, the heat from her body rising as steam into the cold tent interior. She threw off her covers and reached for her sword. Only the silence in her tent and the absolute stillness of the camp outside kept her from yelling the alarm. Shivering in the cold, Tsudao tightened her short sleeping robe and held her katana tightly to her side. No one else had awakened. Kekiesu still snuggled deeply in her own futon, one arm thrown over her pillow.

Silence. For the space of three heartbeats, Tsudao simply listened. There was nothing other than the faint whisper of the wind and the soft crackle of a sentry fire in the distance. Gently, she fell to her knees, placing the katana on the floor in front of her and leaning over the blade as a wave of nausea struck her. Something was wrong, but Tsudao had no way of knowing what it was—or where.

A heavy wind shoved against the covers of the tent, rippling the thick silk in passing. Tsudao closed her eyes, trying to capture some part of the dream that had awakened her.

The armies of the Lion and the Phoenix still camped in silent peace just north of the Kitsu palace and south of the Dragonfly lands. Within seven days, their clans would once again discuss the possibility of peace with the northern Dragon.

A Lion screamed, raising his sword against the beast. More flames—such as she had never seen before—golden and black, burning even the high stone walls . . .

Her eyes opened to deny the scene before them, and her irises flamed a solid gold. "Kekiesu," Tsudao gasped. "Kekiesu!"

Eight swords slicing through the Empire, corrupting history and stealing the past. The Kitsu family crest hovered before her eyes, searing and blackening from an unknown poison.

Hands held her shoulders, brushing the hair out of her face. Tsudao could not see the tent or the sword that she felt clutched in her fist, but she knew that her handmaiden was nearby. The visions swept over her with the fury of a storm at sea, crashing upon her mind like the shore before breaking waves. One by one, they flashed before her, revealing traumas that Tsudao desperately wished she could ignore. If these visions were the gifts of the Sun, then it was better to live in darkness.

A scream, but it was not hers, and it dissolved into laughter.

Eight swords guided by one master, all forged in the Shadowlands and twisted by the vices of the world.

Tsudao could almost make out faces against the blades— one Crane, one Crab, one Dragon, and more—but she could not master the vision enough to make sense of it.

All she knew was that one of those dark blades was near— and that she must rise to fight against it.

"Kekiesu," Tsudao said, her hair falling in sweat-slick strands around her grim face. "Call for Domotai and Dejiko. The Legion marches."

"Domotai and his men are already in the Kitsu city," Kekiesu reminded her. "They were the honor guard for the Lion ambassadors and remained to stay the night."

Tsudao nodded. "Then he will need our help."

Outside, where there had been silence, a voice cried out.

"To arms!" a distant sentry yelled, his voice echoing through the gathered encampment. "An army assaults the Kitsu! To arms!"

Tsudao looked up into Kekiesu's somber brown eyes. "No army of the Dragon could have made it past our sentries, yet this one is already scaling the Kitsu walls. Rouse the commanders—and quickly! The army we fight is not one of this world, and we have little time."

* * * * *

Matsu Domotai was roused from sleep by the screams outside his room. A tall man, he rolled out of his futon without hesitation, finding his footing like a cat. Although he was a member of the Imperial Legion, his hair was still dyed a thick gold like the mane of the creature that graced the symbol of his house. It fell into his eyes, and he shoved it away with an annoyed hand.

"Domotai-sama!" the cry came from his sentry. "An army attacks Oshi-no Kada!"

"Dragon," muttered Domotai, reaching for his katana. He had no time to put on his armor and less time to ready his guard when he heard another scream outside. In three steps he crossed the chamber and threw open the shoji screen that separated his room from the city street. An arrow whizzed past his ear, and Domotai threw himself to the ground. Beside him on the floor, the sentry choked, another arrow lodged in his throat. Within seconds, the man was dead.

The city of Oshi-no Kada was in chaos. Domotai's small guesthouse stood at the edge of the palace grounds, and his men were scattered through the city. Only the commander and his personal guard—one of whom lay dead beside him—had been given rooms near the Kitsu palace. Domotai cursed the inconvenience. Who knew how many of his men would be killed in their sleep?

Where was the enemy? Another arrow lodged in the wood of his doorway, but Domotai could see no archers. He heard screams in the street and the rough shouts of the city guards as they fought, but in the darkness, he could see very little.

Cautiously, Domotai moved forward, thrusting both of his swords into his belt. The light material of his pants clung to his skin in the cold night air, reminding him that winter was not far past. A lantern hung at the roadside, and faint shadows rushed past in the night. Friend or foe, he could not tell. People shoved past him, peasants screaming for their children in the chaos, and there was a loud explosion to the east.

Eastward were the tombs of the Kitsu, last resting place of the greatest Lion heroes. Another scream sounded down the street, and Domotai could make out the outline of a struggle against the faint light of the streetcorner lanterns. He ran, hand on the hilt of his katana, ready to face the danger. Ten samurai stood on the street beyond, and Domotai recognized three of them as men of his own command. Drawing his sword, Domotai charged to their aid, hardly turning to take in the enemy they fought against.

When his sword cut open the flesh of a creature that had ripped out the throat of one of his men, Domotai understood the danger surrounding them. It was barely human—tusks curved up over its lower lips—yet it wore armor in an ancient style, the gaudily decorated enamel plates woven together with ropes of hair. The creature stank, the sickly smell of a filthy beast combined with the clinging stench of death. Its face had once been human, but now the noble features were twisted and marked with soil, its eyes maddened with the Taint of the Shadowlands.

Savage claws tore at the samurai, and where they drew blood, the flesh curled back as if blackened by foul poison. The creature howled as Domotai sliced into its ribcage from the rear but did not cease attacking the man it had brought down until the samurai was dead. Domotai raised his katana again, praying that this strike would end the creature's life, when he saw the first blow begin to heal. The flesh around the wound puckered and turned yellow, pus running down the creature's side as the wound shrank and blistered. Domotai cut downward even more solidly, his blade tearing through tendons and bone, and severed the creature's head from its body. He could not save the victim beneath it, but he could ensure that this half-human beast was condemned to the pits of Jigoku forever.

The body fell to the ground, limbs still twitching, and the face snarled again. It seemed for a moment that the creature would simply reattach the severed head, but after a moment of struggle, the beast howled and its body exploded into ash.

Domotai stepped back in shock, shaking his head to clear it of the horrible vision he had just seen, and he heard other samurai nearby, briskly shouting commands. He turned, wiping his sword on his pants, and joined their ranks. The samurai stood in the center of the street with lowered swords, circling against the press of their enemies. Recognizing Domotai, they gladly opened the line for the Imperial Commander. One of the Lion samurai cried out, "Sir! There are more than forty of them, headed this way!" The man's face was weary, drawn, and one arm hung limply at his side.

"Where did they come from?"

"The east gates. The eastern sentries were carved like meat, sir! Never even raised the alarm." The Lion wasted no time on pleasantries. He was a hardened war veteran, but the gruesomeness of their enemies seemed to have affected even him. "They're headed for the palace, sir."

"Not the palace," another of the samurai said, raising his blade as more of the beasts rushed them from the shadows. "The tombs!"

Domotai suddenly had three of the beast-men upon him, their snarls and hot breath far closer than he would have liked. The thin streets of the city made for good hiding-places, and the enemy was using them to their advantage. One rushed straight for him, fouling his sword with one arm while its claws struck Domotai's face. He slashed off the arm, but the twitching claws still carved into his cheekbone before he threw the severed arm to the ground. The second, equally careless of its life, leaped for Domotai's legs. His strike barely knocked the creature aside.

Behind him, one of the other samurai swung toward his third enemy, distracting the beast until Domotai could sever its head. With a violent explosion, the creature dissolved much like the first. The injured one picked up its hand, re-attaching the arm at the elbow. Domotai could hear popping beneath the beast's laced armor and could only assume that the limb was reattaching itself.

He kicked the one rolling at his feet, hurling it aside with an enraged blow. Domotai's blade arched back toward his injured opponent, severing its head from as it raised a rusted sword. Although hurt, it was still swift—but Domotai's tested blade cut through the creature's ill-treated one, severing sword and neck in the same instant. It grabbed the hilt of Domotai's sword and jerked it free from his hand.

Pain lanced through his leg, and Domotai screamed. Black claws sank into his thigh as the one on the ground crawled back to him, using Domotai's own flesh as a ladder to pull to its feet. The second Lion samurai plunged his katana into the creature's back, but it only howled in rage. The beast spun and launched out with one blackened hand, clawing the samurai's chest in a bloody rake, killing the man instantly. Thinking quickly, Domotai grabbed the sword hilt that stuck out of the creature's back. He tore upward through the creature's neck. A second blow severed the head, and the creature fell to ash.

Domotai's face stung, and his leg was a bloody agony. He lifted his sword from the ground and turned to see how his men were doing. Three were dead, two more howling from their wounds, and the Shadowlands creatures were clearly winning. Domotai set his jaw, refusing to flee the scene. He waded in among them, carving into flesh with swift strokes of his sword and watching as two of the beasts dissolved.

The heavy sound of cavalry disrupted Domotai's concentration as he pulled one of the less injured samurai to his feet. The beasts roared and scattered, not eager to test their prowess against those with the advantage of steeds. As they ran, Domotai's samurai claimed two more, thankful for the intervention of their allies.

The four men on horses lowered their pikes, and one skewered a screaming beast. Domotai cried, "Behead it!"

The beast clawed its way up the horseman's spear, grinning despite the agony. Already, the spear was turning black where the creature's body had hung, the wood blistering and warping from the taint within the blood. A samurai on the ground wove quickly between two of the horses, cutting off the creature's head, and the body exploded. A helm, crusted with filth and woven together with rotted human hair, rolled to Domotai's feet. Unwilling to touch it, Domotai kicked at the scrap of metal—and stopped in shock.

The ancient helm, rusted and polluted as it was, still bore the Kitsu mon.

"Domotai-sama!" a horseman in the garb of the Imperial Legion shouted. "They attack the tombs!"

Domotai stepped back, shaken by the implications of what he had seen, and nodded. "We must defend the tombs. They hold the ashes of all those who have preserved the Empire's honor, and they shall not be tainted by these . . . things."

"The wizards at the tombs will know more of what these creatures are." The horseman offered Domotai his hand, pulling the commander onto the steed behind him. "But I was trained by the shugenja of our clan before I took up the sword. I can tell you this. They are mentioned in the scrolls of the most powerful shugenja of our clan as the Tsuno— Kitsu lost long ago to the Shadowlands. Now they look upon Rokugan with hatred—especially the Lion." The samurai grew even grimmer. "They wish revenge on the Lion. For them to be here, they must have been brought from the Shadowlands."

The Lion thrust his heels into the frightened creature's sides, driving the horse through the black streets of Oshi-no Kada.

"What do they want?" Domotai asked.

"I can only guess." The Lion mon on the horseman's shoulder rode up and down with his movements. "Possibly to desecrate the tombs of our greatest heroes. But perhaps more. The scrolls of the most powerful Lion shugenja are kept within the tombs, interred with ashes of our heroes. With such knowledge, a sorcerer could become very powerful."

"And a blood sorcerer?" Domotai growled.

"More powerful perhaps than the Masters of the Phoenix. I do not know. I am no shugenja. I am only a warrior, and all I am truly certain of, Captain, is that I must defend my home."

Domotai nodded. "Bring the others," he commanded to his men. "We'll need all the aid we can find."

Bodies lay everywhere—peasant and samurai alike—and piles of ash drifted into the gutters. More fighting erupted on all sides. The once-peaceful merchant quarter had become a war zone. Some of the dead were familiar to Domotai, and he hardened his heart. At least they had died fighting. They had died with honor.

Ahead, the glow of the Kitsu tombs guided their run through the battles. Magic illuminated the air around it, driving back the creatures that sought entry, but the spells of the shugenja would not hold back the beasts for long. Already, the dimming fire of the protective energies flickered under the assault.

"Can we go faster?" Domotai shouted.

"Not unless the Fortunes themselves carry us through the sky," was the man's bitter response. "When we arrive, we'll need to find the general of the Tsuno as quickly as possible.

Without a leader, the Tsuno will turn into ravening beasts."

Domotai clapped the man's shoulder. "That is good."

"The best advice I can give you, sir—other than to take your men and get them out of here."

"I can't do that," Domotai said. "I may be a member of the Imperial Legion, but I am still a Lion."

"I thought you'd say that." The Lion grinned. "I'm glad to hear it. Here we are."

The road to the tombs was lined with ancient oak trees, their stalwart branches curving in graceful lines over the main walkway. During the autumn, the leaves fell upon the ground in a rainbow of orange and red, with bright yellow sparks to enflame the view. Now that the winter had stripped them of all color, the oaks seemed like twisted black shadows against the velvet star-covered sky. The tiny buds of spring were invisible in the gloom, and creatures leaped from limb to limb with howls of bloodlust. The light of the temple streamed in golden rays through the trees, showing the path. The light was brighter than sunlight and seemed to sear the flesh of the beasts where it touched them—but still, thousands of the Tsuno gathered on the very steps of the Kitsu tombs.

The horses pounded down the alleyway formed by the spreading oak trees, and Domotai sensed rather than saw the creatures swinging from limb to limb. The Taint was spreading along the branches of the ancient guardians, twisting the trees into shadows of their former selves. Any Crane would have cried at the loss of such magnificent trees, but Lions did not cry. Lions took revenge.

The horse screamed as something fell upon its rump, collapsing its rear legs beneath the sudden weight. Domotai was thrown forward, and he heard the rest of the riders pulling up their beasts, trying to avoid the fallen pony. The samurai with Domotai rolled swiftly to his feet, blade free of its scabbard in a second.

The tombs were only a few yards farther down the path,

but between the tomb and the soldiers were a thousand more of the Tsuno. Their claws were bared, teeth blackened and feral, and their breath hung in the air like thick trails of greenish smoke. Armor clinked with a menacing echo as they slowly came forward to encircle the five horses and ten riders. Domotai saw that his men's faces held barely controlled terror.

One of the horses screamed, rushing into the slowly closing circle of Tsuno. The men on its back drew their swords, releasing the reins. It was useless to try to control the beast—and too late to be of any use. Domotai screamed in fury as the monstrous Shadowlands creatures surrounded the horse. The beasts growled, their rusted blades cutting the pony's feet from beneath it. One of the men shrieked as black claws cut into him, dragging the samurai from the horse's back and drowning him beneath the wave of Tsuno.

Domotai started to throw himself into the fray after them, but the Lion's hand clamped on his shoulder.

"Sir!" shouted the other samurai. "There's no way you can save them."

Realizing that the man's words held truth, Domotai struggled to keep calm despite the rage building in his mind.

"You have seven other men to command, Captain," the man yelled. "Don't abandon them!"

Drawing his sword, Domotai stared at the Tsuno around them. Again, the golden light shuddered and flickered, dying out for a brief second and then regaining its strength. He beheld the building above the press of the Tsuno and saw bloody coils probing for any weakness in the magic that guarded the secrets of the Kitsu. Some sorcerer guided the assault on the Lion stronghold, but Domotai had no time to concern himself with such things. The Tsuno army tightened their circle, enjoying the panic in their captives.

By now, the rest of the men had climbed off their beasts, aware that the creatures' fear would only put them in jeopardy. They held the reins of the beasts in firm fists, keeping the horses from fleeing into the Tsuno that surrounded them.

"Stay in the light!" Domotai yelled, moving to a patch of golden radiance that shimmered from the Kitsu temple. "They cannot abide its touch."

The others swiftly moved to glowing areas, pushing the horses into the shimmering rays of the tomb's aura.

The Tsuno snarled, lashing out with claw and blade, but they could not get close enough to the samurai to hurt them. The light seared their flesh, blistering their tainted skin. They roared, some springing into the trees to seek other entrances, but for the moment, the Lion samurai were safe.

Domotai turned to the samurai who seemed to know about these beasts. "You say these Tsuno were once Kitsu?"

"So the histories tell us, Domotai-sama," the samurai replied.

"Pray that your tales are correct."

Domotai stepped into another circle of light, his katana lowered and one hand raised. "I see before me nothing but filth," he yelled, "creatures ashamed of the lineage they were once given. You call yourselves Tsuno? Kitsu? You are nothing! I am not afraid of you." In ancient challenge, Domotai leveled his fist at the group, trying to gauge their leaders by the markings on blood-encrusted armor. "I do not fear you!" he shouted again.

The Tsuno paused, uncertain. They were not used to prey that did not run.

"Who are you?" An ancient, hissing voice rose from one of the Tsuno, and the creature pushed through his lessers, who scattered before him.

Domotai, his hand still clenched in the ancient symbol of challenge, faced the Tsuno. "I am Matsu Domotai, son of Matsu Hikieru, cousin of Matsu Tsuko, whose ashes lie with our greatest heroes. You will not have this place. You are nothing. Less than nothing. You are dogs, whipped by your Shadowlands masters and running like hounds where they call you."

Domotai's fear caused his voice to shake, and he shook his head to keep the unruly strands of golden hair out of his eyes. The men behind him muttered uncertainly, keeping to the faint circles of pale light.

The beast was half-man, standing on twisted rear legs like a cat's haunches. Its head was crowned by two curved horns that shone the color of steel, and sharp teeth glistened within its mouth. Its leathery skin was rough with small spiked hairs jutting out at odd angles like the torn fur of some sickly animal. Unlike many of the other Tsuno, this one's armor was well kept, the metal plates enameled with magnificent, though horrible, depictions of death.

Yellow eyes sneered at Domotai, rolling madly beneath a thick, dark mane. The Tsuno, fanged mouth grinning, raised its sword and ran a clawed finger along the blade. The weapon was thicker than a katana and far less subtle. It was easy to see why this Tsuno led the others. It was a butcher, filled with strength and cunning—a madman trapped in the body of a beast.

The Tsuno commander laughed, and it was a bitter, callous sound. "Are you challenging me?" it growled.

"I am. If I win, your men allow my soldiers to pass into the tomb. If you win, we turn ourselves over to you."

"I am Tsuno Kurushimi," a shriveled face spat the words as the Tsuno stepped forward to the edge of the light, "commander of the Tsuno, servant of the One Who Draws Us, Keeper of the Beast. I am the one you must challenge."

The Tsuno horde howled, and the eerie keening sent shivers up Domotai's spine. The Tsuno raised his hand in a silent command, signaling to his soldiers to pass the call.

"I accept," said the Tsuno commander.

A whisper went up from the gathered Tsuno, and they seemed cowed. The ranks parted, and a cry went up from the distant Tsuno soldiers. Something moved near the tomb, and Domotai stepped back into the golden light as he saw the blood shadows that wrapped them around the temple darken with power. As the shadow moved toward the streams of golden light, a woman's laughter—as delicate as the ringing of silver bells—danced in the air. The sound chilled Domotai far more than the roars of the Tsuno.

"What is your name, samurai?" Domotai cried to the Lion as Kurushimi came closer.

"Kitsu Seikigawa, son of Kitsu Shiwa!" the man replied, his jaw locked. He was struggling not to show fear, but it trembled behind his eyes, and his sword shook in his hand.

"When you escape this, I want you to carry a message to my Lady General, Tsudao-sama. Tell her all that you have seen and heard. Tell her that I died well and my soul waits to serve her again in the next life. And more ... you must swear to tell her that the Dragon were not involved in this."

"But sir ..." The Lion's uncertainty wavered in his voice.

"You will tell her!" Domotai shouted as the tremendous oni approached. "There are no Dragon here. Only blood sorcerers and oni. Whoever brought these beasts from the south, they are our true enemies."

Kitsu Seikigawa nodded. "I swear it."

"Then I can fight with honor, and if need be, die in peace." Domotai lowered his sword and stepped out of the light toward Kurushimi.

With a roar, the Tsuno charged.

* * * * *

The Imperial Legion pounded toward Oshi-no Kada, the city of the Kitsu, their shouts echoing across the open plain. Ahead, their unknown enemy had already broken through the gates of the city. Screams from within urged the legion onward, the Lion and Phoenix armies at their heels. Despite the relatively close proximity of their camp to the city, it had taken them hours to reach their goal, and the sky was already a faded gray that heralded morning.

"The Dragon!" shouted the Lion commander, Akodo

Ijiasu from his horse. "Again, they defy our offers of peace! For this treachery, they will pay!" He raced on, not caring that his horse was lathered and sick from the forced speed.

The Lion armies flooded into the gates of the city as the Imperial Legions turned left toward the Kitsu Tombs. Tsudao shook her head ruefully. The city of Oshi-no Kada had once been a bustling place, but now its houses were ruined, torn down by sharp claws. Entire arches had been overthrown, the once richly painted wood shattered and cast in the street like so much trash. The road itself was covered in blood, and more scarlet was painted upon the few buildings that had withstood the furious attack.

Not a peasant remained, and no one cowered by the road to welcome the armies. The city was silent and gruesome. Smoke drifted on the wind from a fire somewhere near the palaces, but Tsudao did not pause to find its source. The Kitsu tombs, sacred temple of knowledge, was just ahead.

The main temple of the tomb rose above a row of burned-out oak trees, its enameled roof glistening with strange wetness. The oaks themselves were shriveled and blackened, and as Tsudao and her men slowed to pass between them, a horrible sight met their eyes. Lion samurai had been hung in the trees. They swayed from the branches like cords of forgotten wood. A thousand bodies, each more gruesome to behold than the last, ornamented the tree-lined path toward the sacred heart of the city. The horses stamped, unwilling to pass among the carnage, but Tsudao and her legion forced them, continuing slowly through the trees.

The Kitsu tombs were a city unto themselves, the stone paths easily wide enough for three horses to ride abreast. Statues of ancient Lion samurai stood guard at the edge of the courtyard, their swords raised in salute—or in warning. Where the stone had once been white marble, shining in the sun, now it was covered in stains and smears of blood, chunks of the stone torn away by claws. Like two veterans of some terrible war, still they stood with chipped swords in the air and faces raised. Beyond them, neat rows of open tombs lined the corridors, each one filled with a small statue of the hero they enshrined.

The ashes of a hundred generations and more were interred here—now violated by claws and blood.

Tsudao heard more than one of her samurai swear in horror behind her. They were unable to continue into the main tomb building. She did not care. Although the carnage proved that even the last defenses of the Kitsu shugenja had been breached, she stepped down from her steed and continued on.

On each tomb, a name had been carved—Akodo Shinju, Kitsu Sosenkiu, Matsu Tsuko. The most revered protectors, ancestors of the Lions. One of the tomb's guardian shugenja had thrown his body over Matsu Tsuko's grave to protect the interred ashes from violation. Tsudao stared for a long moment at the grave, her heart unsure. How was it that these beasts of the Shadowlands had come here? What did they want?

And more . . . where had they gone?

"General!" Akodo Ijiasu called to her from another tomb. "Here!"

Turning quickly, she rushed to his side and tried to ignore the puddles of blood beneath her feet. It was everywhere— more blood than she had ever seen, as if each of the dead guardians had bled a thousandfold. The entire tomb had been corrupted. Bodies lay strewn about the area, some still wearing the blazon of the Imperial Legion. Tsudao's eyes scanned fallen corpses, looking in vain for Domotai. If his body was among them, it was too charred, too mangled to recognize. There would have to be a mass funeral to honor them all.

Ten thousand graves stood in the Kitsu tombs—seventy of the most revered histories of the Empire, and even a ruling Empress of ancient Rokugan. Now, all of their souls were tainted. Contaminated.

It would all have to be burned.

Akodo Ijiasu stood before one of the Kitsu tombs. The statue had been ripped free and shattered. The marble seemed to have been crushed by a fist of astonishing strength. A tremendous blow, collapsing the marble and cracking the stone floor of the tomb, had exposed a small chamber beneath. The bodies of a group of Imperial guards had been laid around the tomb as if in sacrifice to some dark power, their flesh blackened and scarred. Some still moved, their limbs twitching as if resisting the stillness of death. Tsudao could not find Domotai's body among them, but there were thousands more.

Tsudao looked up at the name inscribed upon the tomb and felt a chill. Kitsu Okura.

"One of the most powerful shugenja in Lion history," whispered Ijiasu. "His scrolls were interred with him, lest those without the knowledge to control them should gain access to powers beyond their understanding."

Tsudao looked down into the chamber. It was empty.

"Tsudao . . ." one of the fallen samurai near the chamber struggled to force sound out of a bloodied and broken jaw. "Tsudao-sama."

"This one's still alive," an Akodo called, kneeling by the body. "A Lion!"

"The Dragon . . ." the fallen Lion began, blood trickling from his wounds. Tsudao and the Akodo general knelt beside him, hoping to hear the rest. "Domotai made me swear—" the Kitsu choked, clutching at Tsudao's sleeve— "to tell you . . . th-the . . . Dragon—"

He coughed once, and blood spilled between his clamped teeth. His body flinched with pain, and the rest of his voice was no more than a hiss.

"The Dragon . . ." Nothing more. His eyes turned glassy and his hand fell from her sleeve, landing with a soft thump in the dust of the temple road. The samurai's last breath vanished into the wind and smoke of the city, and his face was a frozen mask of sorrow.

"You see," Akodo Ijiasu stood, turning his face from the fallen Lion. "Our enemies are clear. This was an act of war, brought upon us by the Dragon Clan. Now we have the dying words of a samurai as testimony. The testimony of death is one of the strongest accusations a samurai can make. You know that, Tsudao. I swear that the rest of the Empire shall hear this man's words. The Dragon cannot refute their part in this. The Tsuno and their dark masters have gone to the south, obviously on their way back to the Shadowlands. We will hunt them, and when we catch them—" Ijiasu ground a fist into his palm— "they will pay a heavy price."

Tsudao stared into the eyes of the dead samurai for a moment longer, then turned away.

14 | FORSAKEN BLADE, FORSAKEN HONOR

"Come with me, and I will show you a place where your darkest dreams come true."

The voice was real. The dream was real. Junnosuke opened his eyes, and she was there.

The night was cold, and the moon's thin wedge barely pierced the overhanging shroud of forest. His fire crackled with empty breath, hardly even able to warm itself. Junnosuke, no longer Mirumoto, reached for his sword before he remembered that it was missing, and he cursed beneath his breath at the memory of its loss. He had been a general. He had been a savior, the hope of his clan against a world that threatened to destroy them. Now, with the treachery of his men and the cursed Fortune's luck, he was nothing at all.

Here, at the edge of the Shinomen, he was no more than another ronin, another lost soul, waiting for eternal sleep to give it rest from the past. Junnosuke closed his eyes, feeling the heat of his anger flow within his soul. Three times he had considered some form of dishonorable suicide, but his anger would not let him. He knew that he hovered on the edge of madness, but damn madness. Damn anger, and damn the Empire. He would have his revenge.

"Rise, Junnosuke. There is much to see and little time left in the night."

The voice was familiar, cold and clear as mountain ice, and this time Junnosuke knew he had not dreamed it. He looked up through sleep-dimmed eyes, and in the fragile light of the moon, he saw her, pale and unornamented, her black hair drifting like a cloud around her body. Thin braids cascaded down her arms, serpents in the river of her ebony hair. Her face was that of a spirit, beautiful beyond imagining, and her purple lips curved in a smile.

"Who are you?" he gasped. "I have dreamed you before."

Her eyes half-closed, she reached a finger to stroke his cheek. "There are things I must show you, Junnosuke, dreams you have not yet begun to dream."

He stood, his feet leaden. "Where are we going?"

It seemed almost natural to follow her, and Junnosuke stared in awe as she removed her hand from his face. Her tongue licked a trail of scarlet from the tip of her fingernail, and it was only then that Junnosuke realized he was bleeding.

He took her hand without thinking. There was nothing here, after all, that he would need.

It seemed an eon—or a second—since the woods. Junnosuke peered through the mists, hearing the subtle clank of heavy chains. The ground beneath his feet was fleshy, a strange soil that shifted and sank with each step. He followed her through another forest, but this one was not made of trees, or earth, or anything else he recognized. Strange chains hung like weeping willow fronds from a roof he could not see, and she moved among them in a strange dreamlike dance.

"What is your name?" he whispered, suddenly afraid.

"Shahai." Her mouth shifted with an innocent smile.

"What is this place?"

"This is your past."

He considered that for a moment, unsure what she meant, then another voice called to him from the side. Junnosuke turned, losing the woman in the mist, and peered toward the sound. He took a few short steps through the forest of chain and hanging ropes and saw one of the Imperial Guard. The man was beaten, bruised, crouched on his knees, and held his torn stomach together with a trembling hand.

"Kommai." Junnosuke knew him. He was one of Tsudao's most faithful lieutenants, a samurai of impressive lineage. For years, Kommai had stood at Junnosuke's side within the Imperial Legions, until the end. Until Tsudao had stripped him of his rank. Then, instead of standing up for what was right, Kommai had simply turned his back. Like all the others. Junnosuke's face hardened, and he stared down at the tortured samurai with no pity in his eyes.

The other samurai looked up, extending a hand. "Help me stand," he demanded.

Junnosuke did not move.

Shahai stood in the shadow behind Kommai, her hands outspread. "Junnosuke," she said, "this man serves the Empire. Will you not help him?"

"No," Junnosuke snarled and stepped away. The samurai on the ground gasped. "He is a coward, and he follows a traitor."

She smiled and knelt beside the wounded soldier. Her hands brushed the man's shoulders, and she whispered soft words in his ears. He flinched and clutched at his wound. She did not move, did not release him, and Junnosuke watched as some change settled on the man, driving the sanity from his eyes.

Kommai looked up at him with a terrible, desperate gaze, but Shahai did not pause her whispering, and at last, he fell to the ground with a sob of agony and release. His face shifted, became drawn, and Shahai placed a simple porcelain mask over his features. Once it was in place, Kommai's wound closed, and he settled into sleep . . . or death.

"What did you do?" Junnosuke could only stare in fascination.

Standing, Shahai looked down at her creation with a tender gaze. "I have given him peace."

Junnosuke whispered, "Are you a Kami?"

She drifted past him and did not answer. After a moment, Junnosuke took a hesitant step away from Kommai and followed her.

There were more . . . many more. Most of them he knew from his time in the Legion. One by one, Junnosuke watched as Shahai twisted their thoughts and whispered away their fears. By the time she was done, each of the wounded samurai had fallen into a gentle sleep. Each one wore a serene porcelain mask.

"What happened to them?" Junnosuke asked.

She placed the next mask on a whimpering Lion. "Their leader failed them." Her scent was heady, a light touch of dying flowers on a hot summer breeze. Junnosuke followed behind her, ignoring the strangeness of their surroundings, desperately needing her nearness. "Come with me, Junnosuke." She laughed. "It is your turn, after all."

He looked behind them at the trail of Lion and Imperial soldiers, all sleeping on the fleshy soil. Their hands were folded in repose, and looking at their smooth porcelain masks, Junnosuke could almost believe they were sleeping peacefully.

"What peace can you give to me?"

They walked on, her hand sliding into his. The frank physical contact, so unknown in Rokugan, seemed almost indecent. "I know what you want, Junnosuke," Shahai breathed. "I know what secrets your heart holds . . . and I can get them for you."

Junnosuke eyed her with distrust. "You cannot."

"I can give you Tsudao—and all of those who have betrayed you." The sorceress smiled, baring her neck in a long, slow arch.

"What do you want from me?" His question was sharp, suspicious.

Looking languorously to the side, Shahai answered, "Let me show you."

He followed her, as it seemed he had done all his life. It was that natural, that simple to do as she bade him. Junnosuke did not trust her, but he could not refuse.

She pushed aside a curtain of chain and bloodied silk strips, her pale hand sliding through them and parting them easily. Ahead of her, Junnosuke could see a mockery of a torii arch—the symbol of peace and prayer—but this one was made of bone and covered with blood.

A man was tied to one of the pillars, his arms wrapped about the column like a lover. He was barely conscious, his body covered in open, bleeding wounds, yet he could not seem to die. He was so badly wounded that he could not stand, and he leaned against the post with crumpled legs and arms straining against the raw leather binding his wrists. His chest was bare. Shredded pants hung in tatters from his waist, and only the tattoo of a lion's paw upon his torn shoulder marked his clan and alliance.

That is, until Junnosuke saw the man's face.

"Domotai."

Shahai walked through the arch with a dancer's grace. She moved about the bone column, hands caressing the thousands of femurs and fragments that made up the massive arch. Junnosuke did not know how many men had died to make this monument, nor could he guess. As she moved, touching it, his stomach turned at the thought. Still her smile drew him in, and her eyes pulled him close to her side.

"You are a Bloodspeaker." No longer uncertain, Junnosuke tore his gaze from the man tied to the arch and tried to revile her. "A blood-sorcery user. This place . . . it is a realm of your dark imagination. Not mine."

"Am I worse than he?" She pointed one slender finger at Domotai, and Junnosuke could see the Lion moving feebly against his bonds. "He left you, Junnosuke. He abandoned you when you needed him most. He could have talked Tsudao into keeping you in the legion, but he envied your power. He was jealous of your strength, and your cunning."

She touched Domotai, and the Lion flinched from her pale hand. Junnosuke's eyes grew colder as Shahai continued.

"When Tsudao fought you on the Lion plain, he spoke out against you. He told her to let you live with your dishonor. If he had not spoken, she would have killed you and you would have died an honorable man, revered by your clan, a hero." Her voice was smooth and soft. "He would not even allow you to have that. He has always hated you, Junnosuke. Do you not see that?"

Domotai looked up, hearing the voices. His eyes were bruised and swollen, and the golden hair that was his pride was matted with blood. "Junnosuke!" he screamed, unable to see. "Junnosuke? The Tsuno . . . the Tsuno. You must tell Tsudao—"

Shahai cut him off, her purr silencing the bloody samurai with a force more powerful than volume. "Even now, all he thinks about is her. *Her* honor. *Her* legions." The sorceress stepped behind Junnosuke, her hand brushing his shoulder and caressing his neck. She tilted her head to breathe soft words into his ear. "They should have been *your* legions. Even now, he tries to blame the attack of the Tsuno on your clan. He is eager to ensure that you and everything you have wrought is destroyed. Where did he learn this?" Shahai's hands caressed Junnosuke's shoulders and her breath was warm against his neck. "From *her.*"

"No. Junnosuke, do not listen to the witch." Struggling feebly against his bonds, the samurai went on. "Tsudao gave you your first command. She trusted you."

"A command that *he* took from you." Shahai gestured toward the sleeping figures in their porcelain masks. "These were his men, his brothers. He gambled their lives on the skill of his blade, and he lost. Because of him, his enemy took every man in his command. His pride not only destroyed you, it destroyed everyone he touched. All because Tsudao trusted him and not you."

"She lies, Junnosuke. Oathbrother!" Domotai fought to free himself, but the bonds did not give way. "I wanted to find a way for you to return. I saved your life!"

"You gave me nothing but a life of pain," Junnosuke replied.

"But I?" Shahai smiled. "I can give you everything, Junnosuke. Legions to command. Power at your fingertips—enough to destroy Tsudao and her army." She opened her palm, and within it lay a silver dagger whose blade shone with a wicked edge. "This is yours, Junnosuke," she whispered. "You must choose how to use it. Free him, and you can both go back to Rokugan—he as a hero, and you as ronin scum. Or, you can use it to free yourself."

This time, Junnosuke did not ask the price. "You were my Oathbrother, Domotai. I saved your life in battle, and I returned your father's blade when your enemies stole it from you. You repaid me in treachery. If you are the best that the Empire has to offer, if you are truly samurai, then damn the Empire. And damn you."

Anger, resentment, and bitterness welled up in Junnosuke's soul, and his fingernails bit into his palms and drew blood. Without hesitation, he took the dagger and stepped beneath the arch of bone. Junnosuke's eyes lit with madness and release, and he plunged the dagger between Domotai's shoulders. The blade hissed as it entered Domotai's body, and the samurai's eyes widened with agony.

"Hang there, Domotai," Junnosuke rasped as he slashed the tattoo from Domotai's shoulder. "I will take away your clan and your life. I will crush the Lion and see how you feel when you are the last of them—the last Lion, clinging to the bones of the glories you once knew. Hang on this arch, Domotai, until you have suffered as I have. Until eternity arrives—and beyond." Madness shone unbridled in his eyes. "I forsake you. I forsake the Empire."

Domotai's scream echoed through the darkness. One by one, as the scream faded into bitter sobs, the figures in their porcelain masks rose. In rows they stood, hands on their weapons. Their white faces, serene in their unlife, seemed to glow with the sound. As one they turned to face Shahai and Junnosuke and bowed with the formal honor of a samurai to his master. Shahai's victorious laughter blended with the cries, and the earth trembled beneath their feet.

Turning to the sorceress, Junnosuke extended a hand filled with traces of scarlet. "Give me a sword and an army, and I will serve."

"You have your army, Junnosuke, and soon you shall have your sword."

15 | DARKNESS AND LIGHT

The Imperial troops raced across the low mountains. They had traveled for days across hundreds of miles, desperate to catch their fleeing prey. The Tsuno did not weary, but they were on foot, and even the most stalwart footman could not maintain a lead against the swift steeds of the Imperial Guard. Akodo Ijiasu's Lion forces were behind them, their ponies struggling to keep up with the blistering pace.

A horn to the fore of the army sounded a long and desperate note. They had found the Tsuno, and their enemies were at last turning to fight. The Tsuno armies must have been trapped in the passes of the Akodo. Either that or they had found a defensible position, and the Tsuno no longer feared the charge of the Imperial Guard.

No matter what the reason for their halt, the battle would soon be joined.

Bayushi Paneki and his Scorpion rode at Tsudao's side, their steeds lathered and gasping from the long race. The

Bayushi signaled, and a hawk circling above them, fluttered down onto the Scorpion's hand.

"There are many of them, but they are weary," the Scorpion said as he unrolled a message tied to the bird's leg. "Their general is wounded, but there are new troops here." Paneki's tone was questioning, as if he did not truly believe what he was saying. Looking up from the scroll, he turned to Tsudao. "And a new commander."

"They have allies," Tsudao said, "but they are still weary. If their allies number less than their own troops, the fresh reserves will not aid them against us. But night is coming, and darkness is their ally, not ours."

"Do not fear, Tsudao-sama." She shot a questioning glance at him, but Paneki only smiled. "The night has many friends." Behind him, the Scorpion guard bowed respectfully, their dark lacquered armor making little sound despite the movement. Paneki raised his hand in a brief signal as he dismounted. "I will see you on the battlefield, General-sama."

The Imperial troops marched down the valley's edge into the box canyon, betting that time would aid them. They were relatively fresh, though their weary mounts had to be left behind, and with only a few hours left in the day they could not afford to delay the charge until tomorrow. They had to fight this evening.

Tsudao led the troops, unwilling to command her men into any danger she would not face. The Lion were behind them, and the Scorpion had vanished into the woods surrounding the valley. Although the peaks were not as high or as sharp as those of the Dragon Mountains, they were more forested. Through the thick brush Tsudao could see little movement, but she knew the Bayushi were there.

Below, on the valley floor, the Tsuno had erected a mock shrine of wood and flesh, strapping their captives to its walls and lashing them to hear the screams. Some were Lion. Others, Tsudao knew, were her own men. Turning to the legions that followed her, Tsudao raised her sword in salute.

"Samurai of the Empire," Tsudao called, "you are the First Emerald Legion of Rokugan—a name that carries honor and pride. Your foes are not the enemies of the Lion, or the Crane, or the Dragon. They are the enemies of Rokugan." Her eyes glowed in the light of the sun, and her gold and black armor shone like a beacon. "Will you fight the Shadowlands?"

"Show us the way!" a samurai shouted. The mon on his armor was that of the Crane.

Tsudao turned on him, pointing her fist in his direction. "Brave words. But the men down there—" she nodded toward the valley and the fires that the Tsuno were lighting— "they spoke bravely as well. Are you not the same?"

A murmur went through the crowd, and one of the legionnaires, bearing the mon of the Crab, stepped forward. He was a small man, his long pike standing nearly twice his height, but he stood bravely. "Those men were brave, yes," he cried, "but they did not know their enemy. I know these creatures." The Crab pounded on his chest, turning to his companions. "I know them, and I can defeat them. We will find victory!"

"Victory." Tsudao stepped through the crowd, lowering her arm. Her face was somber. The men parted for her, allowing her to pass and hanging on her words. They had seen her this way, always before a battle, and always when the fight would bring severe losses. "Each of you is my brother. Each of you is my sister. How can I stand and say there is victory, if even one of you should fall? Doji Aisori. Hida Gutsumin. Kitsu Dejiko." Tsudao paused before her second in command and held the woman's gaze. "I would die for each of you."

"And we for you, Princess!" one of the samurai in her command roared, and a wave of assent swept the Imperial Legion. They were small—half the size of any of the armies of Rokugan—but their courage and loyalty went beyond any other in the world.

Kitsu Dejiko knelt, laying her sword on the ground at Tsudao's feet. "I have followed you into battle a thousand times, and each time you have brought me victory. I have no fear of this day, live or die, so long as I have done so in your service."

Tsudao gazed at each of the samurai who surrounded her and saw the same faithfulness in their eyes. She walked through the gathered samurai, noting each face, every scar they bore, and when she returned to the front of the legion, Tsudao drew her father's sword.

Beside Dejiko, Moshi Kekiesu whispered, "She *is* the Daughter of the Sun."

Dejiko smiled, and one of the Crab samurai nodded. "You are right, little Moshi." His voice was a deep bass rumble. "And no one shall take her from us." The Hida's voice faded as Tsudao stepped to the front of the samurai band.

"I have seen your eyes," she cried. Her voice carried across the soldiers like warm wind sweeping a plain. "I know that the heart of the Legion is true. Come! Battle! You will always be by my side!"

With a roar, the Imperial Legion raised their swords, and she led them into the valley.

* * * * *

Fire and sunset lit the valley. The rays of the sun illuminated barren swaths of red and brown cliffside above the twisted forest below. Both sides of the valley were boxed in, and the far end of the canyon rose in a solid wall of stone, flanked by twisted pillars rising from the earth. The Tsuno howled in the trees, and their bonfires spread out around the mock shrine of pain where the captured samurai hung. The Imperial Legions flooded through the wood from the north, keeping their units together despite the rough terrain.

Tsudao and her legionnaires entered the forest warily, trying to maintain a solid front line. It didn't take long for the creatures to attack. Their howls ricocheted from the stone walls of the canyon as they leaped from tree to tree. Tsudao raised her sword and ordered the pikemen to raise their weapons against attack from above. The legion moved onward, lashing out with sword and fist against the steady wave of Shadowlands monsters that attempted to block their passage.

Claws tore at armor and ripped chunks of bark from trees, but Tsudao dodged between two large pines to confuse her enemies. Her sword cut through flesh, and she paused to remove the creature's head before the Tsuno could rise again. She heard her men doing the same, and between the screams of battle she heard others passing along the information they had learned from the Lion.

"Behead them and they will not rise!"

The wide clearing in the valley was choked with smoke. Tsudao and her men regrouped at the edge of the open space. In the center, piled higher than three men, was the shrine built by the Tsuno. It was a vague mockery of a Rokugani temple, tiered with half-stripped trees and tied together with leather strips. Bonfires blazed around it, tended by howling beasts capering in the flickering light. The smoke clung, blocking out the sunset, but Tsudao could still see the faint glow above the treetops.

Tsudao saw her opponents moving through the clearing with abandon. On the tiered shrine, samurai hung stretched against the wooden beams of the mock building, their bodies bloodied and limp. Some still struggled, but through the smoke there was no means to tell if they were alive or if their flesh had been inhabited by the power of the Shadowlands. Unlit bonfires clustered around the base of the taller structure, ready to ignite it at a single command.

"Are you so sure this ground is solid, Tsudao?" There was no concealing the viciousness in the voice that echoed through the bloodthirsty roars of the Shadowlands beasts. Tsudao turned from the battle, facing its source and trying to place the mocking tones.

When Junnosuke stepped from the smoke and flame, his leering face was so repugnant that Tsudao took a step backward.

"When you left me, Tsudao, I was nothing. Lower than the earth that shakes and ravages my Dragon homeland." He had no sword at his side, but four huge Tsuno clustered around him, saliva drooling in long threads from their bared jaws. "However, I think you'll find the terrain here far less to your liking than you had thought."

The ground at Tsudao's feet shook, forcing her back. Her soldiers screamed, and several fell, only to be swarmed by the Tsuno. She saw Dejiko fall to one knee, and the Lion commander's blade was knocked away by a lunging beast. Tsudao gathered her feet beneath her and tackled the beast, knocking it away from Dejiko. It slashed at her, its horns twisting to gouge her, but she shoved it with both feet back into one of the bonfires. It shrieked as tufts of hair burst into flame across its back and arms. Reeling, the Tsuno threw itself on the ground and writhed madly as the earth heaved beneath it. A pale fist burst through the shifting ground and clutched the Tsuno's arm in a vicelike grip.

Tsudao and Dejiko lurched to their feet, the earth exploding beneath them. Another arm, then a third and fourth, burst through the earth to clutch at the shrieking Tsuno and tear the creature to shreds. The earth collapsed, and the beast-man was dragged beneath the surface. A moment later, four bodies climbed from the torn earth, their hands bloodied. They were samurai, dressed in the armor of the Kitsu, wielding swords that had been blackened by their time in the earth. Their porcelain faces, white and smooth in the light of the bonfires, were eerily peaceful.

Junnosuke laughed, and a delicate female giggle formed an eerie, discordant harmony with his dark amusement. "Aren't you happy, Tsudao? We've brought your friends back to you."

Across the battlefield, more zombies tore themselves from the ground. Tsudao saw both Lion and Imperial troops—all those who had fought to defend the Kitsu tombs. Their bodies had been corrupted, their flesh tainted by the dark power of the Shadowlands. Now they were husks of their former selves. Tsudao gazed upon zombies that bore her own sigil. Horrified, she realized she knew every one of them.

Doji Usashi. His bloody arms covered in mud, he roared behind his porcelain mask as he cut into his legion-brothers. His sword, a relic of the ancient Crane-Lion wars, was rusted, tainted, and covered in the blood of his own family as he destroyed them one by one. The Imperial Legion scattered, unsure of how to combat the threat.

Another, Hida Tsichiko, crushed the legion troops with her tetsubo. She had once boasted she would be the last of the legion standing when all around her fell. She brought truth to her words by destroying her own companions. Despite the smooth, uncaring image on her porcelain face, Tsichiko's clothing was soon covered in the blood of her friends.

Dejiko shouted, lifting her sword as one of the nearby zombies thrust toward her with a long spear. Tsudao turned away to help the Kitsu commander, trying not to think that it was Kitsuki Riju whom she was destroying. Riju had been a jolly fellow, player of many games of *go* and a singer of ancient ballads. This creature was not him, no matter how it moved, no matter what its armor said, no matter that the scar upon its wrist was the same. The magic had changed him. It was not the Riju she had known.

Tsudao forced herself to believe that and swung her blade. Junnosuke laughed as Tsudao was forced to destroy the Kitsuki zombie.

The Tsuno charged from the smoke, adding to the confusion, and Tsudao heard her men screaming to regroup at the edge of the woods. The ground continued to tear and break apart as the shallow graves holding the zombies broke open and released a new army onto the field. Through the darkness and the smoke, Tsudao could sense the palpable presence of fear.

The darkness grew deeper as the thickening smoke blocked the light of the setting sun. The flames of the bonfire became strangely blue-gray against the hissing ash. The edges of the tall structure in the center of the valley began to flicker with white and blue flame, whispering hints of despair and agony into the growing night. Tsudao could see her men breaking, fleeing into the night, barely containing their fear in the face of the horrors that rose from the soil at their feet.

"Tsudao," Junnosuke hissed, stepping forward. "Face me."

His armor was no longer golden but rust-red, the color of dried blood. It shone in the strange light, and small faces writhed on its enameled plates as if begging for their freedom. Junnosuke had no sword. He crept toward her with open hands, weaponless. Dark hair, thick with sweat and blood, hung in lank strands at the sides of his face. His eyes glowed with madness and bloody rage. Behind him, through the thick haze, Tsudao saw a woman's form silhouetted against the fires. In her hands she held a cackling skull.

The sight of the woman frightened Tsudao more than Junnosuke's open threat. Something about her form, her laughter, and the movement of her long braids in the rising wind . . .

There was something horribly familiar about her. Familiar . . . and terrifying.

Tsudao stumbled back, and Junnosuke laughed, believing her fear was for his sake.

"Nowhere to run, Tsudao?" he snarled. "No legions to hide behind? Already, my army has feasts upon their flesh. Soon, there will be no more Imperial Legion—and no more Toturi Tsudao."

The attack came faster than any human could have moved. His hands crushed Tsudao's elbow, twisting her arm sharply. She raised her sword, cracking Junnosuke's temple with the hilt, but he barely flinched from her powerful blow. With a twist of his hips, he hurled Tsudao into the air. She landed facedown in the torn soil and mud. Her arm throbbed in pain, but there was no time to pause. Junnosuke leaped after her, his body rising high in the air, his arms spread wide.

He glided down through the smoke-laden air like a bird of prey, and Tsudao threw herself aside. Laughing, Junnosuke rose into the air again, and Tsudao pulled herself up to one knee to deflect the kick with her sword. She stared in awe and shock as his foot rang against her blade. It was completely undamaged by the cutting edge of the katana. The blade should have removed his foot—possibly his leg—but Junnosuke landed lightly on both feet, an insane grin lighting his features.

Feminine laughter, high and mocking, rang in Tsudao's ears.

Tsudao stumbled to her feet, holding Toturi's sword level. "You are filled with the Taint. The Shadowlands have given you these powers in exchange for your soul."

"My *soul?*" Junnosuke laughed. "My soul lies broken on the field, General. You saw to that."

He raised his fist to strike again, but she parried and moved under his arm. Her sword cut against his side, and where it struck, bright orange sparks flew from Tsudao's blade. She heard Dejiko cry out as more zombies flanked their position, but Tsudao had no time to spare. Already, Junnosuke had launched another flurry of open-hand blows, crashing beneath Tsudao's guard and shattering the black plates of her armor.

"Dejiko, get out of here! There are too many!"

The Lion commander spun, her long golden hair swirling behind her as she lifted her voice. "Back!" she screamed. "To the hill! The hill!"

At that moment, a Tsuno plunged for Dejiko, his fist crashing into her face. She crumpled, her body flying back. The Lion fell to the ground, her dark eyes closed and a bruise spreading across her pale cheek.

Junnosuke used Tsudao's distraction to his advantage and

caught her knee with one hand. There was a shattering crunch, and Tsudao fell. She raised her sword, but Junnosuke caught her wrist and ripped the weapon from her hand. He gripped Tsudao's helm, tore it from her head, and hurled it aside.

"You may kill me, Junnosuke—" Tsudao grimaced, still trying to stand despite her twisted leg— "but you will never defeat me."

Junnosuke backhanded Tsudao, his knuckles splitting her eyebrow. Blood trailed from his hand as she turned back to face him.

All around, Tsudao saw her soldiers falling. Zombies and Tsuno tore them apart, scattering the legion like ashes before a wind. Tsudao felt the loss of every man and woman who had followed her into battle—all of those who had died had fallen under her command.

The bonfires crackled, their blue flames swathed by shrouds of black haze. As Junnosuke raised her father's sword to test the edge, Tsudao struggled to regain her feet. He kicked her feet from beneath her.

"A good sword," Junnosuke sneered, as he studied its edge.

The woman, her pale arms raised, her violet and black robes clinging to her body, emerged from the smoky haze behind him. The skull hovered in the air at her shoulder. Tsudao looked up through a scarlet fog, blood trickling into her eyes.

"In darkness, Tsudao," the sorceress whispered, bloody smoke swirling around her gesturing hands. "That is how you shall die."

Suddenly, Tsudao emembered her. It seemed decades ago, when Tsudao was a child, but the woman's pale face had not changed.

"You are . . . Shahai," Tsudao groaned, shaking her head to clear it. "The blood-witch of the Iuchi. You were executed. . . ."

"No, little one." Shahai laughed. "They failed. They cast me out of my father's house, but they could not kill me. Instead, their scorn allowed me to find my true worth within the darkness of the Shadowlands. Soon, Tsudao, you will see what I have become."

"A traitor?" Tsudao snarled, spitting blood at both Junnosuke and Shahai. "You live in darkness. You know nothing of honor."

"Honor no longer rules the Empire, Tsudao—" Junnosuke raised his sword and began to strike for Tsudao's exposed throat— "and it never will again."

As the blade fell, Shahai's dark magic coalesced around them, blotting out every touch of light from the fires, every fading ray of the sun that struggled through the smoke-filled valley. Tsudao felt the light extinguish, and a horrible cold crept into her soul. Shahai and Junnosuke were bathed in a faint, cold glow, and the seconds seemed to slow as her father's sword burned through the air toward her. She stared up at it. For a second, she saw a glimmer of sunlight disappear along the edge of the blade.

No.

She would not die this way.

Light boiled within her, and Tsudao opened shining golden eyes.

Across the battlefield, the clouds burned away, and the sun seemed to gather strength. Shards of golden light shot down where there had been darkness, and through the smoke, the Sun showed his face once more. It tore away the shroud of night. Wherever it touched, the Tsuno screamed, their skin blackening and cracking.

Sunlight flooded the forest, and the sky was suddenly golden and pure. The creatures of the Shadowlands howled in agony. Dejiko, still stunned, stared up as the Tsuno clawed its own eyes. Blood trailed down its face, and Dejiko fumbled for her sword. With a single stroke, she removed the creature's head.

"To arms!" she roared.

* * * * *

Across the field, Moshi Kekiesu looked up into the sudden light, tears sparkling on her cheeks. The true light of the setting sun shone across the bloodstained valley, illuminating every thread of smoke that still clung in the air. The trees sparkled with energy, their limbs straightening with the touch of purity. Kekiesu whispered a faint spell, and the samurai nearby felt their wounds healing.

"The time has come at last. . ." Kekiesu whispered, standing in the sunlight. She closed her eyes and felt the gentle touch of the mother Sun whisper across her skin, raising her hair into the breeze it created and illuminating the entire valley.

* * * * *

The sunlight burst across the mock shrine, extinguishing the dark fires that burned at its base, and each of the porcelain figures stumbled and fell, struggling to rise despite the agony of the golden aura that surrounded them. Shahai clung to Junnosuke's upraised arm, her spell falling to shreds before the sudden dawn.

"We must go," she cried, her face drawn and frightened.

"Not until she is dead!" Junnosuke howled, raising Tsudao's sword once more. Beneath him, Tsudao met his gaze with brilliant golden eyes, and the full force of the Sun shone upon Junnosuke's tainted flesh. He screamed in pain, clutching his face, and blood ran down though his fingers.

"No!" Junnosuke snarled, trying to see despite the pain and blood.

"Not today," said Shahai, dragging him back. "If we stay, the sun will touch our souls. The power of the sun protects her. If we stay, we will die." Her skull's maniacal laughter was a counterpoint to the chanting as she invoked a powerful spell. The light around the sorceress grew stronger, coalescing in golden globes of light that burst into brilliant white sparks. A dark shroud fought against the sunlight, driving back the sparks and extinguishing them where they touched Shahai's black magic.

"Tomorrow . . ." Shahai whispered, and her hand fell. Across the battlefield, the Tsuno vanished. One by one, their bodies became wisps of smoke, and their roars turned to faint echoes—then vanished altogether. A cold wind swept through the valley, and each of the zombies withered and sank into the ground.

A portal tore open where Shahai and Junnosuke stood, and a dark, blood-encrusted plain beckoned through the gate. Shahai stepped through, pulling Junnosuke after, though he still stared down at the broken body of his prey as if sheer malice could drive the life from Tsudao's body. She was surrounded by sunlight, a golden ring that parted the clouds. Small motes danced in the air around her, illuminated by the gleam of the setting sun.

For a moment, long threads of darkness spilled from the portal, twisting and writhing at the empty air as if trying to pull the rest of the world into the nether realm. There was a soft scream, discordant and somehow faded from reality, and then the tentacles withdrew, ethereal blood trickling upon the ground.

Once on the other side, Junnosuke turned back, staring at Tsudao as blood ran like tears down his sunken cheeks. Pausing only a moment to consider, the tainted Dragon raised Tsudao's blade in a mocking salute.

"We will meet again, Tsudao," he said as the portal slipped away.

* * * * *

The Scorpion knelt over the general's limp form, feeling for a pulse on her bloodstained neck. It was there, faint but strong. Tsudao still lived. Her face was drawn and bloodied, and one leg was twisted like a child's broken toy. No sword lay in her hand, and the scabbard at her side was empty. They had taken her blade, but they had not taken her life.

Although she was unconscious, she still had a serenity that touched even his cold, hardened heart. He stared down at her for a long moment, considering the alternatives as he brushed a lock of long black hair away from Tsudao's face. Something in her features reminded him of a statue he remembered as a child, when Amaterasu still held the Sun within the canopy of the sky. Tsudao—the image of the goddess of light—lay quietly upon the cold earth, beautiful, serene, and still.

It was the will of the Fortunes that she lived, and it was not his place to defy the Kami. No matter what Naseru would say. . . .

With a soft sigh, Bayushi Paneki gently lifted Tsudao's body into his arms and carried her from the field.

16 STRIPPING AWAY ILLUSION

Kekiesu knelt before Tsudao and wiped the sweat away from her mistress's brow. Four days had passed since the Battle of Dawn's Valley (as it was becoming known), and still Tsudao had not awakened. The legions whispered the story of their victory and the strangeness of "dawn at twilight"—the strange miracle that had driven away the Shadowlands creatures from the field. Kekiesu wrung the cold rag out in a bowl of water and replaced it on the lady's forehead.

"Kekiesu-san?" Paneki's voice, just outside the tent. The maiden stood, checked Tsudao's covers once more, and then went outside to greet him. Paneki's gold and scarlet robes were informal, his pants black beneath the long hem of his shirt. His vest was in the traditional style, and black Scorpion mon were patterned into his sleeves. A thin golden mask barely covered his features, reminding all who spoke with him that his words could not be trusted.

Kekiesu brushed a strand of black hair out of her eyes

and straightened her maiden's foxtail. The hair hung halfway down her back against the green robes of her own clan. She knelt beside a small stream that flowed near the imperial encampment and washed out the small wooden bowl. He followed her in silence, knowing that the Moshi shugenja would speak when she was ready.

At last, she sat back on her heels and sighed. Her heart-shaped face was filled with concern, and she bit her lower lip.

"Tsudao has not awakened," Kekiesu whispered, answering the unspoken question in Paneki's eyes. "It is likely that she will require some time to heal the damage done to her. To draw the Sun herself from a night sky . . . the candle within her soul has burned low. We must allow it to awaken again on its own."

Paneki nodded.

"For now," Kekiesu continued, "we must discover what magic was used to allow the blood sorceress and her allies to flee the field. Only the most powerful spells can defy the power of the sun. I did not believe such power existed."

Paneki's eyes narrowed in contemplation as he leaned against one of the weapon racks placed outside the general's tent. "But you do now?"

"I must believe what I have seen."

The Bayushi nodded. "Then we must prepare to fight against it. The only weak enemy is an unprepared enemy."

Around them, the encampment stood on the plains just north of Dawn's Valley, where peasants had already begun to leave tokens. The mouth of the valley was littered with sheaves of grain, small black and gold ribbons tied to the trees, and scrolls of praise to the Fortunes and the Kami. Some of the soldiers had begun to tie similar scrolls to the openings of their tents, thanking whatever divine agency had rescued them from certain death.

"Tell me, Kekiesu, how did they escape us? There were no other exits to that valley. My men guarded both walls, and the Lion held the opening of the canyon. There should have been nowhere to flee."

"I told you, Paneki-san. I do not know." Kekiesu looked down, scrubbing the bowl furiously and not meeting his eyes.

"Hmph." The Bayushi grabbed her arm, making her drop the bowl into the dust, and pulled the handmaiden around to face him. "You know more than you say."

Kekiesu shoved Paneki, breaking free of his grip. "What I know, the Sun has given me." Her eyes flashed.

"And my own studies lie in shadow. Between us both, we should be able to discern their secrets and break their powers. Tsudao lies unconscious in her tent. Do you believe she wants us to remain still? To ignore this threat until she returns to us? Or do you believe that we must also fight this battle with all we have—and when she awakens, we will have something to show for our effort?"

Kekiesu watched him for long moments, her eyes narrowed.

"There is a ritual that can tell us more," Paneki said. "You know of it. I believe you can cast it." His voice was strident, impassioned, and he stepped within inches of Kekiesu. She did not move, refusing to be bullied by his presence. Kekiesu raised her chin and stared into the Scorpion's eyes as he continued. "She cannot defeat this threat without us. Her father stood alone against it. Look what happened to him."

"I will not hear you speak so about the Emperor." In deference to the dead, Kekiesu did not speak Toturi's name.

"Then hear me speak about his daughter." Paneki's eyes were dark and shadowed behind his thin golden mask, but his face was sharp and foxlike. "Were you not the one who told her that some threats cannot be defeated with a sword?"

Kekiesu gaped. Her private conversation with Tsudao . . .

Paneki grasped her again, more gently, and Kekiesu did not move away. "Then realize that when she awakens, her first thought will be to find Junnosuke and destroy him. Where will she go? To the Dragon, perhaps. Or to the villages that shelter ronin. Or perhaps she will go to the Shadowlands

REE SOESBEE

and seek the source of his dark power. What will happen to your mistress then?" Paneki's hand upon her shoulder was firm. He shook her lightly, whispering, "What will become of Tsudao if she goes into the Shadowlands after him?"

"She will . . . she will be infected by the Taint. . . ."

"And the law demands that no samurai who bears the Taint can rule."

Kekiesu stared, her rose-colored lips parted in horror. "She would never rule. The Empire—"

"Would have only three heirs. Whether she found Junnosuke or not."

"It cannot be."

"It *will* be, if you and I do not stop it. Tsudao's long slumber is a blessing. It will allow us to discover the truth and set her feet upon the proper path. Help me, Kekiesu." Paneki's hand was warm upon her shoulder, and he pulled the young handmaiden to him. His breath brushed her cheek, and the wooden bowl fell from her hand. "Only you can perform the *Ooyake michisuji*. You know the spell. You must perform the Ritual of Open Paths."

"No," Kekiesu protested. "It does not exist."

"It *does,* and the Moshi have held its secrets for generations."

"That is not . . . not true."

"Kekiesu, do not lie to a Scorpion." Paneki smiled. "We already know the truth."

Kekiesu slumped in his hands. "There is such a ritual, but I cannot perform it. It has not been cast in generations. The spell calls upon unpredictable kami, spirits of both future and past. To invoke it means that you must twist your own future by their whim. It is too dangerous. There is always a cost when one seeks dangerous truths."

"If we do not pay the price," Pankei said, "then Tsudao will. The Moshi have held their secrets close for many years, but you are not betraying your family. I already know of the ritual. You are a powerful shugenja and the only member of your family within a thousand miles. If you do not help me, then you have already forsaken her. She will destroy herself."

"No," Kekiesu stepped back, shaking. She placed her hand on his breast and stood for a silent moment. "No, that will not happen. The Ritual of Open Paths . . . we will experience the past again, but from a different perspective. If we do this, then we will have to go back into the valley in order to draw upon the moment of their escape." Kekiesu looked up again, and her eyes met his with warmth and hope. "She must live. For the Empire's sake."

"With your help . . . she will." His voice was soft in her ear, yet the sound gave her strength.

"Then we must begin at once. Come, let me show you the way."

* * * * *

The Valley of Dawn was empty now, its forested basin quiet. The thick pine trees that had hidden the army of Tsuno swayed in warm spring wind, and the earth seemed to have been turned by plows rather than torn apart by porcelain-masked zombies. If Kekiesu had not known this was the sight of a horrible battle, she would never have guessed. On one arm, she carried a laden basket covered in a thin silk scarf. With the other hand, she brushed the tree limbs, pushing them aside as she and Paneki passed beneath the overhanging forest.

It was beautiful here, almost serene. Kekiesu reached up to a branch of the pine, noting that the ends of each needle had turned a brilliant shade of gold. All around her, the forest seemed permanently touched by the sun's power. It welcomed them with the faint rustle of branches and the scent of a forest dell.

Paneki followed close behind Kekiesu, his hands tucked into the sleeves of his robe. Together they walked into the valley and toward the clearing near the canyon's end.

The shrine-like structure that the Tsuno had built was

destroyed. Each of the samurai who had hung from that terrible mockery had been buried with full ritual as fallen warriors. The few Crab shugenja left in the Imperial Legion had spent hours scouring the area, incense braziers wafting the sweet scent of myrrh and rose through the once-tainted valley floor. After three full days of chanting and ritual, they had declared the area re-sanctified, all traces of the Taint removed.

Still, some sense of the horror remained. Looking at the burned clearing, a shiver crept up Kekiesu's spine, and she wrapped her arms around her body. Paneki stepped close behind her, his hand gently touching her shoulder.

"What is it?" he whispered.

"Nothing. I felt . . ." Her brow wrinkled. "This place holds too many memories. Hurry. We must be swift, or we will be discovered." She shook off the eerie feeling, turning her trained senses to matters of the spirit and away from fears of the flesh. "Where did you find her body?"

Paneki studied the landscape critically, then pointed. "There."

They approached the spot slowly, picking their way through torn ground and around incense-laden areas where the Crab had held their rituals. When they reached the small hillock, Kekiesu set down her basket and moved away from Paneki. She knelt and touched the ground with her hands. She was very close to the center of the valley, only a short distance from the location where the base of the false shrine had stood. Closing her eyes, Kekiesu reached out with her mind, sensing any trace of Tsudao's presence. The world spun slightly around her, twisting through corridors of scent and sound toward the trail that she sought.

There. Her mistress's presence. And another, a man . . . and another woman, but this one cold and empty, with little of true life left within her.

"You are right, Paneki," Kekiesu whispered. "Swiftly, hand me the basket."

Tearing away the silk cover, Kekiesu withdrew her ritual implements, placing them in a half-circle on the ground around her. There was a small knife, three sticks of incense, several small candles, and a series of golden chimes shaped in a circle like the rays of the sun. Lastly, a single long stick of blackened wax covered in strange golden kanji, which Kekiesu half-buried in the ground between them. Paneki knelt opposite Kekiesu, uncertain how to assist her.

"Place these candles around us, at every quarter of the circle," she directed, and he was quick to do as she bade. "The incense sticks go in the center, like so, and the chimes are mine. Hold the knife in your left hand, and when I tell you—and *only* when I tell you—cut it in half. Your strike must be precise, Paneki, and it must be clean, or else the ritual will not cease, and we will be dragged forever into the mists of uncertain time." Kekiesu looked up at him, her eyes dark and somber. "You must be ready. If I begin to lose control, only a cut of that knife will save us. But only cut it when I tell you. Do you understand?"

Paneki nodded, unafraid. His hand clenched around the hilt of the white-handled knife, and he slowly withdrew it from its sheath. The blade was not made of metal nor of gold as he had suspected. Instead, it was formed of crystal as pure as mountain water, glassy and clear. Even to his untrained eye, the blade sang of magic and ritual, and his face seemed oddly distorted in its crystal edge.

"We are the Children of the Sun, sons and daughters all," Kekiesu said, holding her hands above the incense. "As this world was given life from flame, so it will return to flame one day. Before we lived, before Rokugan rose, before the Kami appeared in the heavens, the Sun danced and the world was born."

As she chanted, her fingers began to glow. One by one, the candles around the edge of the circle sparked and ignited into flame.

"I call upon the Mother Sun, Amaterasu, and her incarnate

successor, Yakamo the Bold. I call upon the holy light of day, the brilliance of noonday heat, and the pure flame of truth. Guide us in our quest." The light of the candles grew, and even though the sun shone high in the heavens above them, the light of Kekiesu's candles began to cast shadows of their own. "Hear me."

Something wavered in the earth around them, a faint tremor that only Paneki seemed to feel. Power flowed through the circle, and Kekiesu lifted her hands toward the sun as if gathering sheaves of grain.

"Listen to me, delicate Kami of time, fortune, and fickle luck. Bind yourselves to me, and show me paths that have already been trodden. I seek the path to the past, to open the passages of what has been."

The incense in the center of the circle smoked as if it were held under a thick piece of glass for too long. In only a few seconds, it burst into flame and passed into glowing coal. Smoke rose from the sticks of incense, and the scent reminded Paneki of long summer days in his childhood. He had never smelled that clear, earthy scent before, but it spoke of days by the river and nights staring up at the sky, dreaming of the day he would become a man.

Kekiesu smiled and closed her eyes. "Hear me."

She spoke a third time, closing her arms over her shoulders as if holding something close. "I call upon dream itself, the future that is unknown and unknowable. As the past is tied to the present, so too must it be one with those days yet to be. Though we seek the past, the days that have moved beyond us, we call to the future to hold our paths open, that we might return. So knowing, we offer ourselves as sacrifice for the truths we call forth. May the kami of past and future both hold us in their care."

As she finished the last words of the spell, the black taper in the center of the circle trembled, and the earth beneath them rocked. The candles did not shiver, their flame did not move—and suddenly it was as if their flames were frozen in crystal. Paneki stared at one of them, willing the dancing flame to move, but it remained completely still.

Around them, the valley changed, and Kekiesu opened her eyes in half-aware trance. "Time moves without us, Paneki-san," she whispered. "We are in a time that is not time, a space that has no ties upon this realm. Now we must turn time back, to the moment of Tsudao's fight with Junnosuke. Only there can we find the answers we seek."

Paneki opened his mouth to ask a question but closed it again before the words escaped him. Instead, he said, "Tell me what to do."

Kekiesu reached out to the taper that stood in the ground between them and deftly broke the seal at its top. She pulled, and a thin golden thread unraveled into her hand, still tied at one end to the taper. Now Paneki saw that the cord was wrapped around the black tallow, sunk into its coated sides and covered by the kanji runes that were painted on the surface of the waxy stick. Kekiesu pulled away gently, and a bit of the cord unraveled from the stick, wax flaking to the ground. The earth heaved as she did so, and the sun leaped backward in the sky.

"Draw the cord," Kekiesu said, handing the cord to Paneki as it unwrapped from the stick. He caught it in one hand and drew it across his body, watching it unweave from the tallow. He then handed it to her on the other side. Around them, the sun sank into the morning sky, and a brilliant dawn flashed past into darkness. She drew upon the cord again, twisting down the spire of the tallow, and more black and red wax fell to the ground as the golden thread came free. The night passed in a matter of seconds, then day sprang from twilight and into noon.

Crab shugenja walked backward across the plain, chanting and drawing incense-laden smoke into their braziers. They opened their hands, and shards of jade leaped from the ground back into their pouches, their heavy staves breaking the ground back open instead of tamping it down with each step.

Paneki stared in awe as he was handed the thread once more. He drew it around again, offering it back to her as the dawn once more turned into night. Another day—more Crab littered the field, and chanting peasants fluttered past in half-realized motion, their speed transfigured into flickers of motion at the edge of his vision. Again the Crab walked past, and a great pyre burst into flame in the center of the valley. The flames burned slowly, picking up speed and brilliance as the wood fell from their hungry mouths. The pyre swelled, and men carrying torches extinguished the flames. The bodies of the dead were lifted from the wooden dais and placed upon the field around them by cowering slaves. Bit by bit, the golden cord unwound.

Paneki saw himself, walking toward them. In his arms he carried the limp form of a woman, her black and gold armor stained with blood. He set her on the ground before them, touched her face gently with one finger to place a dark hair across her cheek, then slowly backed away.

"Here," Kekiesu whispered, not noticing the flush on Paneki's face.

"Now we will see them," she murmured, holding the thread aloft and twisting it away from the tallow in tiny fragments. The world ground to a halt, then was silent. Tsudao lay upon the ground before them, and a man stood over her with her father's sword. His red armor was the color of dried blood, his eyes maddened with vengeance and blood lust. A delicate woman stood behind him and cradled a laughing skull in her pale arms. The sorceress's eyes were dark and eager. Her smile was that of a lover, savoring a kiss.

"Good-bye, Tsudao." Junnosuke's voice was but a pale echo of its former self, laden with the passage of time. He raised Toturi's sword for a final strike, and Shahai's laughter sang, high-pitched and musical, across the war-torn field.

Darkness—burst apart by a golden explosion of light. Tsudao lay upon the ground, her hair swirling in a brilliant aura of radiance, and Junnosuke staggered back. Shahai screamed and pulled at Junnosuke's arm. He raised his hands his face, blood streaming down from his seared eyes. The light around the sorceress grew stronger, coalescing in golden globes of light that burst into brilliant white sparks. A dark shroud fought against the sunlight, driving back the sparks and extinguishing them where they touched Shahai's black magic.

"Tomorrow . . ." Shahai whispered, and her hand fell.

The golden cord froze, and the scene around Kekiesu and Paneki took on a strange shimmer. Behind Shahai, a portal tore open, and they could see a dark realm of mist and twisted features. Kekiesu gasped, staring into the gate as if she had seen the mouth of madness.

"Kekiesu!" Paneki burst out. "What is it? What do you see?"

Her eyes grew fearful, and a low keening escaped her throat as she stared into the portal where Shahai and Junnosuke stepped. As if summoned forth by her wail—or perhaps warned by it—dark tentacles slid out from the opening and reached for them.

The tentacles were not responding to things that had once been. They were aware of Kekiesu and her companion. One struck at the candle nearest to the portal, extinguishing its flame, and Kekiesu screamed. Two more coiled past the opening of the circle, twining around Paneki's shoulder and pulling at him with incredible strength. The samurai struggled to remain within the circle as Kekiesu howled in pain. Another tentacle struck her, its black, sticky coating searing her pale arm.

"Paneki!" Kekiesu shrieked. "Cut the tallow!"

Without hesitation, Paneki turned and raised the crystal blade. The tentacle around his arm tightened, pulling his hand back, but as the crystal knife touched them, the tentacles jerked away as if scorched. Paneki cut at them, pushing the ethereal limbs back so that he could lift his arm once more. The tentacles smashed into the ground before him, reaching eagerly for the stick of tallow.

Paneki drew the knife before him, screaming with all the power of his chi. He struck, and the tallow parted cleanly before his stroke.

The world turned black and spun around them. All Paneki could hear were Kekiesu's screams, echoing in the darkness that surrounded them. Without releasing the knife, he reached for her. She struggled, fearing the tentacles, until he pulled her against his chest and held her close. Realizing that it was Paneki, Kekiesu clung to him and shivered like a willow in a strong stream. He closed his eyes, pressing his lips to her soft hair, and whispered her name.

When he opened his eyes, they were back in the empty clearing. The Valley of the Dawn shone around them in the sunlight, free of all the signs of battle and all the bloody marks of the days that had passed. The candles around them were extinguished, the tallow severed cleanly in half. The golden thread had turned a sickly greenish color, hissing on the ground as it disintegrated from the touch of the pure sunlight. Kekiesu still lay in Paneki's arms, whispering a soft prayer to the Sun as she clung to him.

"Kekiesu," he said. "You have done it. We are returned to the Valley of the Dawn."

She opened her eyes, fearing to see what lay around them. A fearful smile crept across her face when she realized that he was speaking the truth.

"You see?" Paneki smiled. "No harm done. The cost was not so high, after all."

"Oh, no, Paneki-san." Kekiesu pulled away and trembled, biting her lower lip in worry. "That was not the cost. We will still pay for the truth we have determined. Those tentacles that attacked us were something else. Something even more foul that came out of the place where Shahai took her armies." Kekiesu shook her head. "I did not think such things were possible. We were not part of that time. Nothing should have seen us, yet it did."

"What was it?" he asked.

Kekiesu looked up at him. "I cannot say *what* it was, but I do know where it came from. I looked beyond the sorceress's magic and saw where they fled, but the news is graver than any I would have expected. They did not go to the Shadowlands, Paneki, but to a place far worse. A place beyond this world, and beyond any other. It is a nether-realm, a dark plane of existence known as the Realm of Slaughter. If Shahai has the power to carry an army across all the planes of existence, then either she is far more powerful than we expected, or she has aid such as I've never seen before. A power long thought lost. . ." Kekiesu's words trailed off and she shook her head. "He is dead," she whispered. "He must be."

"Who, Kekiesu?"

"No." Her voice rose, on the edge of hysteria, and Paneki drew her close until she regained control. "It is impossible! Toturi killed him. It cannot be."

"Tell me, Kekiesu," Paneki demanded.

"Only one power has ever been known to have such control over the hells surrounding Rokugan," she whispered. "There is only one being who has ever been known to travel the Plane of Slaughter freely." She stared up at Paneki, and he could see naked fear in the young priestess's eyes. "That creature was Fu Leng himself."

"Fu Leng is dead," Paneki reassured her. "The god of the Shadowlands is dead."

"He is banished from this plane, yes," Kaikiesu breathed in fear, "but not truly dead, nor forgotten. If his followers gain enough power, they may be able to reach him, no matter how far away his spirit lies. If they do that, the Empire will be destroyed."

* * * * *

My Master,
You were correct. I should never have doubted you. I know that now.

Tsudao awoke shortly after we returned from the Valley of Dawn, her eyes as golden as the sun. She is weak and says that she remembers little of the battle. Still, I believe the incident has educated her, if nothing else. She spends her mornings meditating now, facing the east—the dawn and the sun.

The Imperial Legions head south, toward the Shadowlands and the Shinomen Forest, that mythical forest of magic and power, to seek a passage into the realms beyond. According to the Centipede's research, the Shinomen Forest is the only place in the Empire where the nether realms touch our own. The shugenja say that we may be able to open another entrance into the Realm of Slaughter and follow after Shahai and Junnosuke. I can only guess what we shall find. It is a place where dreams walk and dangers hide in mists. The nether realms are close there, indeed. But you know that, I believe, far better than I. It is also the site of Toturi's death, and Tsudao cannot be convinced to separate the two. If we cannot find what we seek there, Tsudao is determined to go to the Shadowlands to hunt down Junnosuke and retrieve her father's sword. He is still our pawn. As you had foreseen.

Whatever may come, Tsudao will face Junnosuke again, and this time, only one will survive the conflict. The Season of War will continue, no matter what the outcome. As you have commanded, so shall it be. I will watch, and wait, and bide my time.

I know my duty.

B.P.

17   EDGE OF THE STARS

The Shinomen stood, as it always had, steadfast against the storms that brewed in the south. Though their fierce winds ruffled the tops of the ancient trees, the fury of the storm would not even be noticed by the quiet dells and thickly clustered branches of the lowest trees. It was a land unto itself, watching as the tides of the Empire ebbed and fell. The paths that led into the forest's shadowy groves were dark and mossy, each step sliding ever farther into myth.

The trees were tall oaks whose branches hung low against the ground. Their roots spread for miles in every direction, knotting the ground with their gnarled knuckles. Winds rose in the deep fells and dark valleys within the forest's shadow, whispering of dreams unknown to man. Within the Shinomen Forest, all things that were lost to time could be found . . . even secrets best left forgotten.

The legion camped just north of the forest, several miles from the edge. Although none of the samurai claimed to believe in the murmurs of dark sorcery and mystic beasts within the forest, the commanders thought it best to camp in the open fields rather than despoil the forest's stillness. Of course, that was not the reason, but it allowed everyone to save face, and so the tents were carefully raised some distance from the trees. As for the scrolls of blessing and protection that hung from the entrances to each tent . . . no one saw the need to comment or complain about their presence.

Toturi Tsudao sat upon her command stool and stared at the grim horizon. She watched the storm above the trees until long after night had fallen. She seemed carved from stone, frozen upon the earth as the legion moved around her. None disturbed the general's thoughts or disrupted her silence. She sat with her chin balanced upon a tightly clenched fist. With golden eyes, she stared into the dark recesses of the forest as if determined to steal their secrets.

Black and gold armor hung on a stand nearby, but no sword rested within the stand in the honored place at its side. Only an empty walnut holder stood there, empty of the samurai's most precious burden.

Tsudao rolled the small ivory statuette between her fingers, feeling every ridge and curl in the storm-lion's mane. It roared silently in her palm, refusing to be cowed. For a moment, Tsudao wondered about her father's last thoughts as he stood on this very road, before this very forest . . . and met his death.

What would he think of her now?

Again, his voice echoed in her memory. *"You will not wield this sword, Tsudao-chan. Perhaps one day, if you prove your honor, the sword will wield you."*

Now her father's sword was in the hands of a traitor. A ronin. A man who had sold his very soul for vengeance. She had driven Junnosuke from the Empire, but in so doing she had lost the one tie she had to her father's spirit. Was that the cost of her destiny? To lose her father's sword but gain an Empire? Where were the truths hidden in this riddle?

Kekiesu's voice joined with that of her father. "*What if your blade cannot carve away these wars?*

Why, now that she could no longer deny the truth, had the dying light of the Mother Sun blessed her? Amaterasu was dead now, her spirit lost in the realms of the kami. Her successor, the bold Yakamo, ruled the day with a hand of jade and swept darkness from the sky. Tsudao had not asked for this power, nor for the burden it carried. What did it mean for Rokugan?

What did it mean for her claim to the throne?

"Sezaru," Tsudao whispered, the small stone lion clenched in her hand, "my wise brother. Where are you now, when I have more questions than answers?"

Her eyes narrow with anger and with regret, she stared once more into the darkness of the forest. Something lay within that forest. Something she must find to ease the burden of her father's soul. Sezaru could not do it. In his quest for truth, he had left the Empire to rot and burn. Naseru she simply did not trust. And Kaneka . . . Kaneka, for all his valor, was a fool. The samurai of the Empire would never follow him. They would tear themselves apart before they bowed their heads to a ronin.

Rokugan's Emperor had been killed by something that lived within the Shinomen, and Tsudao alone could seek its true face. She bore no sword and would wear no steel. But when she returned—if she returned—by the Sun and the Seven Fortunes, she would bear the truth—or some part of it. Enough to lay her father's soul to rest. Her father's memory was more important than all the lands, all the samurai, and all the honor in the Empire. Toturi must be avenged—whatever the price.

As she looked into the Shinomen, Tsudao felt ever more the lost child. She wondered if the choice between her father's soul and the Empire would truly be that easily made. . . .

* * * * *

Tsudao gave orders for the legions to remain camped upon the plains surrounding Ryoko Owari, the famed City of Green Walls, until she returned. Kitsu Dejiko shouted, railed, and nearly broke the code of bushido when Tsudao told her that she would be remaining behind with the troops. In the end, the Kitsu commander knelt before her general and asked softly—so quietly that it would break a Crane's heart—if the general would allow her to follow. Tsudao would not listen and did not answer.

Kekiesu and Paneki stood together outside the encampment, both garbed for travel and bearing weapons. Paneki wore the two swords of a samurai, while Kekiesu held only her staff. Tsudao stared at them for a long moment, debating if she should command them to stay, then changed her mind. She did not have it in her heart to deny Kekiesu's request, and to turn away Paneki would solve nothing. He would follow, come what might.

Tsudao shrugged, shouldered her knapsack, and entered the Shinomen Forest at the first rambling path she could find. The wood was cool and quiet, the ancient oaks spreading their wide boughs over the sky in a blanket of green. The path beneath Tsudao's feet crunched softly with the sound of secrets being told, each dried leaf and fallen twig snapping in muted percussion. Kekiesu stared openly, amazed at the size of the trees, hardly noticing the path that guided them onward. She kept closely to Paneki's side, brushing near him as they avoided huge root tangles and low-hanging limbs.

"These trees are as old as the Empire," she breathed.

"Older," Paneki replied. The hush of the forest was so great that none of them wished to break its silence. "The legends of this forest are known in my clan, very well. The Naga live here—spirit creatures, half-man and half-serpent. They were a peaceful people who wished to live their lives in solitude and meditation, so I am told."

"My father told me of them," Tsudao said in assent. "They were sacred creatures, but they came from a time long before the Empire. Before the Kami fell from the heavens, back when the Shadowlands were green."

Paneki nodded. "When the Shadowlands fought in the Empire, the Taint was so great that it awakened the Naga, and they fought beside our fathers to save the world from darkness. I was but a child then, and Kekiesu was not yet born."

"I remember only images—great serpents in my father's court. They spoke of dreams. . . ."

"Yes," Paneki agreed. "They lived their lives in silent sleep before the Shadowlands awakened them, and when the threat was past they returned to their forest to sleep again. If we are lucky, we will not find them, for to awaken them could be incredibly dangerous."

"What would such evil be doing in a place of dreams and dreamers?" Kekiesu's eyes were round with a thousand questions.

"I do not know," Paneki glanced away. "I know only that their dreams haunt this forest and that if we are not careful, we too will fade into sleep and never be seen again."

Quietly Tsudao said, "Legends."

Kekiesu and Paneki exchanged glances, and Kekiesu replied, "I would not be so sure. The tales of the Great Sleep are very specific . . . and the presence of such magic could explain why the nether realms are so close in this place." She closed her eyes, concentrating on a sense beyond sight or sound. "There is a powerful source within this forest, one sheltered by many spirits. It may be these Naga I sense, but—" Kekiesu paused, wrinkling her brow— "there is something else."

"Come." Paneki took Kekiesu's elbow, gently calling her back to the mortal world. "It is not safe to remain still for too long, lest we are noticed." He peered up into the leafy boughs of the oak trees and continued down the path.

"Wait." Tsudao stopped. "If your power can tell us where these Naga sleep, or if it can guide us—"

"To open yourself up to the forest is dangerous. It can be deadly if she senses something beyond her ability to understand." Paneki was strident. "We must keep moving."

Kekiesu moved past Tsudao and Paneki, lifting her staff over the roots that twisted upon the ground like writhing snakes. She held her hand open in front of her, reaching out to the source of the strange presence within the forest. She closed her eyes once more, twisting her body to the right as if swaying in a breeze that Tsudao and Paneki could not feel.

Paneki stepped toward her, frowning, but Tsudao glared at the Scorpion and he did not touch Kekiesu. The shugenja walked down the path as if in a half-trance, turning into the woods and extending her arm. "There . . ." she whispered. "We will find what we seek if we go this way." Kekiesu opened her eyes and looked back at her companions. "I have a feeling time is short. There is an active presence here, and it is aware of us. Already, it searches the forest. We cannot hide for long."

Tsudao stepped forward, passing Paneki and nodding to her handmaiden as she entered the deep groves of the forest. "Then do not pause, my friends. Destiny will not wait."

The Shinomen grew thicker as they continued, the tall trees growing closer together as their branches wove tightly above them. Soon, no sky at all could be seen, and only a faint glow shimmering faintly though the thick leaves showed them the way. The oaks here were as large around as six men and shrouded in thick, clinging vines and warm mist. Tsudao picked her way along roots as wide as roadways, crawling under where they arched into the curtain of vines that hung down from the treetops to the ground. The vines hung in curtains, waterfalls of thick green canopy that blocked all view, preventing any wind from disturbing the inner sanctums of the forest. Twice more, Tsudao paused to allow Kekiesu to find their way. They did not pause for food or rest, aware that danger lay all around them.

After many hours, the pale light around them faded, and

Tsudao looked up into the treetops to see only a misty darkness. Outside the forest, the sun had set, and night had gathered the world into sleep. The forest was unchanged. Luminescent mosses shed a dim glow upon canopies of green vine and passageways curving beneath high, arched branches.

The wild grasses and thick brush upon the ground muffled their footsteps, and it seemed for a time that they walked through an eternity of silence. None of them wished to draw attention to themselves or to break the mystic spell that hushed every birdsong and creature within the forest. The entire Shinomen hung as if between worlds—silent, shrouded and asleep.

Tsudao paused as a faint scent lingered in the air around her. It was bittersweet, oddly pungent, and she could not quite place its origin. Signaling to Paneki and Kekiesu, she climbed up onto one of the arching roots at the base of a gigantic rowan tree and tried to find the source of the disturbance.

To the south, a building rose from a low valley in the wood. It was square, made of stone, and Tsudao thought for a moment that it was a watchtower, so cunningly were its walls designed. The darkness prevented her from seeing more. Climbing down, Tsudao murmured softly, "To the south. There is a building."

The others nodded, following her as she led the way. Behind her, Paneki walked beside Kekiesu, exchanging a concerned glance for her hopeful smile.

The forest opened, and beneath the mossy ground Tsudao could feel hard stone under her sandals. Cobbled tiles, broken and unattended, were scattered along the edge of the dell as if an ancient road had once curved into the valley. Now, it was broken and overgrown with moss and trees, but once it had commanded a view of the surroundings that must have been impressive.

In the dell itself, a building rose from the mist—tall and

square, its stubborn rock walls refusing to decay. From the rise where the road had been, Tsudao could see the entire building, from foretower through to entrance of the walled courtyard beyond. Kekiesu took a single look, then staggered back into Paneki's arms, hiding her face in his shoulder. Tsudao furrowed her brow—unafraid but unsure.

A thousand bodies lay piled upon the parapets and stacked around the walls of the small keep like cords of wood. Blood stained every inch of stonework, tainting every bush and tree that tried to grow on the cursed ground. The earth was rust red around the keep, and the leaves upon the nearest oaks had turned black with loss and pain. Tsudao stared, grasping little beyond the carnage at first. Once her mind had adjusted to the horror of the sight, she began to notice the details of the scene.

The bodies were not human. Serpent tails on human torsos, the creatures whose bodies littered the keep had odd, greenish skin. Their empty faces were snakelike, with slitted eyes and long, forked tongues. Even the blood that had been spread throughout the dell was a strange brownish-green.

"Naga," whispered Tsudao. "They are all Naga."

Paneki nodded, keeping his face half-turned from the carnage below. "These Naga must have guarded those within the Great Sleep. I have heard of such places—where some few remain awake to tend their dreaming race. But the Shinomen was their home. No beast within it would have attacked them."

"No beast," Tsudao agreed, pointing at the stacked bodies and blood smears upon the stone. "Something that walks upright—a being that knows and relishes pain—did this."

"The legends say the Naga are a peaceful people." Kekiesu shuddered. "Why would someone destroy them? They weren't a threat. They are all sleeping."

Suddenly, a horn blew in the forest. It rose in pitch, sounding a mournful, eager note. Paneki reached for his sword. Tsudao took a martial stance, only too aware of the empty scabbard at her side. Kekiesu clung to her staff with wide, frightened eyes. Beyond the trees, the sound of birds' wings rustled, growing closer and doubling in size until it sounded as if a thousand crane were taking flight. Louder and louder it came. Within minutes, Tsudao could hear the noises more clearly. As shadows leaped from tree to tree, closer and closer still, Tsudao peered intently to identify the oncoming threat.

"Those aren't birds," she said, knowing that it was no use trying to hide their presence. "Those are Tsuno."

Hurtling through the trees, the Tsuno came with slavering jaws and sharp fangs. The rustling of the leaves around them made the sound of birds' wings as they swung from limb to limb high above the ground. Their claws sank into the thick wood, spilling sap like blood from the sleeping forest. Laughter echoed, breaking the mystic silence of the Shinomen as the Tsuno approached.

"Have they seen us?" Paneki growled.

"Undoubtedly." The horn sounded again, this time much closer, and Tsudao could hear the blood-lust in the screams of the creatures. They had only a few moments to prepare for the attack. Tthe Tsuno would soon be upon them, and they would be outnumbered nearly a hundred to one.

"Kekiesu?" Tsudao said, but the shugenja shook her head.

"The presence of the Taint here is strong, my lady. The spirits are weak, and if I call on them, I may mistakenly summon the Taint to myself and forsake my very soul." Kekiesu shook her head quietly. "I am of little help to you here."

The princess set her jaw, and fire lit in her golden eyes. "Paneki, Kekiesu, follow me. We must enter the keep. Only with stone walls around us can we hope to survive. Out here we are carrion for the Tsuno's feast."

"In there?" Kekiesu's fear grew, and she made a superstitious sign above her brow. "With the dead?"

"We flee or we die." Tsudao said, "Now, *go!*"

Too frightened to disobey and seeing no other alternative,

Kekiesu fled down the hillside toward the bloody tower. With a curt nod, Paneki followed. Tsudao gauged the Tsuno's rapid approach and followed her companions.

They entered the stone archway of the watchtower as the horn sounded again. It was very close, and the howling creatures hovered in the trees around the dell like vultures above a battlefield. Several shrieked in mad cacophony, flexing their claws and tearing at the air in threat. Tsudao and her companions did not hesitate but continued into the courtyard and through, to the keep beyond. Leaping over the mutilated bodies of the dead, Tsudao tried not to think of the gore that surrounded her. She kept her eyes on the entrance into the keep, praying that it would hold against the Shadowlands beasts.

The building beyond the courtyard consisted of a single room, tremendously wide and three times as high. The ceiling was carved in imitation of the arching forest branches, the walls covered in strange tiled writing—a single, twisted line, dotted with gems and sparkling jewels. Although the outside stank of blood and rot, incense had been lit within the inner sanctum, keeping the stench at bay. And for good reason.

A thousand Naga—or more—lay clustered upon the warm stone ground of the small keep, their bodies entwined in sleep. Long serpentine tails twitched softly as they dreamed within each other's arms, and Tsudao recognized men, women, and even small Naga children. Kekiesu stood farther inside, surrounded by the dreamers. With wide eyes, she stared into a pool filled with water at the center of the room. Paneki leaned against the doorway, peering outside, his harsh breathing rasping in the relative silence.

It was quiet. The horns of the Tsuno had stopped, and even their screams had stilled into chanting and cursing just outside the keep. It was as if the Tsuno feared to follow them into this chamber—as if something kept them at bay. Magic, thought Tsudao, or sensibility. If the Naga were to waken, they would wreak a heavy vengeance on those who had trespassed within their forest—particularly if such interlopers were creatures of the Shadowlands.

"What is this place?" Tsudao whispered.

"It is a sleeping chamber," Kekiesu knelt beside one of the Naga maidens, afraid to touch the dreaming woman's emerald hair or pale skin. "The Tsuno fear to awaken them. But some spell has been cast here. I can feel it." The shugenja looked up at Tsudao with anguish. "Something is terribly, terribly wrong."

Tsudao approached cautiously, looking first at the sleeping Naga, and then at the pool in their midst. It was large, wider than her armspan, and did not seem to have a bottom to its swirling depths. The pool was a part of the building, as ancient as the rest of the structure, but a new addition had been built that was far more recent.

Buried to their hilts around the edges of the stone basin were eight large swords that reeked of corruption. Gems pulsed scarlet in their hilts, and their blades dripped blood.

"Eight swords . . ."

Tsudao froze, remembering the vision she had seen long ago. *Eight swords slicing through the Empire, corrupting history and stealing the past. Eight* . . . and one soft voice, *and He who Rules them.* Her father's face as he left the gardens of Otosan Uchi. The Steel Throne, its pristine beauty marred by the touch of an oni at Winter's Court . . .

"By the Sun . . ." Tsudao whispered, suddenly afraid.

One of the swords began to pulse with a black aura, its shadow growing and twisting along the ground. The shadow slithered into the pool as if compelled by some strange intelligence, and the waters of the shrine blackened and boiled.

"Tsudao, what's happening?

"Wake them." She spun on one heel, her hair flying out behind her. "Wake them!"

Kekiesu obeyed, first shaking the Naga woman, and then landing a stinging slap upon the Naga's cheek. Through it all, the Naga slept on. Her serene countenance did not change at all. Paneki drew a knife from his belt, drawing it across the palm of one of the Naga lying in torpor by the doorway. Greenish blood sprang from the wound, but the serpent-man slept on, undisturbed.

The waters of the pool grew more and more red, and mist began to rise from the Naga's conjoined breaths. As each breathed the deep slumber of dream, wisps of smoke drifted from their mouths, swirling toward the pool and gathering into a darkening cloud of smoke. A greenish mist rose from their bodies, swirling ever inward toward the boiling pond. Mouths opened, whispered in dream and shadow, and smoke rose from the Naga's voices, from their breath and their slumber, filling the chamber with wisps of power that raised the hair on Tsudao's arms. The sword continued to glow, its mates humming softly in time with the power arising within the chamber.

"Tsudao-sama—" Paneki crept away from the sleeping Naga— "I don't know if we're safer in here than were were outside. I'd rather take my chances with a threat I understand!"

"The Tsuno aren't here to kill the Naga," Kekiesu said, backing away from the pool. "They're guarding them—protecting them while they sleep. They only killed the ones who were awake. The guardians." The shugenja passed her hand through the mist as it swirled toward the pool, her face lighting with realization. "The nether realms—they are close here. Close to the Shinomen . . ." Turning to her mistress, the handmaiden cried, "I understand! Tsudao, this is how our enemies keep the dark realms near our own. They do it through sleep, through dreams. They travel through dreams, and the Naga are their source. So long as the Naga sleep—"

"The Shadowlands can walk freely through the Empire," Tsudao finished.

"But why is the gate opening?" Paneki stood in the shadow of the doorway, his hand on his sword hilt. "Did we trigger it somehow?"

As a tremendous shape began to materialize within the smoke above the pool of water, Tsudao answered. "The gate isn't opening for us to go to them, Paneki. It seems they are sending something . . . to us."

The Bayushi samurai stared outside, watching the Tsuno mass in the trees and on the forest floor surrounding the keep. Their horn rang again, this time with a mocking, cawing sound.

"We must go."

"Go where?" Tsudao snarled. "I will not run from fate, Paneki-san, and we have a better chance here, against this threat, than in that forest, alone."

Although she had no sword, Tsudao turned to face the massive creature emerging from the pool. As she turned, her eye fell upon a spear, cradled in the arms of a sleeping Naga. The shaft was of blackened wood, strong and firm, and the blade shone like a pearl from beneath the deepest ocean. It was not much, but it would do.

The beast rose from the water. It opened a tremendous fanged jaw and bared rows of sharklike teeth. Over nine feet high and nearly as thick, the oni had a bloated belly covered in thick, scaly hide. Rich redness cascaded down its back and over muscled arms as it emerged from the pool. It roared, and the sound was like shattering glass falling into thick tar. A long greenish tongue snaked out between its teeth, licking the floor and leaving poisonous trails of drool. As it clawed its way out of the water, four tremendous arms separated from the body, the upper two bending back into sinister wings of flesh and membrane. The rear legs were haunched like a dog's, covered in a fine gray fur that was matted and rotting, lumps of hair falling from its body in clumps. A tail sprouted between its rear legs. Long and spiked, it looked like a torn fleshy strip covered in metal shards, and it lashed through the air in wild, chaotic patterns. The oni yowled again, teeth bending back in its mouth to allow the tongue to glide over the ivory fangs. They glistened, and the tongue snaked out once more, searching for an enemy to drag into the beast's mouth. The head was no more than a skull, thinly covered in fleshy scales, and baleful eyes glared out from two sunken eye sockets.

Tsudao crouched, spear in hand, and faced the creature. The portal behind it shimmered and grew, and through the gateway Tsudao could see a wasted plain. She knew that place. It was the land where Shahai had taken Junnosuke—the place where her father's sword had gone—and only the beast stood between her and the gate. Certain of her path, Tsudao let out a tremendous war scream and charged.

The oni spun, its tail lashing through the air. Tsudao leaped forward, flipping high over the strike. She landed squarely before the oni's belly and drove the spear at its thick hide. The oni moved shockingly fast, jerking away from Tsudao's thrust before her weapon could pierce it.

Behind the beast, Paneki struck, his knife slashing at the oni's flesh. The skin parted, and a long line of red tore open from the dagger's strike. With a furious roar, the oni lashed at Paneki, its hand connecting with the Scorpion's shoulder. The strength of the blow hurled Paneki from his feet and sent him spinning through the air. He landed with a sickening crunch against a far wall of the chamber and did not move.

The oni, even angrier than before, turned back to Tsudao. It tested its wound, smiled a terrible, blood-encrusted grin, and attacked. One clawed hand struck out at Tsudao, but her spinning spear parried and slashed at the beast's wrist, drawing a thin line of blood from beneath its matted fur. It roared in fury, and Tsudao took her stance swiftly. She stared down her spear at the vicious beast, and before it could strike again, she moved past its claw, pressed the butt of her spear against the ground, and launched a ferocious kick at the side of the oni's head. Her entire body tensed from the blow, but the creature hardly shifted. It smiled. Tsudao rolled back to her feet, carrying the spear in her hands.

She charged again, but this time the oni was ready. It clawed at her, but she parried—and fell directly into the beast's feint. Its thick tongue curled around her arm, tearing flesh with its acidic spittle. She did not allow herself to cry out in pain but instead reversed her spear and jammed it into the tissue of the creature's tongue, driving it through the flesh and tearing through the muscle ligament. The beast roared, but its tongue did not release her. Despite the spear wound, it wrapped its claws around Tsudao and drew her to its mouth.

Kekiesu screamed and held her hands before her. Fighting back her terror, she chanted sacred words of prayer. In this dark place, the light of the Sun was hidden from her, so she had only one option. She drew power not from her patron, the Sun, but from her own spirit—a dangerous venture and one that could easily kill her.

Tsudao screamed as the demon's claws pierced her skin, and Kekiesu shuddered as she completed the spell. A ball of flame launched from her palms. It streaked across the room as Kekiesu crumpled from the power she had expended. She fell to the ground, her face white and drawn and her eyes rolling back into her head. Unconscious even before the spell struck its target, Kekiesu did not even see what she had wrought with her sacrifice.

Flame detonated in the creature's eyes. It released Tsudao to grapple at its eyes, clawing blood from its own flesh as the golden flame spread across its skull. The oni spread its membranous wings, batting wildly, and the fetid wind of its breath swept through the chamber. Tsudao landed heavily, still clutching her spear. Although her handmaiden lay on the mosaic floor, Tsudao had no time to see if Kekiesu was all right. She rocked back onto her shoulders and kicked to her feet in one smooth motion.

The oni peered through scorched flesh and bloody bone and extended its claws once more. Its tail slammed into the floor with enough force to shake the building.

"Paneki-san!" Tsudao screamed, tying a strip of her pants around the wound in her forearm. "I need you!"

He stood as silent as a stone by the doorway, his eyes filled with a strange sense of uncertainty. She could not tell if he feared the oni or if his indecision was brought about by some other means.

"Paneki!" Tsudao shouted again. The Scorpion shook his head, staring at the oni as if expecting something to occur.

Cursing the Scorpion for a coward, Tsudao launched herself at the beast once more. The pearl-bladed spear spun in her hands, its dark wooden shaft sliding with infinite precision as the blade thrust one, two, three times into the oni's stomach. The cuts were more than pinpricks—blood rolled down the creature's body—but it continued to fight. Roaring in fury, it slammed its hands into the ground to squash Tsudao, but she already leaped away, pushing off the oni's own shoulder to land beneath its ribcage.

"There are no openings," Tsudao rumbled. Her trained eyes searched the creature's armor, its movement—anything—to find an opening. A Crab might have known some ancient method of defeating the portal guardian, but Tsudao was not a Hida. She was a Toturi by blood, a Lion by training, and the only way she could fight was to put all of her heart and soul into every strike. Yet the creature still stood.

It lunged again, this time drawing its tail through the air in a mighty zigzag and crashing the iron-coated lash where she stood. She dodged again but felt a great weariness in her muscles. The wound on her forearm was beginning to slow her down, and exhaustion from the long march would soon set in. Yet even as she noticed this, she noticed something else—the creature was slowing, as well. The wound Paneki had caused seemed blackish, the flesh pulled back as if seared, and the beast was limping.

Still it fought, desperately trying to ignore the sickness that invaded it. Its tail whipped across the ground, forcing Tsudao to dive over a pile of sleeping Naga in order to avoid the spikes, and another claw descended upon her. Tsudao held the spear braced against the ground beneath her and the oni gripped it, its own eagerness to clutch Tsudao forcing the tip of the pearl spear deep into its palm, through the muscle and bone, and out the other side. For the first time, the oni howled in real pain, drawing back in surprise as its hand dripped thick black blood onto the floor of the sacred room.

Kekiesu's limp form lay silent and quiet, her hands burned from the power she had released. The pool in the center of the room boiled over, the waves red with oni blood. Tsudao tried to roll away from the beast's grip, but this time the claws landed to either side of her body. Although she tried to kick out of its grasp, the oni sank its claws into her ribs and lifted her from the ground.

It drew her to its sharklike mouth, eager to sink its teeth into the princess's flesh, but Tsudao writhed and kicked at its hoary face. Luck was with her, and her iron-shod sandal sank directly into its eye. The oni jerked back as she felt her foot sink into sticky wetness, and blood burst from the eye socket across her legs. Half-blinded, the creature threw Tsudao across the room in rage. She struck with a heavy impact against the stone wall. Sparks flying across her vision, Tsudao slid to the floor and gasped for breath, her sore ribs aching with the force of her landing. She did not wait for it to spring at her again, but pushed to her feet with an enormous effort. There had to be another weapon . . .

She heard the creature stumble and turned to look. It fell to one knee. The wound Paneki had given it was wider than before, and the edges sizzled with sickness. Blood trailed from the gash, a blackish-green slime that seemed poisoned and foul.

Paneki was at her side, lifting her from the floor.

"Where have you been?" Tsudao gasped, wincing at her wounds.

"Finding you a sword." He pressed a weapon into her

hands, and she felt the raw power of the blade shiver against her skin. "You were in no danger. The creature has been dead for minutes, General-sama." Paneki smiled. "It's just too stupid to realize it."

Tsudao glanced down at the knife in Paneki's hand and saw that it was covered in thick black poison. The oni screamed again, lashing its tail, but it was too sick to fight anymore. It staggered and grasped its throat, forcing Tsudao and Paneki back. The oni's blood ran freely from its many wounds, but still it struggled to destroy them.

"Then let me finish it," Tsudao said resolutely. She stepped forth to the sickened oni's side and drew forth the strange sword that Paneki had found among the Naga bodies. Her draw was a swift, pure *iaijutsu* strike she had learned as a child from the old Emerald Champion, the Emperor's right hand. As the blade came free, Tsudao spun on the balls of her feet. Using the oni's own hand as leverage, she pushed the strike through to the creature's exposed throat.

The blade sang in release as it sprang from the sheath, and a greenish glow shimmered along the ancient weapon's edge. Jade! The blade was forged not of steel, but of the purest jade—the ancient foe of the Shadowlands. It hummed in Tsudao's hand, eager for combat, and sank into the demon's flesh as easily as if it were parting the water of a flowing river. The creature staggered once more, its roar formed more of pain than of anger, then toppled to the side with a terrible crash. The earth around them shook, and the demon moved no more.

"Kekiesu!" Tsudao remembered, pushing her way through the sleeping Naga to get to her handmaiden's side. The Moshi was awakening, her eyes fluttering in dizziness. "Kekiesu, you must get out of here."

Tsudao looked up at the pool and the swirling gateway that hovered, open, above the water.

"Tsudao . . ." she whispered as she struggled to stand.

"Here," Paneki said, and the two shared a gentle smile.

"You are too weak to make it through the gate," Tsudao said. "I must go alone."

"No, Tsudao-sama." Bowing her head, Kekiesu climbed to her knees and faced her mistress. "I am sorry to refuse you, but I will not return. Nor will you go alone. You are wounded—you both are wounded. I am no more incapacitated than you. We go together."

"Then we should go swiftly," Paneki said. "The portal is closing, and we may never have another chance."

Tsudao heard the ring of stubbornness in Paneki's voice and saw Kekiesu's unwavering loyalty in the handmaiden's eyes. Gripping Kekiesu's hand in commiseration, Tsudao nodded.

"Come on," she said. "There is no time to waste."

Tsudao turned to face the wavering portal as her two companions gathered their equipment. It was wider than a man and twice as tall, hovering mistlike above the Naga pool. Helping Kekiesu, Tsudao walked out into the center of the pool, then stepped through the portal and into the land beyond. The mist wavered and glowed faintly, carrying the two women into the darkness of the void.

Paneki wiped the blood from his sword onto his torn pants and stared after the two women as the gateway began to shrink and dissolve. He hesitated as if making a crucial decision, then cursed softly. "Damn honor, damn the Empire, and damn me, as well."

With a sigh, he strode into the portal just as the gateway closed.

18 | REALM OF NIGHTMARE

*Y*ume-do. In dreams, a mind can wander from reality to myth and back to where existence seems but a pale flash within centuries of history. In the realm of Yume-do, a samurai can forsake honor, forsake his true nature, and let his mind wander into the restlessness of sleep. The realm of dreams is a place without reprisal, without limits and laws, where minds roam like children, exploring the consciousness around them. Yume-do is a land where dreams and nightmares come true, where everything can exist.

There are said to be no portals to Yume-do. No god guards its gates. No laws forbid entrance to the unsanctified. To enter the land of dreams—to go to Yume-do—all one must do is lie down, close his eyes, and drift into sleep. The land is but a peasant's tale, a myth told to children who fear the night and cry in the darkness. To true samurai, those who scoff at lies and hidden fears, it is a fable.

It is real. And it can be reached.

But as Shinsei the Prophet once said— *Samurai may march in pairs, but we dream alone. . . .*

* * * * *

Moshi Kekiesu stood on the edge of a seashore that ran along the edge of a twisted jungle. The sky was blue and clear, and the ocean was so blue that it shone almost transparent in the brilliant sunlight. Birds of every color swept past, their wings sparkling like jewels beneath a brilliant sky.

"Yume-do," Kekiesu whispered. "It is so beautiful. Don't you—?" But as she turned to see Tsudao's reaction, the shugenja realized she was alone. Her scrolls and her staff were gone as well, and there was no sign of the portal that had carried them into Yume-do.

The salt sea whispered against the sandy beach, wiping the white sand clean over and again. Like a child's chalkboard, free of lines and imperfections, the sand extended in immaculate purity for miles in each direction. There was nothing to show her north from south, nor east from west. The sun hung in the sky like a jeweled orb, perfectly centered over Kekiesu's head.

"Hm." Kekiesu stepped toward the ocean, feeling her sore muscles ache from the battle. The spell she had cast to aid Tsudao had drained most of her power. The sun shone high above her, and Kekiesu felt the gentle surge of spirit that was the blessing of the Shining Mother's radiance. "This is the realm of dream," she murmured, drinking in the light. "Even the Sun dreams. The Kami dream, the wind, all things that live and know, and seek enlightenment—all the world dreams. Why should she not be here with me? I am her child." Kekiesu spread her arms wide, feeling the energy flow through her.

If only she had her scrolls, she might have found a spell to ease her journey. Or, she frowned, to find Tsudao, which should be more important. To think of herself right now was an infraction of bushido, the code that every samurai followed. One's lord should outweigh all of one's troubles. All of the burdens we bear are nothing without the gratitude and respect of those we serve. Kekiesu sighed, wishing that her heart would accept that and be still.

Every step she took was an agony, but Kekiesu began the long walk down the beach. North or south, it did not matter. She walked in the direction she had been headed, her footprints leaving dark marks upon the perfect sand of the beach. She cast a gentle spell to ease the pain of her muscles, but it would not last.

It seemed that she walked for hours, at times dragging each step forward, forcing herself to keep walking. Once, she stopped long enough to bathe her bleeding feet at the edge of the ocean. Tears of pain stained her cheeks, but again she stood and continued.

At last, after an eternity of pale sand and glimmering sun off waves, Kekiesu heard a shrill scream. She turned, her dark hair fanning out behind her, and stared into the depths of the ocean. The sky had grown darker, the sun hiding its immobile face behind a fan of clouds, and the sea was darker and less friendly. In the waves, some distance out, Kekiesu saw a small girl, screaming and waving above the rocking water. She had swum too far out into the ocean, and now the undertow was dragging at her legs, pulling her under and sweeping her out to sea.

"Help!" the soft voice came. "Please, help me!" She was no more than eight, her wide eyes terrified of drowning in the undertow that dragged her out to sea.

Without thought, Kekiesu reached into her spirit. She began the incantation, summoning the Kami of wind and hoping it would be enough. The wind picked up around her as she cast, behaving strangely, but it did as she commanded. A zephyr swept across the ocean, lifting the child and slowly bringing her back toward the beach.

Kekiesu hurried into the waves, walking out until her body

was submerged. She reached with pale arms to take the weeping child and held her tightly as the little girl wrapped her arms around Kekiesu's neck.

"Shh," Kekiesu comforted her, walking back toward the beach with her burden. Her feet ached, cut now by sharp coral that tore against her legs beneath the surface of the sea. The child was safe. That was all that mattered. She fell to her knees at the edge of the water, the waves crashing against them both.

"Thank you, thank you . . . I can't find anyone. I've been so alone, and I just wanted to swim, but the waves—"

"Yes," Kekiesu wiped wet hair out of the girl's eyes. "I know. I lived by the sea as a child. It is a dangerous place to play, and you are lucky I was here."

"I am, I am," the child sobbed, gripping Kekiesu's neck again.

"Ssh, there. All is well." Kekiesu soothed the child, sitting beside her. When the girl had quieted, Kekiesu looked down at her feet, now torn and bleeding badly. A whisper of spell, and the sores healed, but the pain came from deep cuts that even her magic could not ease. With a sigh, Kekiesu tore strips of cloth from her robe and wove them around her bare feet.

"You're hurt," the girl whispered fearfully.

"I will be well soon."

"When?"

"When the Sun grants it." Kekiesu replied with the common answer of her youth, remembering the days when nothing happened fast enough to suit her. Those days were long gone, buried beneath the formal, ritualized training of a priestess, but her heart still asked the same questions.

"Why doesn't the Sun grant that it happen now?" The girl's face was innocent, trusting, and Kekiesu couldn't help but smile.

"What is your name?" she asked.

"Toturi Tsudao," the girl replied. "I am the daughter of the Emperor, and one day, I will rule."

"I . . . I have no doubt," Kekiesu murmured, uncertain. Was this truly Tsudao as a child or simply a dream of her mistress? There was no way to tell, and in the realm of Yume-do, they might both be the same.

"You do not believe me?" The little Tsudao stood, pantomiming a martial stance. "I am going to be the boldest warrior the world knows. When I am grown, I will command soldiers, and I will save the Empire. Just like my father."

The child's eyes shone at the mention of Toturi, and Kekiesu stared in amazement. What strange dream was this, she wondered, to show her such things?

"Of course." Kekiesu bowed slightly, giving honor to the imperial princess. "You are the Daughter of the Sun. You can do anything."

"The what?"

"Daughter of the Sun," Kekiesu smiled. "You are the chosen one, gifted with the blessings of Amaterasu. Her chosen heir upon—"

"No." Tsudao said resolutely. "I am the daughter of Toturi and of no other. Take back your lies. I will not allow your heresy to taint my blood."

Kekiesu stared in open shock. "Heresy?" She raised a hand to point at the glowing orb in the sky. "That is the Sun. She is the all mother, bringer of life upon Rokugan. She is your m—"

"No." Again, the child denied Kekiesu's words. "My mother is Toturi Kaede, the Oracle of the Void, and my father is the Emperor of Rokugan. I am nothing else."

"You are the Daughter of the Sun." Where once this had been a pleasant discussion, something dark moved beneath the surface of Tsudao's words, troubling Kekiesu deeply. In her mind, she remembered Tsudao's argument on the Dragon plains. *"Kekiesu, listen to me. I am mortal, as are you. As are all who have descended from the Kami. I am no more than this."* Those sharp words of rejection echoed in the child's arrogant shouts. Kekiesu felt keenly every time that Tsudao had denied her place in the world, the times when Tsudao had rejected the Sun, turned away from her destiny and the gifts that were rightfully hers as the true Daughter of the Sun. Tsudao had made a mockery of Kekiesu and all the Moshi clan by rejecting their beliefs without even considering that they might be true. Kekiesu's brow furrowed, determined to change the young Tsudao's mind. Perhaps, if she could just make the child see her place, she would save the true Tsudao from failing her destiny and offer her peace within the real world.

Perhaps this was the meaning of the dream—that she must guide Tsudao, teach her, and show her she was wrong before it was too late.

"You *are* the Daughter of the Sun." Kekiesu was unrelenting, her body stiff. She pointed again at the light in the heavens. "She has chosen *you* to be her heir. *You* bear her gifts. You *are* her child."

"I am not!" Tsudao screamed. She hurled a rock at Kekiesu. "I am the daughter of Toturi!"

"*And* the Daughter of the Sun. I am your handmaiden. Amaterasu—"

"Amaterasu can fall into the Shadowlands, for all I care," the child yelled, "and may she take you with her! There is no Sun! There is only the Empire!"

Kekiesu felt her cheeks redden with anger at the child's blasphemy.

"My father can kill a thousand men with a stroke of his fan. He has defeated oni, and he has crossed into the realm of death and returned!" Tsudao's pride made her small face glow, and she pointed an accusing finger at Kekiesu. "Your goddess has done nothing. She burns the land and turns her face away from those who need her. Where was she when Fu Leng conquered Otosan Uchi? Where was she when the Hantei were destroyed? Where was the Sun when Rokugan needed her?

"The Sun is nothing. You have no power and no strength.

You are nothing, Kekiesu. You are not a true samurai, not born of a true clan, and even your goddess is nothing but a pack of lies, bound with golden thread." Tsudao stamped her foot. "I am daughter of the Emperor of Rokugan, and by bushido, you must obey me. You will give up this false goddess and reject her teachings, or I will have your entire clan destroyed."

Rage controlled Kekiesu's actions, and before she knew it, she had begun to summon the power of Amaterasu. At first, it was a gentle spell, one meant to calm them both and to prove that Kekiesu's magic did exist. Yet as she drew upon it, her own fury rose. How dare Tsudao speak this way about the mother of all life? How could she demand that Kekiesu turn her back on all that she had ever known? Reject the Sun? Never. Not if the world were to die and fall upon her.

She would never turn her face from the truth. Not even for Tsudao.

Flames burst forth from Kekiesu's hands and engulfed Tsudao. Realizing that her anger had gained control of her powers, Kekiesu fought to stop the spell—but it was too late. She had succumbed to the greatest shame a shugenja could know: she had allowed her emotions to taint the purity of magic. Kekiesu watched helplessly as the spell's power grew, roaring in white-hot flames around the child. It raged out of her control, fueled by her anger and pride. The flames leaped along the beach, turning the seashore into a white-hot inferno of blazing power that rivaled even the brilliant light of the Sun above.

"Make it stop!" the young Tsudao screamed, the flames burning her clothing. Her hair burst into flame, and she shrieked. "Please!" In agony, Tsudao cried out for her father, but there was no answer. "Kekiesu, please make it stop!"

"Amaterasu," Kekiesu fell to her knees, tears streaming down her face. It was too late. "I cannot . . ."

The words were no more than a mist of breath. She covered her mouth with both hands, sobbing as she watched Tsudao writhe within the furnace of the Sun.

Then the fire leaped up toward the heavens, and she could see no more.

* * * * *

By the shore of a white sand beach, a broken shugenja knelt in the waves, her eyes filled with bitter tears. For a moment, she considered throwing herself into the waves. It would not be a quick death, but it would be all she deserved. There was nothing left. She had killed the Daughter of the Sun. It was a dream, yes, but in her heart she had truly done the deed. The spell was hers, the anger, and the charred ash on the whispering wind was the aftermath of her pride.

"Come with me, fallen one," whispered a soft voice, "and I will make you forget the pain."

A pale hand moved gracefully behind a cloak of black braids, and a gentle finger swept away Kekiesu's tears.

* * * * *

Paneki stared at his surroundings, his face white and cold.

"Beautiful?" he sneered, gesturing broadly out at the curving, twisted hallways of brick and stone. "You call these dungeons beautiful, Centipede? They stretch for endless miles, chain upon chain, and the tortured screams of the damned echo from every restless stone. Beautiful?" Paneki scowled. "Horrifying. These are the hallways of the cursed souls from Traitor's Grove, not the dreams of the Scorpion."

He looked to the side, where he had heard an echo of her voice, but he saw nothing.

"Kekiesu-san?" A long, silent moment. "Tsudao-sama?"

Again, no answer. He could have sworn he'd heard Kekiesu's voice. Either Yume-do was toying with him, or Tsudao had arranged to leave him behind. He seriously doubted the princess had the resources or secrecy to do the second, so he would assume the first option. For now.

"Yume-do." Bayushi Paneki adjusted his swords in his belt. "I'd rather be in Jigoku. Hell would be preferable to the dreams of the Scorpion."

The corridors of the dungeon stretched out in every direction, weaving through each other like a spider's web. Paneki walked down them with a solemn step, pausing to stare for a moment at a pair of bloody manacles chained to the wall in one of the open rooms. A soft wail echoed down the stone hallway, sending a shiver up his spine and making him reach unconsciously for the hilt of his sword.

Frowning, he pulled his hand away. The tears in his clothing covered bloody gashes from the oni's whiplike tail. They stung when he touched them, and the cold air of the building seemed to seep into his flesh.

The hallway twisted to the left, and he followed it, slowing when the passage opened out into a wide chamber. It was built of stone and had the cold clamminess of underground caves. Shaped into the sides were prison cells with iron bars that reached from the high ceiling down to the floor. Other prisons stood throughout the room. They were circular and had no apparent doors or openings. Paneki stared at them, wondering how prisoners were placed inside—for there were prisoners within the cells. Some of them still seemed human, but others writhed like living lumps of flesh, pawing at the bars with broken and twisted limbs. They howled from time to time in cacophony. The discord ached in Paneki's teeth and set his mind on edge. Torches, flickering and dim, lit the edges of the room, and the occasional lantern hung like a flickering star across the long, narrow ceiling.

"Bayushi Paneki." The voice was solemn, slow. Familiar. It came from somewhere across the massive chamber. Steeling himself, the Scorpion moved among the cells, staying out of the grasp of the prisoners within the bars. He watched every shadow, his mind insisting that more than one moved to follow his motion.

Paneki passed a wailing stump of a woman in one of the

barred cells, and stepped lightly around a patch of blood congealing on the brick floor. The darkness around him seemed to thicken as he approached. Certain that his imagination was playing tricks on him, Paneki stepped into a patch of shadow. Something cold and smooth swept past his legs into deeper darkness, and he jumped back—but it was gone before he could draw his katana.

"So easily frightened of shadows but so eager for the night." The same familiar voice spoke from behind him. Paneki spun to face the speaker. Standing in a patch of light between two writhingly full cells stood Hantei Naseru. His gold and green robes were spotless, reflecting the light around him like a soft aura of gold. A crown of golden chrysanthemum leaves, the symbol of the ancient Hantei emperors, graced his stern brow. One eye stared soulfully at Paneki, the other was covered by a black patch of shining obsidian. His hands, long and delicate yet filled with strength, smoothed his robes firmly.

Paneki immediately dropped to one knee before the imperial prince, touching his fist to the floor with a quick salute.

"Ah, yes," Naseru had a smile of ice and snow. "You *do* remember me, after all."

"You are the imperial prince, Hantei Naseru-sama, the son of Toturi," Paneki said, not wishing to be asked. "You are known as the Anvil and the keeper of law."

"And your master's master. Certainly you did not mean to leave that out?"

Paneki flushed, looking down at the fitted stones of the prison floor.

"You serve your Champion well." Naseru's smile was cold. "Yes, I know Bayushi Yojiro is quite pleased with you. You have done all he has bidden—and he has bidden you to do my will. But then again, you always knew that you worked for me, did you not?" Naseru's silken voice paused for a long moment then continued, "I thought so. You are a thoughtful man and a clever man, but not a traitorous one. Thoughtful men know better than to dangle their loyalties on a fragile string. Men without loyalty must jealously guard their backs as they offer their allegiances to the highest bidder, and their word of honor is worth no more than dust. But I know you, Paneki, and you are *faithful*."

Naseru steepled his fingers, crossing the room in long, slow strides that took him to the edge of the iron bars.

"I have seen you with them and seen how you share your learning and wisdom. How touching that the little Centipede girl loves you—and you know that she loves you, Paneki." Naseru's brows shadowed his glance. "A great prize to be used one day. The handmaiden of my sister, completely within the palm of our hand. When the time comes for us to kill her, I will let you twist the knife. It will be a gift, Paneki, for your honorable service. I am made quite certain of that by your actions, Paneki. You are an *honorable* man."

The prison cells around the edges of the chamber took on the appearance of hungry mouths, iron bars stretching from the ceiling to the floor in sharpened grimaces. The frozen stone ached beneath his bent knees. Paneki tried to keep his head lowered respectfully. The hairs on the back of his neck rose with his master's every step.

"What is the judge of a true samurai, Paneki-san? Do you know?" Naseru turned to regard him as if he had almost forgotten the kneeling Scorpion was there.

"Bushido, my lord."

"No." Almost lazily, Naseru touched his fingers to his chin. Paneki knelt in silence, allowing Naseru to play his game. It was a test of patience, and patience was a Scorpion's first lesson. At last, Naseru rumbled, "The judge, Paneki, is his lord. That is the last judge—the *only* judge—of a samurai's faithfulness. His honor. His loyalty."

Swifter than Paneki would have thought possible, Naseru slid a blade from his hand and pointed it at the Scorpion's bared throat.

"Yojiro is my lord." Paneki spoke of his Champion with

respect and fear.

"*I* am Yojiro's lord," Naseru said, "and Yojiro sent you here to perform my will."

"I have not failed you," Paneki said through gritted teeth. "Yojiro sent me to ally with the general, to win Tsudao's trust—"

"But you have known all along that your true orders would be to destroy her. Why else gain her trust, if not the better to plunge the knife into her back when the time was right?" The voice was smooth and reasonable, and Paneki could not deny it. "Whatever your orders may have seemed, you have always known what their outcome would be."

Paneki lowered his head. A long moment passed, then he nodded once. It was true.

"Tsudao still lives?"

Paneki nodded but did not dare say more.

"Do I sit upon the throne of Rokugan?"

A pause, and Paneki responded, "No, Naseru-sama."

"The season of war does not fill the rivers of Rokugan with blood, Paneki." A sigh, and the knife pressed more deeply into Paneki's neck. "I am displeased."

"I have done as I was commanded."

Naseru's sharp growl of fury cut him off. "You did not do *enough!*"

Paneki trembled, not from fear of death or the blade, but of Naseru's anger. The Hantei were known for many things, but they were not renowned for their mercy.

"You serve the Scorpion, and the Scorpion serve *me!*" For a moment, the anger bored through Naeru's eyes. "I have given you chance after chance, test after test, and still you fail."

From the floor before him, Paneki saw snakelike tendrils rising up between the stones. He stared at them, not comprehending. They twisted together into iron bars that reached upward.

"You said you wanted what was best for the Empire."

Paneki choked, trying not to think of the other cells and what would become of him. "You said you served the Throne!"

Naseru stepped back as the iron bars cemented themselves into a prison of stone. "You should know by now, Paneki-san." His face began to melt, and his hands twisted, turning black. His eye turned black and smooth, matching the shining obsidian that balanced its appearance. "I serve *myself*."

Both of Naseru's jet-black eyes blinked and stared in amusement as Paneki fell back against the restraining prison wall. Writhing beneath the surface of the skin, Naseru's fingers thinned and became sharply clawed. His entire visage changed, and Paneki recognized the smile from children's tales and the black paintings of the Crane.

It was the face of Fu Leng.

Paneki drew his katana and swung it with violent rage against the bars that held him captive. The sword met and rang with a sharp, loud note—then shattered like glass. Paneki staggered backward, the hilt of his broken katana hanging limply from his hand. He sagged to his knees, not wishing to believe the vision before him, as the beast that was Hantei Naseru threw back his head in a cruel, cold laugh.

"Stay, faithful servant, and know that I will always trust your blade." The mocking face sneered, and fragments of Paneki's broken katana turned to crawling, poisonous scorpions beneath his feet. "I know your mettle, Paneki, and I always have."

The figure turned and walked into a smothering darkness, swallowed by the shadows and wails of the tortured throng. Paneki clung to the iron bars, feeling them writhe beneath his clenched fists, and let out a scream that rocked the dungeon with its fury. He had been tricked—tricked and used. And there was nothing he could do to change it.

Nothing at all.

He had traded his honor and his loyalty for nothing. He had committed the worst sin a samurai could perform.

Bayushi Paneki had given his soul to a dishonorable lord and betrayed a true one to evil.

"I swear to you," Paneki snarled into the empty chamber, his knuckles whitening against the iron bars, "I did not know. . . ."

* * * * *

In the darkness of the prison, a woman's voice called to him. It seemed first to be his mother, but then changed to the silken tones of Bayushi Kachiko, the spirit of his clan. At the end, he believed it to be Tsudao, calling him once more to fight the oni by her side. He saw himself fleeing the temple, knowing that the Tsuno would not hurt him—then stopping, struck by doubt, forcing himself to return in time to save her life. Either way, she was doomed . . . and so was he.

The soft voice whispered, and the bars spread apart, writhing in protest. A woman stood outside his cage with open arms. In her embrace, she held hope. Freedom.

Revenge.

He reached for her, and the prison fell away.

* * * * *

Tsudao breathed deeply, the scent of spring and warmth filling her lungs. "Scorpion? I'd have never thought the Scorpion were so interested in battle—or history."

She looked around at the wide battlefield with tents and banners flying. On a mountain in the center of the field stood a tall keep, its walls white as marble and its high towers shining with golden light. It was a castle built by kami, on the dreams of the samurai who served their lords, of all the Emperors who ever loved Rokugan—a magnificent palace, built upon the honor and glory of bushido.

Tsudao hardly noticed when neither Paneki nor Kekiesu replied, so entranced was she by the view before her. Tents of every era, from modern silk to ancient hide structures littered the area. Swords and armor were laid out upon their stands, representing every clan, every generation—even some she had never seen before. Their iron masks scowled down at the encampment like silent sentinels.

Tsudao crossed the area slowly, pausing to look inside the tents and stopping beside blazing campfires. The entire encampment seemed empty. Though the grounds were well tended, the tents held no chattering soldiers, no generals planning for battle. Maps lay on display, and small ceramic men held tiny spears as if to charge across the wide tables. A cold breeze crept through the empty field between the tents and the high palace. The only thing moving was the grass, bowing to honor the wind's passage. Through twisting paths, around large and silent tents, the imperial princess walked. Her calls of greeting met no response.

The camp was empty. Tsudao looked up at the banners above the tents and recognized many of the names emblazoned in bold kanji upon the silk—Hida Kisada, Doji Hoturi, Akodo Arasou. Heroes of ancient times, all known for their bravery and courage. Matsu Tsuko, and more . . .

As she paced among the eerily silent tents and burning campfires, Tsudao began to recognize many of the sets of armor as those of her own men. She saw Kitsu Dejiko's favorite spear and the elaborate armor for Matsu Domotai's horse.

Yet she was alone.

She left the somber encampment and walked onto the battlefield. There, Tsudao saw marks of recent fighting, but the fallen armor lay empty upon the ground, the bloodied swords ignored on the broken turf, and there was no sign of bodies. No calls of wounded soldiers met her ears. She looked up into a clear blue sky and realized that there weren't even any crows. Everything was silent and empty. No movement, no sound, no life.

Tsudao, her brow furrowed, followed the road toward the

palace. Why show her a battlefield with no battle? The jade katana of the Naga still hung at her side, but it was a false comfort. It could never replace the sword of her father. The thought steeled her, and Tsudao marched determinedly across the eerily silent plain. She would find Junnosuke, and she would make him pay.

Long, thick steps led up to the castle. The mountain it stood upon was solitary, rising from the center of the wide field in singular formation. The castle upon it shone, white walls glistening in the bright sun, but there were no soldiers pacing its walls. No doves sat upon the curving rooftops, nor did horses grace the stables halfway up the path. Tsudao's dark hair clung to her neck and shoulders from the heat and exertion of the climb. The silence seemed almost oppressive, and the long march made her legs and back ache. When the wooden gates of the palace proper came into view, she blessed the Fortunes and prayed she would find someone inside.

She needed to find a gate. Shahai and Junnosuke had come through Yume-do, but they had not stayed here. The plane of dreams was nothing more than a transition from life to the realms beyond. It was a portal in itself, an entire plane of doorways, each leading to its own destination. Where had the sorceress gone, and how had she managed to bring an entire army through in one dream? Neither Kekiesu nor Paneki had managed to remain with Tsudao once they entered Yume-do, yet Shahai's army marched with her across the plane of dreams . . . to where?

The oak gates of the palace were closed, but a gentle touch caused one of the massive doors to swing slightly. Tsudao pressed her palm against the doorway and pushed the high gate ajar. Inside were the inner courtyards, very much like those of the imperial palace, but more functional. Weapons were lined up on racks to each side, and more armor stood on stands where soldiers might have marched.

A sound echoed from inside the palace, and Tsudao spun.

One of the golden doors that led into the main building swung slowly open, as if something had recently pushed it.

"Hello?" called Tsudao, but there was no answer. She frowned. Someone was playing a game, and she had no choice but the follow along. More whispers, just at the edge of conscious thought; she could not quite make out the words.

Inside the palace, a whisper led Tsudao down the long hallway to the great doors of the throne room. Like the outer gates, these doors were solid oak, but they were ornamented with elaborate scrollwork of jade and gold. Tsudao touched the gates, but they did not move. She pushed harder, certain that the sounds she heard were emanating from within the doors of the chamber, but again they did not swing inward. Feeling like a child, Tsudao planted her feet against the floor and pushed as hard as she could. At last, the door moved. It swung first an inch, then two, and then at last, with a croaking groan, the door slid inward enough for her to slip through. She pressed the scabbard of her sword against her body and eased through the narrow opening.

She was standing in the throne room of Otosan Uchi, and hot rays of golden sun shone through the windows above the dais. It felt as if she had stepped into a part of her own childhood, and Tsudao felt suddenly out of place in the large chamber. She walked along the wooden boards, feeling each familiar creak and whisper of the room, and inhaled the scents she had known all her life. It was Otosan Uchi. This was home.

"I have waited so long for you, Tsudao," her father's voice said.

She started and stared up at the dais. Seated there—how had she not seen him before?—upon a dark throne made of iron and steel, was Toturi.

"Father," Tsudao said numbly, staring at him. This was a dream. It was nothing more than a trick of Yume-do, a hallucination of her mind. But as Toturi opened his arms to his daughter, Tsudao could not find it in her heart to stay away. The three steps between them were crossed in less than a second, and Tsudao threw her arms around her father with tears staining her cheeks. She clung to him, feeling his reassuring strength holding her tightly as it always had when she was a child.

"Father, I've looked everywhere, and I can't find you." The words slipped from Tsudao's tongue before she knew what she was saying. "The truth of your death is out there. I know Shahai is involved. I know she knows the truth—who did it, why, how—but I can't find it. I can't get to her. Yume-do stands in my way, and I can't make it through."

Toturi simply held her, his hands softly petting his daughter's long dark hair. "It doesn't matter now, Tsudao-chan," he whispered. "The Empire is far away, and I am here. Forget all the things that trouble you. Together, we shall find the truth."

Tsudao felt her tense muscles relax. Pulling back, Tsudao stared up into her father's kind eyes and said, "But the Empire needs me. I have so little time. The Dragon and Lion stand at war, and the Phoenix use their powers for revenge, not peace. Even in the south, the Crane and Crab threaten a civil war, and the Shadowlands—oh, father, the Shadowlands . . . I fear they have infiltrated Otosan Uchi itself."

"Shh. Do not think on such things. Your brothers can care for the Empire, and we shall discover the answers you seek. We have all the time in the world, Tsudao-chan." Toturi smiled. "Somewhere here, on Yume-do, someone is dreaming of the truth. We will search all the dreams, until we find that truth. Stay with me, and we will find it."

"My brothers . . ." Tsudao shook her head, brushing away the hair that fell into her wide eyes. "Sezaru will never turn away from your spirit, Father. It is all-consuming, and he would follow you into Jigoku itself to find the truth."

"Sezaru is a priest, with a priest's sense of responsibility. You are a samurai. Your bravery will carry you farther than his prayers ever could." Toturi spoke proudly. "I need you more than I ever needed Sezaru. He may search the entire world, ask all the Kami of the heavens, and speak with each of the Oracles in turn, but he would never have had the courage to come here and find me. He is driven to discover the secrets of the world. I cannot turn my throne over to one destined to fall to the Taint by his own greed and power-madness." He shook his head. "Sezaru cannot be my savior."

"Kaneka . . ." Tsudao ignored the stern look in Toturi's eyes. "He feels the pain of your death more keenly than anyone. We had time—our entire lives with you, Father. Kaneka had nothing. He will search for the culprit of your death with raw vengeance. They took away our past. They stole his future."

"Kaneka sees *only* the past, Tsudao. He has no future, outside of avenging the pains that were visited upon him when he was a child. Nothing is more important to him than the scars he bears, except for his own arrogance. He has no honor. Kaneka's ambition is everything to him. He would destroy us all in an attempt to rule and leave the Empire a ruin of ashes and blood." Toturi shook his head and brushed his daughter's fondly. "I was not there for him when he needed me. It is his destiny to fail me, as I failed him."

"And Naseru?" said Tsudao. "Simply because he bears the name Hantei does not mean he is not your son. Toturi blood is in his veins. Only his honor forces him to keep the Hantei name, out of respect for the last of their line. He, of all your children, knows the Empire best. His life has been spent between the two worlds of the Hantei and the Toturi. He has seen both and knows the merits of each. Naseru could use his contacts, his allies. He knows secrets we cannot fathom. He may already know the truth—"

Toturi held up both hands in mock protest, a serious tone in his voice. "Naseru wishes only for the Steel Throne. He does not care about the Empire. He only wishes to keep it from the rest of you. For him, it is a game. If he wins, I doubt he would know what to do, and his mind would see traitors and spies in the every shadow. His suspicion would carve the Empire to shreds. No, your brothers cannot help me, Tsudao. Only you can. You were always my strongest child, my true first-born."

"There is no one but me. . . ." Tsudao shook her head and lowered her eyes. She frowned, realizing this for the first time.

"The Empire is not your responsibility, Tsudao. I am your father. Does that not mean more to you than peasants and political games?" Toturi lifted his daughter's chin, but she looked away.

"I am all there is," Tsudao said without pride. She looked once more at her options, and thought of each of her brothers in turn. Stepping away from Toturi with a strange shiver, she looked at her father. "The Empire cries for me, and all I could see was you. The Dragon and Lion went to war, and I was so obsessed with finding your killer that I nearly turned my back on them."

"Tsudao . . ."

"No, Father. You are right." She spoke slowly, her voice halting. "I was always your strongest child. The most like you, of all that were born from your line. You taught me that the Empire stands upon the shoulders of the strong." A long moment passed, and Tsudao said, "I have been weak."

"No."

"In all this time, searching for the blade Junnosuke took from me, I never realized that *I* was your sword." Something young and innocent died inside her heart, but Tsudao released it and let it pass. All swords were forged in fire.

"Tsudao . . ."

She froze, closing her eyes. At last, she opened her eyes and turned to him, seeing him truly for the first time. "Good-bye, Father."

"Stay with me." His eyes were sad, hurt by Tsudao's rejection, but she stepped back.

She looked at him once more, memorizing every line of

his face. Each wrinkle he had won through his stubbornness and courage. His eyes, a caramel brown, shone with love for her—love and understanding.

"I must choose. The truth . . . or the Empire?" Tsudao shook her head. Each step she took away from him was another twig on his pyre, and her breath was short with pain.

"Tsudao, no."

Tsudao stared for a long moment at her father then turned away. As she walked out of the throne room, a brilliant flash of white light permeated the entire room, spreading from the other side of the door.

"I have learned, Father, that one cannot always achieve everything. Sometimes, people must choose between two things. Like two forces who meet on the battlefield, it is inevitable that someone will die." Tsudao swallowed, staring into the impenetrable light with shining eyes. "I would rather have my own dreams die than see the Empire fall. If that is the price I must pay . . . then so be it. I know that one day, you will understand."

She stepped into the light and was free.

19 | THROUGH BLOOD AND PAIN

No!" the sorceress screamed. "She will not turn her back on me. I will not let her!"

She began a spell of binding, drawing Tsudao through realms unseen and unknown, forcing her spirit to obey. Only through blood could the sorceress twist the barrier, but in the Iron Citadel there was no lack of pain to fuel her power.

"Scream, damn you," Shahai hissed to her prisoner, knife slicing through flesh and deep to the bone. "Scream and call her to me."

* * * * *

The whiteness surrounded Tsudao, blinding her and forcing her to close her eyes against the torturous purity that enveloped her. She surrendered herself to it, knowing instinctively that it would take her wherever she needed to go. It was the border of Yume-do, the barrier between reality and dream. She stepped forward, eager to find her way out of the nether world.

"Tsudao!"

The scream rippled through her. It was Kekiesu's voice, and she was in pain. Tsudao turned toward it, dreading what she would find. These realms were not her chosen battleground, but she had no choice. She could not abandon her friends. The white light around her rocked and shifted, but Tsudao held her course.

Eight swords rise in the Shadowlands. . . .

Tsudao's own words haunted her memory. In a flash of insight, she saw eight powerful oni, recently summoned from the depths of the Festering Pit. She saw their master, for but an instant, and then Shahai's face rose from the darkness. The sorceress was laughing. . . .

. . . in nightmare, a battle . . .

In a drift of dream, the light faded and was gone.

Tsudao opened her eyes to darkness and horror. The ground at her feet was forged of iron, broken and cracked by numerous upheavals, and the arched ceiling of the huge room was made of the same material. Eight tall columns held aloft a massive ceiling, and light filtered down through a massive scarlet stone that hung at the top of the arched dome. Dark rust, like blood, stained the walls and pooled at the bottom of the eight huge pillars.

Darkness hovered at the edge of her vision, concealing the far walls of the massive room. To one side, Tsudao could see a spotlight of scarlet, like a ray of light stained with blood, concentrating its energy on three crumpled figures. They clustered around a pedestal that could only be the Steel Throne. It was truly the throne, but how had it come here, so far from Otosan Uchi? Tsudao stared in shock—taking in the ugly splotches that stained the throne from top to bottom. Taint. The oni. It had infested even the symbol of the Empire and dragged it here for Shahai's amusement.

The first of the three around the throne was unmistakably

Matsu Domotai. Tsudao stared, stunned to see him here. Her heart had hoped that he had lived through the attacks at the Kitsu Temples, as his body had never been found, but to see him here, twisted and bleeding at the whim of the Shadowlands was almost worse. Domotai was broken and chained, his arms twisted in strange angles. One shoulder had been savaged, and darkness festered at the edges of a deep wound. He was chained to the right side of the throne with thick iron manacles. They cut into his wrists and wept blood onto the iron floor. He did not move, nor did Tsudao know if he was alive, but her heart hoped he had withstood the worst of it.

Beside him, lying to the right of the Steel Throne, was Moshi Kekiesu. No chains held her down, but the Centipede priestess did not move when Tsudao called her name. She simply stared at her hands, as if mesmerized by them, and flexed her fingers, rubbing at them as if wiping away some stain only she could see. A fresh wound smeared blood onto her pale white cheek, a cut from some savagely sharp knife. Shuddering and whimpering, Kekiesu wept at the foot of the throne, unable to react to the world around her.

But the worst of all was Bayushi Paneki. He stood behind the throne of his own will, his eyes black and pained. He stared down at Tsudao in full control of his faculties but did not step forward when she met his eyes. Something dark had reached him, twisted his loyalties, and told him lies that he believed. When Tsudao raised her voice to call him to her side, Paneki shook his head and turned his eyes away.

The plane of dreams had changed them all.

"Sweet princess, I almost thought you were leaving us. It would have been such a pity. There are so many webs left to unravel. So many games left to play."

Iuchi Shahai lounged against the pillar closest to the throne, stretching her lithe body against the tall iron pedestal. Her violet and black robes shimmered in the scarlet light, and one hand still held the sharp knife that bore Kekiesu's blood. A catlike smile played about her features.

"Moshi Kekiesu, Bayushi Paneki, and Matsu Domotai are coming with me." Tsudao's voice was firm and uncompromising.

Shahai purred softly, the knife glinting against the iron pillar. She drew it down along the iron surface of the wall, listening to the faint echo of steel. "I don't think they want to go."

Tsudao's hand brushed the hilt of her sword, and she took a step forward. "What have you done to them, Bloodspeaker?"

"I only listened to their dreams." Shahai lowered the knife, staring at the stain of blood upon the blade. "That was more than you ever did, General, and they've repaid me with their loyalty." Her eyes flickered up to Tsudao's face. A smooth smile whispered about the sorceress's lips. "An *undying* loyalty."

"No." Tsudao shook her head. "Whatever they have bargained to you, I will buy back."

"With what, Tsudao?" The lack of honorific was like a slap in the face, but Shahai's voice was pleasant and soft. "With your own soul? How interesting. But you see, I already have the blood of emperors on my side. The throne can only have one master, and that master shall be the Scion of Hantei." Shahai stepped away from the pillar and walked slowly up the steps to the Steel Throne. "There is nothing you can offer that I want."

Tsudao slowly drew the jade katana at her side, and the greenish blade shone with purity in the scarlet light of the room. "If there is nothing I can give you, then I will simply have to take them." She stepped up the first stair toward the dais as Shahai lingered on the arm of the Steel Throne.

"Go ahead," Shahai spread her hands. She turned toward the three samurai that clustered around the throne. "Take them."

Her laugh rang out across the chamber, and she lifted the bloodstained knife, weaving it in an intricate pattern in the air. The image glowed, shimmering faintly with red, malicious light, and Tsudao saw something change within the eyes of her companions.

Matsu Domotai stood slowly, as if drawn by unseen strings. Chains hung from his arms and legs, dragging across the floor with zombie-like slowness. He stepped down, away from the throne, and blood tricked from his open wounds. Taking a length of chain in his hands, he snapped it like a garrote and came at Tsudao with empty eyes.

Tsudao took her stance, the jade sword before her, as Bayushi Paneki stepped to Domotai's side. Kekiesu stood as if forced by some restraining power but hid her head in her hands and wept uncontrollably. Tsudao grimaced. Whatever power Shahai had over her friends, Tsudao had to accept that they were not in control of their actions. They had no compulsion about hurting Tsudao, nor did they seem to care about their own survival.

She would have to fight to win.

Domotai's chain swung around his head in a wide arc, the metal links clattering as they gained speed. Paneki crouched beneath the loop of chain, knife weaving from hand to hand as the two samurai moved closer to Tsudao. Kekiesu stepped to the front of the Steel Throne, her hands lifting into the air as tears slid down her cheeks. Unlike the others, she seemed completely unaware of her surroundings, whispering words of prayer as if reciting a litany that held no meaning.

"Paneki, Domotai, fight it! Fight her!" Tsudao shouted. "I know that your soul is stronger than this. Don't let her control you!"

"It's too late, Tsudao," Paneki snarled, striking out at her with the knife and forcing her to back away. "You don't understand what we have become. If, by killing you, I can regain my honor and destroy the past, then I have no choice. You must die."

The chain spun toward her, and Tsudao sprang away from the slithering coils. Metal sparked against the iron floor of the chamber, and the chain smashed just inches from her feet. It recoiled around Domotai's head, lashing out once more and forcing her to leap over the snapping, writhing length. When she did, Paneki was there to block her landing. He shoved the knife for her ribs, and Tsudao was barely able to block his thrust with the length of her blade.

She threw herself against him, knocking the Scorpion to the ground and rolling under another lash of chain. Domotai's metal whip coiled around Tsudao's leg, yanking her back toward him, and she scraped against the floor to gain a grip. Pulling against the grasp of Domotai's leverage, Tsudao cut downward with the jade katana, severing the chain in a burst of greenish sparks. Domotai staggered back as the weight on his chain was released, and Tsudao kicked to her feet.

Paneki leaped under her sword and struck again. Tsudao caught his hand and twisted his arm roughly to try to force him to drop the knife. Grinning, the Scorpion leaped, turning as his arm twisted and regaining his feet as Tsudao's grip on his wrist slid away. He shot a vicious punch to her face, cracking against her jaw and sending Tsudao staggering. Before he could take advantage of her momentary shock, Tsudao had the jade katana up again, pointed at his breastbone and ready to take his life with a single thrust. Paneki twisted away, losing ground, and circled once more.

Suddenly, from the dais, Kekiesu screamed in an unearthly, haunted voice. Her incantation ended, and a rush of crimson flames exploded, knocking Tsudao and Paneki to the ground. The flames burned Tsudao's flesh, searing her skin. Only Domotai seemed immune to the explosion, and the chains whirled ever faster in his hands. Searing silver lights glistened within the flame as it roared up and down the dais stairs, and Kekiesu seemed to give herself entirely to the magic, screaming words of power above the roar of the flame. When the spell had finished, she sank to her knees, tears rushing down her face.

"Kekiesu!" Tsudao screamed as the flames singed her skin.

"Remember! I know you can fight her! You can make this stop!"

Make it stop. Tsudao saw Kekiesu shake her head, clinging to the sound of Tsudao's voice. Opening her eyes, the Centipede turned toward Shahai and stared up with rage at the bloodspeaker who lounged upon the Steel Throne. Tearing her eyes from the combat, the Centipede shugenja allowed the magic to pass through her once more. Tsudao watched as power poured through Kekiesu's fingers, dousing Shahai in a shroud of brilliant light.

"You made me kill her!" Kekiesu screamed. "*You* did this to me!" The fire released from Kekiesu's spell turned back upon her, shrouding the Moshi priestess in a cloak of flame.

With a scream, Shahai raised her hands, blocking the heat of Kekiesu's attack with a field of dark energy, but the power of Kekiesu's spell pressed through.

Tsudao dodged her opponents' blows, desperately trying to see the duel of magic occurring across the room as Kekiesu and Shahai poured their magic into each other. Shahai lashed out with the power of blood, and a vile black serpent appeared around Kekiesu's wrists. Tsudao heard Kekiesu shriek as fangs tore into her flesh. The Centipede fell as the serpent bound her in its coils. Screaming, Kekiesu landed at Shahai's feet, then, with a choking gasp, she lay still. Its duty complete, the snake vanished.

On the floor of the chamber, Paneki's knife whistled down once more and sank into Tsudao's leg. Ignoring the flash of pain, she swung with the jade sword and saw Paneki's hand withdraw, covered in blood. A fierce kick dislodged the Scorpion, and he flew back into Domotai's chain. Gripping the chain, Tsudao twisted it around Domotai's body as the samurai struggled to regain his freedom. She plunged her sword through the links as the chains wrapped tightly around his back, sealing them with the fulcrum of the jade sword. The chains groaned against the solid piton that now held them taut, but they did not break. Domotai hung limply from his prison, his bloodied body no longer resisting. So long as Tsudao left the sword to pin Domotai to the ground, he would not be able to fight—but Tsudao now had no weapon of her own. She stepped away, making her choice, and left the sword behind. She could not kill her friends.

On the throne above them, Shahai laughed.

Tsudao ignored her and turned aside Paneki's blade with a brutal blow to his wrist. The blade spun. Tsudao caught the hilt and hurled it across the room. It was lost in the shadows on the distant side of the chamber.

"Paneki," Tsudao said, "you have done nothing wrong. Stop fighting me. I need you."

The Scorpion kicked at her, trying to knock Tsudao's feet from the stone stairs. "I have betrayed the Empire. I have served a false lord."

"A dream, nothing more." Tsudao caught his hand and jerked the Scorpion to her side. She pushed her face into his. "You are caught in a nightmare, Paneki. Fight it!"

"Naseru . . . told me to betray you, to leave you!" he screamed. Paneki's torment shook his body. "To let you die! I was his pawn. Don't you see? I thought I was following Yojiro's commands—my Champion's commands—but I was a pawn for Naseru. I trusted him. I trusted them both. They said the Empire would be forged upon the anvil of war. With your death, the clans would rise against one another, carve away the weakness, and begin a new Empire. A stronger Rokugan. But it could not happen, not so long as you were there to make peace. I cannot let Rokugan die because it could not see the enemies that stand before it. If you will not fight, then you will die!"

Paneki struck at Tsudao with a familiar, black-coated knife and buried the blade in Tsudao's chest. The blow was slightly askew, tearing into shoulder muscle and breast rather than piercing the heart, but it sank deeply. He released the thin blade in horror as the point scraped upon her rib cage. Through all his anger, all his fury at himself for failing his lord, he had sought to kill her. Now that he had nearly done so, the depth and reality of his treason shook him free of the emotions controlling his actions. Paneki staggered back and clutched his head in his hands. With a terrible scream, he wrenched himself free of Shahai's spell and stared up at Tsudao with wide, shocked eyes.

"What have I done?" the Scorpion whispered. "We are trained all our lives to obey, to honor the throne, and yet I ... I have ... Kami save me ... Tsudao ..." He stared at her in anguish, his mind at last free of the darkness and dreams of Yume-do.

Tsudao slowly drew the knife from her breast, clamping her fist over the thin entry wound to stop the bleeding. "Was it poisoned, Paneki?" she asked quietly. "Like the oni?"

The Scorpion staggered back with blood on his hands. He nodded, realizing his surroundings for the first time. "It was a dream, wasn't it, Tsudao? I betrayed you for a dream. I saw Naseru speak to me ... the words of my Champion. He ordered your death, and I thought I must obey him to regain my honor. But that could not have been. It was a dream."

"Just a dream, Paneki-san, and nothing more." Tsudao whispered. She looked down at the wound. "How long do I have before this kills me?"

"Not long," Strangely calm, Paneki's arrogant demeanor crumbled. "Not long at all."

"Then I had better finish what I came for." Tsudao turned and limped up the stairs toward Shahai. She handed Paneki the knife that had wounded her. "Take care of Kekiesu, Paneki-san."

He nodded grimly, taking back the blade with careful hands and moving quickly to the fallen shugenja's side.

The imperial princess turned and fixed her gaze on Shahai. Her leg was deeply cut, and the blood from her chest stained her once-pristine gold and black kimono. Tsudao's hair hung wild around her face, the long strands blowing softly around her even features. With fire burning in her golden eyes, the daughter of Toturi walked up the stairs. She held no sword, no weapon of any kind, but her hatred gave her the strength to carry on.

"Now, Shahai. You have no more pawns, no more toys to throw in my way. I assure you, there is no spell you can cast before I get my hands around your throat."

The sorceress backed away, fear shimmering in her eyes, but she lifted one pale hand to her mouth to suppress a high-pitched giggle. "We're still playing my game, princess," the bloodspeaker said. Her eyes were wide, her lips curled into a child's mocking laughter. "Never forget that."

"It may be yours, bloodspeaker," Tsudao stood over the throne, her expression one of resolute courage, mixed with a tiredness born of suffering. "But it would appear I am the victor."

"No, Tsudao. This game is over." Suddenly, her head was forced back by an inch of steel that brushed against her skin. The razor point of a glistening blade hung just inches from her throat. Tsudao froze, still prepared to strike. She stared up the length of the threatening katana into the mad eyes of Mirumoto Junnosuke.

"You lose."

20   SWORD OF JUSTICE

Shahai laughed, her musical voice echoing through the grand hall.

Above the Steel Throne, a skull chattered. It hovered in the air like some strange bird, dancing on the winds that drifted through the chamber, and its mad howl ricocheted from iron walls. Shahai looked up at it, enjoying the bone smile upon its featureless face, then lowered her eyes to Tsudao. Dark, sooty lashes brushed Shahai's colorless cheeks, and a childlike smile curved her blood-red lips. She lounged on the arm of the Steel Throne, her dark robes cascading over the Emperor's seat to the floor. One bare leg curved over the arm, down the front of the throne like a lover's caress, and her long black hair shimmered across the high back and elaborately forged side.

Before the throne stood Toturi Tsudao. Her clothing was ripped, one leg showed a wound through the torn pants, and a deep cut on her chest oozed blood. The sword at her throat reflected bursts of red light.

Mirumoto Junnosuke stood at the side of the throne. Golden armor shimmered on his body, the scales covered in strange runes that flickered with each echo of Shahai's laugher. He smiled an insane grimace, clearly enjoying the position he held.

Lower on the dais, a wounded Scorpion guarded his two tortured companions. The Moshi shugenja seemed all but catatonic, her fallen body crumbled at his feet. Another samurai, this one beaten and bloodied beyond mercy, lay still, wrapped in a cocoon of chain. Paneki held a sharp blade in his hand as he stood over them, staring at the Mirumoto with death in his eyes.

"My poor princess," Shahai whispered, tracing Tsudao's face with her eyes, enjoying the sight of steel against her white throat, "it has come to this. Killed by her father's sword. How very tragic." She sighed. "I'll adore hearing the stories the Crane compose about your death." The sword drew a thin line of blood. "Kill her slowly, Junnosuke," Shahai purred. "There are so many ways to torture a woman of honor . . . and the sweetest bone to break is the one that holds their spirit. To draw it out like marrow, to see it wasted on the floor while she screams . . . that is a fitting end for a princess, don't you think?"

Shahai lifted her hands, stretching back upon the throne and opening herself to the magic that drifted all about the chamber. She began to chant, closing her eyes in supplication to the dark powers that drifted through her soul.

"I call upon Iuchiban the Old, thrice chained and twice freed. Hear me!" Power trickled down Shahai's arms, lingering to arch between her extended fingertips. "I call from this dark plane, through the dreams of Yume-do, the nightmares of tortured men and the screams of wounded on forgotten battlefields."

The sorceress's voice echoed in Tsudao's ears like the beat of a *kotei* drum, calling to something she had forgotten, something that lingered at the edge of memory—hidden, but not lost.

"I call on the name of Fu Leng, who has brought this into being—he whose power reaches from beyond the grave." Shahai lifted her hands to the ceiling, and a dark spatter of blood trickled down the walls of the chamber, covering the rust with slick, wet tar. "I call from the edge of victory, to the Scion of Hantei. Come to me now and see what I have wrought in the name of our Dark Father!"

A darkness, vast and powerful, grew within the hall, and a shiver crept down Tsudao's spine. Something traveled through dream, through nightmare, to reach them. Called by Shahai's summons, it walked the borders between the planes. Someone was coming, and he was more powerful than Tsudao could ever have guessed. Perhaps she'd been a fool to believe Shahai could be defeated, to think Junnosuke would easily rise to the bait. Now she would have to fight them both—before this new entity arrived to seal their power. A face swam before her mind, and a name . . . *Hantei.*

Tsudao closed her eyes, trying to block out the visions that crept upon her. Here? Now? She shook her head, painfully aware of the blade cutting into her flesh. Shahai's voice faded, and the vision came in even more clearly.

The Scion of Hantei . . . and eight new children of vice and evil, eight new beasts within the Shadowlands.

Tsudao opened golden eyes and saw a vision before her. Eight tall oni stood in a semicircle around a dark man. His black robes shifted in a howling wind, and his hands lashed out against the Empire with power. Eight oni risen from the deepest pits of the Shadowlands, each carefully constructed from all that was vile and corrupt, one for each of the eight clans of the Empire . . .

With an icy stab, Tsudao realized their purpose at last. They would be the downfall of Rokugan and the beginning of an Empire of Pain. With no one to guide the clans, to fight the evil as it arose, the Empire was doomed. These oni would sweep across the Empire and devastate all that they touched. No one clan could stand against them, and with no one to unify them, Rokugan would fall.

I am the Sword.

The scream howled from the pillars of the citadel, shattering the scarlet stone above. Golden light shimmered across the dais, scattering shadow and driving away darkness. The powerful voice rose, and Tsudao suddenly recognized it as her own.

Shahai's spell shattered like the bloodstone above them, her voice dying away beneath the savage roar of Tsudao's soul. For a fraction of a second, she held the spell together by will alone, desperately seeking to open the gate she called forth. Junnosuke turned toward her, staring in awe as blood trailed down the dark sorceress's face, bleeding like tears from her eyes.

In that moment, Paneki moved. Too quick to follow, he kicked Junnosuke's hand, tilting the sword away from Tsudao's neck. It was not much, but it was enough. Freed of the threat of Junnosuke's blade, Tsudao launched a furious attack against the former samurai, her hand chopping viciously at his throat. The blow landed, but it only served to push him down the stairs. Paneki threw himself after Junnosuke.

With a snarl, Junnosuke twisted away and leaped for Kekiesu's body, his weapon plunging down to end her life. Again, Paneki jumped in the way, hurling his body over hers before Junnosuke could pull his strike. The cut drove into Paneki's arm, severing tendon and cutting to the bone, but it did not reach Kekiesu. Before Junnosuke could strike again, Tsudao was on him. She spun him away from Paneki before Junnosuke could send another blow to sever the Scorpion's head.

Shoving her fists through his defenses, Tsudao pounded his sides, where only lace protected him from her assaults.

The golden armor groaned in protest but held against her blows. Junnosuke spun to face her, and Tsudao saw her father's katana arcing toward her face. She ducked and allowed it to pass by, then shot forward to drive her shoulder into Junnosuke's side. Off-balance, Junnosuke went down, landing with a heavy crash.

Tsudao jumped quickly, ignoring Shahai's screams of protest. Junnosuke was her first threat. She would deal with the sorceress later. Junnosuke regained his footing and settled into a martial stance before Tsudao reached him.

Junnosuke swept the sword in a savage arc, forcing Tsudao to step back. He thrust toward her chest, but Tsudao dodged the blade and caught his arm in her hand. With a brutal blow from her elbow, she heard the snap of bone.

Her foe screamed and spun toward her, levering a kick to her wounded leg. It connected with a violent impact, and Tsudao crumpled, her injured leg unable to bear the strain. Junnosuke clung to the sword, backing away for a moment.

"Do you think that you can hurt me, Princess?" Junnosuke snarled. In the shattered rays of the blood-red stone, Tsudao saw the bones of his forearm rejoining, his arm growing straight and strong once more. Black ooze trickled down from under his armor, covering his hand. In moments, his wrist moved normally. He snarled, raising the sword once more.

Tsudao climbed to her feet, all of her will forcing her leg to bear her weight. The wound in her chest ached, and numbness was spreading through her joints. She shook her head, aware that her time was short.

"Come, Junnosuke. I'm not as impressed with your Shadowlands tricks as you seem to be. If you are too busy staring at yourself to fight me, then surrender. I'll be sure to have the Crane find you a mirror for your execution."

He roared in fury, storming toward her. Tsudao worked fast to dodge the tremendous blows that fell in a flurry to all sides, leaping back and forth, in and out of Junnosuke's range. All the while she taunted him, goading the ronin into an even greater fury.

No matter, though. The ronin's swordplay was excellent—far better than Tsudao would have thought him capable of. He did not tire, and Tsudao's reflexes were growing ever slower. Only her incredible anger gave her the edge she needed to stay alive, but it would take more than that to defeat him. Tsudao fought with the ferocity of a tiger, but she had little time. Already, she could feel the venom at work in her veins, slowing her heartbeat and stiffening the muscles of her body. The world grew colder with each passing second.

"You will die, Tsudao." Junnosuke's voice was filled with madness. "I will have your blood, and when I am done, I will have the Empire as well. The clans are nothing more than weak, pathetic children before the power of the Shadowlands . . . and they will die."

Tsudao didn't doubt him, and rage built in her heart like the breaking of night into dawn, but it wouldn't help her. She was dying, her body exhausted and the poison claiming the last reserves of her will. The jade sword shone in Domotai's chains, mocking her empty hands, but to recover it, she would have to free him—and this time, she would have to kill the Lion. She could not do that, even if it meant she would have no weapon to fight Junnosuke.

There was little she could do. Poisoned, beaten, and losing blood, she felt her body weakening with each beat of her heart. Junnosuke stood above her, smiling and ready to continue the battle. He would rush her once more, and this time, Tsudao would run out of courage. She was defeated.

* * * * *

By the side of the dais, a fallen Moshi Kekiesu watched her mistress fighting against Junnosuke. Though unarmed and unarmored, Tsudao still managed to hold her own. She reached up to take Bayushi Paneki's hand, drawing the Scorpion to her side.

"Give me your knife, Paneki," Kekiesu whispered hurriedly. "Please."

Paneki opened his mouth to argue, but the serious look on her face stopped his words. Silently, he handed her the poisoned blade. Kekiesu drew it between her fingers as if testing its strength. Raising palms stained with Tsudao's blood, the Centipede priestess nodded. It would do.

"What are you doing?" Paneki said, touching the Centipede's cheek with gentle fingers.

She looked up at him with a half-smile, then turned away. "Saving her life."

"Blood magic?" Paneki whispered, clutching his arm where the deep wound from Junnosuke's sword had nearly removed it. "Kekiesu, no—"

The shugenja shook her head, silencing him with her eyes. "Not blood magic. A simple reversal of energy—hers to mine, her wounds to my own. A magic of spirit, not blood, Paneki. It is the only thing that will save Tsudao."

Kekiesu shut her eyes and closed her palms around the narrow blade. Words of sorcery flowed from her lips. As she chanted, the knife began to glow with a faint golden energy. Paneki knelt beside her, the arm of his shirt covered in his own blood. He could not fight to save Tsudao, but he watched as the two warriors struggled across the floor of the Iron Citadel. Junnosuke chased and struck at Tsudao, but she wove through his attacks and assaulted him with fist and kick, still unable to get through the golden samurai's armor.

"Whatever you're going to do, Kekiesu," he breathed, "do it quickly."

The blood between her fingers took on a light of its own, transforming into liquid gold. Kekiesu whispered to it, calling the spirits of the sun to reach out across the barriers of Yume-do. The magic answered. It swept into Tsudao's blood and into Kekiesu's body, transforming them both into golden light. Transformed into sunlight, their darkness removed, a mystic communion between Kekiesu and Tsudao was forged.

"There will be no death this day, mistress." Kekiesu's breath drifted through the sunlight that danced on her skin as a similar glow began to shimmer around Tsudao. Far across the floor, the light of the Sun joined their flesh, made their minds and bodies one for a single moment. Kekiesu smiled, feeling the love and sorrow of her decision. "Not for you."

Sharp pain lanced through Kekiesu's body. Terrible agony rumbled in her soul, but she would not scream. Paneki bent over her, gripping her hands and calling her name. Another shiver of agony stripped through her, nearly tearing a scream from her throat.

"H-help me . . . Pa-Paneki," Kekiesu whispered. "If I . . . s-scream, the s-spell . . . falls . . . to blood. We . . . w-will . . . be consumed." Her hands grasped his, and she desperately sought solace in his eyes. "Give m-me . . . your cour—" her back arched as pain spasmed through her body— "your courage! H-help me . . . to . . . to be silent . . . or . . . we . . . w-we—"

Paneki pulled her to him and placed the hilt of his knife between her teeth. "Do not fear, Kekiesu." His voice was tightly controlled. "I will guard you. You will not fail."

Kekiesu looked into his face and knew his thoughts. They were written upon his dark brown eyes. Paneki knew that if he joined the fight with Tsudao, his wounded arm would fail him, and he would die. He could not help Tsudao, nor recover his honor through battle. His fight was here with Kekiesu, and he would not give up until it was finished.

Another shudder rocked Kekiesu, and the pain shot through her spine. She bit down on the handle of the knife, allowing the magic to begin its transfer. Paneki hovered at the edge of her vision, and the feel of his hands on hers was the only reality that invaded the envelope of bitter golden pain. There would be no screams, despite the agony that tore apart her flesh. There would be no death for Tsudao, no pain, no more poison . . . but the cost would be high.

It was the price of such a spell, binding her own body to Tsudao's, but it was a price that Kekiesu was willing to pay.

21 **THE COURAGE OF STEEL**

Golden light danced across her skin, stealing the pain from her wounds and pouring strength into weary muscles. Tsudao stumbled to one knee, her body afire with pain and instinctively recoiling from the magic at work on her flesh. She felt a warm presence in her mind, smelled a soft scent she had known almost from birth, and knew that Kekiesu was with her.

Remember, Tsudao, her handmaiden's voice whispered in her mind, *each of us has the right to choose our time to die. Now is not your time. Rise and show the strength your father gave you.*

Light flooded through her, and Tsudao raised her hands. The wounds began to knit and heal, reforming into seamless flesh. The pain of the poison that had taken her breath and stolen her strength ebbed within her, the burning of its presence within her blood subsiding. Within moments, it was gone, and Tsudao knew she was whole once more.

She looked up into the face of her attacker and saw Junnosuke's eyes widen in fear and realization. Tsudao was pure. Her body wiped clean of exhaustion and pain, her system free of the poison that had weakened it, she raised golden eyes to meet his dark ones, and in them was no trace of fear or resignation.

"Junnosuke," Tsudao said, feeling her strength returning with each passing moment, "I have fought you with every breath in my body—not because I wanted to, but because you forced me. Because of *your* choosing. Your path led us to this place, and only your path can lead us from here."

Her eyes glowed with the restoration of her life, and one by one, each of her wounds sealed, the blood drying and vanishing upon her golden skin. The ronin in his golden armor seemed pale beside the true light of the sun, his breastplates dull and bronze by comparion.

Tsudao pushed herself to her feet and stood in an open stance before a dumbfounded Junnosuke. "Are you ready, Junnosuke-san?" she asked, as the ronin took a stumbling step backward. "Or are you going to run from this challenge as you have run from every other challenge in your life?"

Junnosuke's eyes widened as she spoke, but it was too late to back down. The golden blood in her veins pulsed with the purity of sunlight. For this moment, he could not harm her, and he would listen.

"You were born a samurai, Junnosuke, with all the burdens and honors that station offers. You threw it away because of your rage and your hatred. You stepped on your own honor and broke it in two. Now look what you've become, Junnosuke—a pawn for the Shadowlands, nothing more than the lowest snake that crawls through their Tainted grass." Tsudao reached a golden hand toward him. "I saw you when you stood over your troops when you defended the Dragon lands. I saw they loved you. You were a hero to them until you let your own pride blind you."

Tsudao took another step toward Junnosuke, and he

stepped back, unable to tear his eyes from hers. Her words seemed tore into his soul, and Tsudao saw doubt and fear coloring his features.

Behind him on the dais, Shahai rose from her throne, curling her hands into clawed fists. "Junnosuke! Destroy her! I command you!"

"You never lived like a samurai, Junnosuke." Tsudao's voice was clear and sharp, uncompromising, but it carried a hint of compassion, and the man could not break her gaze. "You have murdered innocents, betrayed your commanders, and broken every oath you ever gave. Your sword is tinged with dishonor, and your soul has been twisted by the Shadowlands. When the Dragon Clan looks back on their son, Junnosuke, they will say he did not live like a samurai."

"No!" hissed Junnosuke, swinging his sword at her.

She dodged it easily, fully aware that the golden glow touching her skin was fading. The spell was ending, leaving her whole—but vulnerable once more. She felt renewed and refreshed, her wounds had vanished as if into dream. Whatever it had been, Kekiesu's spell had worked.

"Look at me, Junnosuke, and see what you could have been!"

"She lies, Junnosuke. Destroy her!" Shahai snarled, raising her hands to compel him. Whatever magic she tried, it did not succeed, and Tsudao saw Junnosuke's body flinch and recoil from the puppet strings of Shahai's spell. Yet he resisted. Tsudao prayed it was a sign that her words were reaching him, that somehow, he understood the path she placed before him.

"Do not let her make you crawl," Tsudao whispered, and she saw Junosuke flinch.

"What does an imperial princess know of crawling?" Junnosuke's face was haunted, but his eyes never left hers. "What do you know of pain and failure?"

"I know samurai, and I know that when I leave this place, I will carry the tale of Shahai's black magic upon your soul. But you must tell me, how will this story end, Junnosuke?

With your failure? With another broken sword, and another blow to your family's honor? Will you fall to the Shadow-lands, or will you fight them as your family has fought them for a thousand years?"

Junnosuke's movements were feral, his sword shifting for-ward and back as if seeking an opening. He did not answer, but his mouth opened in pain and anguish, unable to respond to Tsudao's words.

"You've never lived like a samurai, but you have one final chance," Tsudao said, her eyes searching his. "Tell me, Miru-moto Junnosuke, can you die like one?"

"You do not know me!" Junnosuke screamed, his rage a sound of pure heartbroken anger, echoing from the room around them. He raised the sword high above his head. "You do not know how I will die!"

Junnosuke tore his eyes from Tsudao, his hands shaking on the hilt of the katana. Behind him, the sorceress sat on the arm of the Steel Throne and raised her hands to prepare a spell. She was too late. With a bellow of blind rage, Junno-suke threw himself up the stairs, his sword stretched out before him like a pike.

Tsudao's entire training demanded she move away, but she forced herself to stand still. Something in Junnosuke's eys told her that he had made his decision, and she would not deny him the right of blood. He struck fast and hard, driving the sword toward Tsudao with the intensity of a lightning bolt.

But at the last possible second, he twisted his strike.

Gripping Junnosuke's wrist, Tsudao pulled his sword for-ward with all her strength, lending her weight to his blow. The blade passed so close to Tsudao's body that it tore her black shirt. The wind of his *kiai* shout blew Tsudao's hair in a wild fall around her face, half-covering her savage grin. In that perfect instant, she stared deeply into Junnosuke's eyes and saw death within them. He had made his choice. It was not enough to repay her for her father's loss, but for a single moment, Tsudao felt avenged.

The sword slid past Tsudao, forced with the strength of two warriors to strike behind her and into the belly of the Steel Throne. Tsudao stood chest to chest with Junnosuke for an instant and at that moment realized that somewhere in his heart, a true samurai had been born.

A terrible scream erupted through the hall, filling the corridors and chambers of the iron citadel with blood as Junnosuke's killing blow buried itself deep into Shahai's heart.

Junnosuke staggered backward, his hand releasing the hilt of Toturi's sword as Shahai's spell unraveled. The webs of black magic spun and wove like tentacles between the blood sorceress and her pawn, spreading magic and blood through the room in horrible dripping strands. Without thought, Tsudao gripped the hilt of her father's blade, drew it free of Shahai's body, and reversed the stroke. The sword moved fluidly in her hands, spinning in her grasp, perfectly balanced for her movements. It felt clean and pure in her hand, steel singing with renewed honor.

Shahai shrieked, a high pathetic sound, and her hands began to bleed of their own violition. "Junnosuke!" Her voice was as brittle as glass, and her body shook with the death-wound she had been given. "Do you think it is so easy to betray us? To leave—?"

Her hands moved through the air as if she were tearing paper, and Junnosuke screamed. Although his blow had torn open her body, her magic still spun like the web of a spider, volleying from her hands toward Junnosuke. It coiled around him like a snake, out of control and wild with Shahai's pain.

Junnosuke fell to the floor, his body bursting open. Coiled strands of magic tore into his skin, feeding on his blood as Shahai's magic took on a life of its own. The sorceress fell to her knees, looking up at the raging magic with a half-dazed smile. She fed more of her lifeblood into it, watching as the spells exploded, shaking the very stone of the corridor in which they stood.

"You ... will die, Junnosuke!" she rasped as the black shards of spellcraft shattered and fell to the ground like an obsidian rain. Shahai smiled weakly, her madness shining in dying eyes and blood trailing like inky blackness from her fingers and the terrible hole in her chest. She poured all of her soul into the black magic—then set it free with her dying breath.

The citadel shook, as if some tremendous strike had leveled one of the upper towers. The chamber swayed, each of the stone pillars cracking with sharp bursts of sound, and the reddish light from the high ceiling turned dark and sickly.

The shards of power cut Junnosuke's flesh, feeding on his pain, and he coughed up blood. His golden armor was rent and torn from Shahai's abuse, and he seemed nothing more than a broken puppet upon the ground. Tsudao tried to reach for him but could not approach the raging spell. At the end, Junnosuke looked up at her and smiled, a last remnant of his humanity—beaten, bloodied, but unconquered. He died while Tsudao was trying to reach him, defying Shahai's magic to the end. He died with honor.

"Tsudao-sama!" Bayushi Paneki's voice rose over the terrible shrieks and wild explosions. His voice faltered, hoarse with emotion, then called to her again. "Come quickly! Kekiesu ..."

Carrying her father's sword, Tsudao turned away from the Steel Throne. As she approached her companions, she saw Kekiesu's limp body, blood seeping out from beneath her clothes. The stain was directly over her heart—right where Tsudao's own wound had been.

"Kekiesu!" Tsudao screamed. "Oh, Fortunes, no!"

"We have to get her out of this citadel!" Paneki reached to lift Kekiesu but winced when her slight weight tore at his injured sword arm.

Tsudao slid her father's sword under her belt, raised.

Kekiesu to her chest, and pulled Domotai to his feet. Tsudao held the two companions close, then lurched forward. "Quickly, follow me."

Around them, the citadel shook and burned, and a cacophony of magic swirled around them, tearing at their ankles and trying to suck them back into the black flames. Tsudao held Kekiesu close, praying to the Fortunes for their release, and Paneki raced ahead to find the path that would lead them out of Yume-do.

Paneki tore at the iron gates, pulling apart the massive bars as Tsudao approached. The iron was barbed, and his hands were bloody from the effort, but beyond them lay a wide swath of ground that shimmered with sunlight. The borders around the gate were shifting and twisting, severing the citadel from Rokugan. They struggled to close, to part the realms forever, but Paneki stood between them, letting his own body be all but crushed in their grip rather than allow the gates to close. He struggled to hold them, refusing to allow the realms to part.

"Take her through!" he shouted through clenched teeth.

"No, Paneki! You cannot stay. You must follow us."

"I intend to, Princess," Paneki said with a hint of his ironic smile, "but after you. Go!"

Tsudao pushed through the gates, feeling the fierce pressure of the iron bars against her skin as she forced her way past. She stepped into the gulf beyond and felt the softness of grass against her bare and bloodied feet. As soon as she felt the pressure of Shahai's spell-realm leave her, Tsudao knelt upon the sunlit grass and placed Kekiesu on the ground. She could not leave Paneki behind.

Turning, she saw the portal from the far side—a twisted hole in reality that glimmered with bloodied edges. The Scorpion stood between two iron gateways, his hands bleeding from the effort of holding them apart. Tsudao reached for him, grasping Paneki's hands in hers, and pulled Paneki through the high iron bars.

There was a terrible rending sound, as if the world sought to heal a wound it had been given, and the edges of the portal turned to blackness and blood. In the distance,

Tsudao could hear a high-pitched shriek—Shahai's forsaken soul, howling in vengeance and agony—and then the portal closed with the sound of falling stone and collapsing architecture. The last vision Tsudao had of the land beyond was of blood and raging, uncontrolled magic, tearing apart the very walls of reality where a great citadel had stood.

Paneki gasped, and Tsudao could see where bruises from the gates would mark his chest and arms. He had literally stood on the borders of reality and held worlds together. Tsudao's heart swelled with pride. He had proven his honor.

Then she looked beside him, to the bodies in the grass at Paneki's side. Although he was wounded, Domotai was breathing steadily. Kekiesu's chest rose and fell in erratic, shallow bursts. The Scorpion brushed a long lock of Kekiesu's hair away from her heart-shaped face, his eyes dark and concerned. Tsudao knelt beside them. The Scorpion lifted the Moshi shugenja into his arms tenderly, as if he were afraid that the motion would cause her to break. Tsudao looked at Kekiesu's body and suddenly understood the spell that the shugenja had cast. All of the wounds Tsudao had taken in the conflict were reflected on the Moshi's broken body. Kekiesu's lips were blue from poison, and her body was light from loss of blood. The girl's skin was pale, her eyes half-closed, but her fingers twined against those of the Scorpion samurai.

"She used her magic to take your injuries." Even though he struggled to contain his emotions, Paneki's voice revealed an ocean of pain. "You were healed . . . but she is dying. The poison is killing her."

"Kekiesu . . ." Tsudao gripped her handmaiden's shoulder, touching her face in concern. "No. There must be an antidote. Something—"

"As I told you, General," Paneki said gravely, "there is no time."

Golden sunlight shimmered through trees around them, dimly lighting the grassy dell. They were in the Naga forests, somewhere near the edge of the great trees that guarded the deep groves of the Shinomen. No sound broke the silence, no bird sang or flittered among the trees. They were alone, with only the golden sunlight to kiss their cheeks and shine down upon their tears. The iron citadel of nightmare, once corrupt and tainted, was gone forever.

They had won.

Kekiesu's eyes fluttered open, and Tsudao stared down at her friend with sorrow. "Kekiesu-san," Tsudao said, "why did you do it?"

"You ... are the Daughter of the Sun," Kekiesu replied, as if there were no question at all, "and you must live." She turned to Paneki, her eyes speaking without words. She lifted his hand and kissed it, then placed his hand over Tsudao's, weaving their fingers together. "Stay with her, Bayushi Paneki, and walk ... where I no longer can. Serve her with ... your heart, and remember me. The love I bear you both ... unites your souls. You are one. Walk ... as one. Forgive and ... move on. I know you will need ... each other in the dangers to come. It is not good for either of you to be ... alone."

"You can't leave me, Kekiesu-chan." Tsudao's voice broke, and her features were etched with loss. "I've never been without you. My whole life, you have been beside me. What will I do if my handmaiden is no longer here?"

Tears sparkled in Tsudao's eyes. Kekiesu reached up toward her mistress with a gentle hand and brushed them away before they could fall.

"I have been beside you ... in the realm of dreams, Tsudao-sama ... beyond the gates of heaven and of hell. I know ... the path, and the road is ... is clear ... before me. I will sleep in Yume-do ... in peace. I will never be far ... from you. ..."

Placing her head upon Paneki's chest, Moshi Kekiesu closed her eyes. As quietly as she had lived, she passed away, sinking without argument into dreamless, eternal sleep.

EPILOGUE
NASERU'S BURDEN

Journal Entry, 28th day of the Horse, 1159

Today my sister came to my chambers in Otosan Uchi. I have never seen her as she was today, and I think some great change has come upon her. The Dragon and Phoenix still fight in the north, and their war may last a generation. But that is not the tale she came to tell me—not the story of war or of the clans to the north that spill their blood upon the ground. She speaks to me of stranger things, of darker stories and grimmer outcomes.

At her side was a Scorpion I know well. He would not meet my eyes.

They had traveled, she said, through the very heart of Yume-do, the realm of dreams. There, they saw sights beyond imagination—and dark revelations for the Empire. I do not doubt it, though I wonder if the lessons they learned are as real as they believe. In the realm of Yume-do, not all epiphanies can be trusted.

Junnosuke, she says, is dead. A pity. He was a most engaging man, but I knew he would fall in time. Her eyes, those brilliant golden eyes that could only belong in my sister's face, are strange when she says it. She asked if I knew him, if he followed my command.

I am samurai. I do not lie. The answer must be yes. He was my pawn, and I drove him to his death. Even in the end, he was useful.

Am I in league with the Shadowlands? Her question was simple. The answer is so much more complex than she can possibly understand. It was a long moment before I responded, and when I did, I was guarded. But I was not raised by our father. I am not a Toturi, who carries his heart in his hand and offers it to the world. I am a Hantei, raised by the Steel Chrysanthemum and given life in the forge of pain and persecution. I have been scorned by the Empire for keeping the oath my father made—that one of his children would bear the Hantei name. I know the difference between appearance and truth. Tsudao would never understand.

I told her that I have only loyalty for the Empire, and she accepted that as an answer. She is samurai. Samurai must believe words over evidence. Whatever she saw in that dark place, my word is still my bond, and to Tsudao, that was the truth of the matter. Her questions are at an end.

I do not know if her companion thinks the same.

My sister spoke of a "Scion of Hantei" within the darkness, within the Shadowlands, someone who has taken my name. Eight oni stand by his side, she says. Tsudao fears for the future of the Empire. It is well that she should.

Tsudao knows now that her place is not to discover the truth but to defend the Empire. Though we still contest for the throne, I have won a victory. Others will discover the truth of our father's death, wasting their time with idle mysteries while the true issue rots before their blind eyes. The Empire itself is at stake. I have time for nothing less, and there is nothing greater. Tsudao understands that.

Something that Tsudao said remains with me as I watch the world pass outside Otosan Uchi's protected windows.

"The manicured gardens lie in perfect harmony—a world of natural beauty, shaped with the precision of man. Come what may, we will see that Rokugan is preserved and properly cared for, as a gardener cuts away the errant limbs."

Her words haunt me like the image of snow upon the bushes and the trees. I remember when the leaves fell, and the bare branches reached for the sky in protest. Today they are green and lush. Tomorrow they will be bare again.

Hantei Naseru, Anvil of Rokugan.

FORGOTTEN REALMS®

Sembia

The perfect entry point into
the richly detailed world of the
FORGOTTEN REALMS®, this
ground-breaking series continues
with these all-new novels.

HEIRS OF PROPHECY

By Lisa Smedman

The maid Larajin has more secrets in her life than she ever
bargained for, but when an unknown evil fuels a war between
Sembia and the elves of the Tangled Trees, secrets pile on secrets
and threaten to bury her once and for all.

June 2002

SANDS OF THE SOUL

By Voronica Whitney-Robinson

Tazi has never felt so alone. Unable to trust anyone, frightened
of her enemy's malign power, and knowing that it was more
luck than skill that saved her the last time, she comes to realize
that the consequences of the necromancer's plans could shake
the foundations of her world.

November 2002

FORGOTTEN REALMS®

The latest collections from best-selling author R.A. Salvatore

Now available in paperback!

THE CLERIC QUINTET COLLECTOR'S EDITION

Follow the tales of scholar-priest Cadderly as he is torn from his quiet life at the Edificant Library to fulfill a heroic quest across the land of Faerûn. This one-volume collection includes all five of the original novels, complete and unabridged, and an introduction by R.A. Salvatore.

A new collectible boxed set!

THE ICEWIND DALE TRILOGY GIFT SET

A handsome hardside case houses the first three tales of Drizzt Do'Urden ever published – the novels that started it all! Follow the renegade dark elf and his companions as they pursue evil from the windswept reaches of Icewind Dale to the farthest edges of the desert. A must-have for any fan or collector.

September 2002

The War of Souls

The sweeping saga from best-selling authors
Margaret Weis & Tracy Hickman

The stunning climax to the epic trilogy!
Dragons of a Vanished Moon
Volume III

War and destruction wrack the elven homelands as Mina
marches on the last stronghold of the Solamnic Knights.
Driven to desperation, a small band of heroes allies with
a Dragon Overlord to challenge once and for all the
mysterious One God. And through it all, a kender named
Tasslehoff holds the key to the past—and future—of Krynn.

June 2002

The New York Times bestseller
now available in paperback!
Dragons of a Lost Star
Volume II

The charismatic young warrior-woman Mina leads a loyal army
on a march of death across Ansalon. Against the dark tide stands
a strange group of heroes: a tortured Knight, an agonized mage,
an ageless cleric, and a small, lighthearted kender. On their
shoulders rests the fate of the world.

An all-new series of novels based on the greatest roleplaying game of all time.

Come to a land of adventure where goblins attack in hordes, spiders overrun local villages, and rich lords deceive the righteous. Every hallway holds dangers. Every door could be trapped. And inside every room, monsters, treasure, and glory await those brave enough to kick in the door and claim their prize. It's a 200-page dungeon crawl with your favorite heroes from the DUNGEONS & DRAGONS® roleplaying game.

The Savage Caves
July 2002

The Living Dead
August 2002

Oath of Nerull
September 2002

City of Fire
November 2002

The MAGIC® Legends™ Cycle Continues!

Explore the danger and intrigue
behind some of the most popular
MAGIC: THE GATHERING® characters
with these new titles:

Hazezon

Legends Cycle, Book III
Clayton Emery
The last in this exciting trilogy

Full-scale war seems imminent as Johan continues
his march into the southlands. Hazezon, Jedit, and
Adira must stop him at any cost.

August 2002

Assassin's Blade

Legends Cycle Two, Book I
Scott McGough
A new cycle begins

The head of the emperor's assassins plots the death
of several regional monarchs, kings, and leaders. The
emperor's champion disagrees with this dishonorable
tactic and works to stop the assassins. In the midst of
this turmoil, war seems inevitable.

December 2002